The Scorpion's Tail

a novel by

Sylvia Torti

CURBSTONE PRESS

Printed in Canada on acid-free paper by Best Book/Transcontinental
Cover design: Susan Shapiro
cover artwork: © Maria Tomasula, "As No Gives Way To Yes" 2002,
oil on panel, 10x8 inches; courtesy of Forum Gallery, New York.

This book was published with the support
of the Connecticut Commission on
Culture and Tourism, National
Endowment for the Arts, and donations
from many individuals. We are very
grateful for this support.

NATIONAL
ENDOWMENT
FOR THE ARTS

Connecticut Commission
on Culture & Tourism

Library of Congress Cataloging-in-Publication Data

Torti, Sylvia, 1968-
  The scorpion's tail / by Sylvia Torti.— 1st ed.
    p. cm.
  ISBN-10: 1-931896-17-8 (pbk. : alk. paper)
  ISBN-13: 978-1-931896-17-7
  1. Chiapas (Mexico)—History—Peasant Uprising, 1994—Fiction.
2. Indians of North America—Mexico—Fiction. 3. Americans—
Mexico—Fiction. 4. Women biologists—Fiction. 5. Young women—
Fiction. 6. Mayas—Fiction. I. Title.
  PS3620.O68S37 2005
  813'.6—dc22   2005007503

published by
CURBSTONE PRESS   321 Jackson St.   Willimantic, CT 06226
      phone: 860-423-5110   e-mail: info@curbstone.org
                http://www.curbstone.org

Acknowledgements:

Many thanks to those who commented on this work: Betsy Burton, Anne Collopy, Joan Coles, Bill Coles, Lissy Coley, Don Feener, Franz Goller, Bob Hunt, Margot Kadesch, Lynn Kilpatrick, Dorothee Kocks, Carlos Martinez del Rio, Felicia Olivera, Margot Singer, Cheryl Strayed, Manuel Suarez, Vincent Tepedino, Anna Torti, Frances and Dardo Torti, Stephen Trimble, and Nicole Walker.

For relentless encouragement, I am grateful to Joan, Bill, Nigella, Franz, and above all, my mother. This book exists because of Don.

I thank Alexander Taylor at Curbstone Press for his editorial suggestions; the Hedgebrook Foundation, Sacatar Foundation, and the Writers at Work literary conference, which all provided support.

for Don

The Scorpion's Tail

CHAPTER ONE
Chan Nah K'in

Listen. Time is coming straight at us. Soon it will begin. For now, we sit in the middle of this night and wait. Cold clouds sink over the valley when the sun goes in, and now in darkness Ocosingo is covered in heavy wet air. For so many years, the cold made us suffer. Now, it excites us, makes us ready for morning. And with Pacho on one side and Álvaro on the other, I hardly feel the cold anyway. We huddle together and listen to the fog-dampened sounds of the night. We are ready, but we must wait for time.

Not so long ago the forest touched this town. The white buildings were shaded by a thousand trees. Mahogany and cedro stood above everything, guano and escoba palms below those. Everywhere, even on the dirt streets, the light was green and the air was cool, earthy. My mother remembers it like that, when town was a three-day walk up from our village through big trees. Now there are only cows and grass in the valley, dust in the streets, and in the steep canyons, where water flowed below the big trees, there are only rocks. Nothing grows there anymore. The forest has become small, like an old woman bent over on herself, and every day the rivers flow a little less. This town and the people here make my mother angry, but I've known it always like this. It's hard to be sad or angry about what you don't remember.

When the earth is revealed again it will be a different place. I sense change. I can smell it coming. The first day of the new year will be the end of all that has been, the beginning of everything. Like rains that mark the end of the dry *Ya'ax K'in* months, the stink of the past will be washed from the ground and carried away by the river. We will breathe in the sweet scent of a new world.

We sit in silence, the three of us. There is nothing more to say. I know their stories and they know mine. I know they're nervous about how it will go. Álvaro stands up and paces in and out of the fog behind us. It's not the cold; he's impatient. He has always been this way. Like me, he wants time to hurry up, to reach us.

It feels good to have my brothers Pacho and Álvaro waiting with me. We're not of the same people or language, but still, they are my brothers. I grew up with them and they with me. I was seven, maybe eight, when my mother joined the movement. People in our village laughed at her. Her father said she was confused.

"Problems come when the gods are angry," he explained. He squatted next to the incense burner in his palm-roofed temple behind the house and talked in a low voice to the gods. He asked forgiveness, guidance, direction. He fasted, drank *balché* and didn't sleep. After many days, he had an answer. "We must ignore outsiders, avoid conflict, move to a new place."

My mother didn't agree. "Moving is the old way. When you come to the end of the forest, where will you go?"

"The forest goes forever. It always will," he told her.

"You *know* it doesn't go forever. Besides, this is my home. I want to stay. If we go, they'll be cutting our trees at our heels. Mahogany for our canoes. Ceiba that connects the worlds. Palms for nuts. If we stay, we can fight."

He shook his head, but didn't respond. She continued.

"You don't find tapir in the highlands. They need the forest, and so do we. In the same way, those people, the Tzeltales, the Choles, they can't live here. It's not their place."

"Fighting doesn't please the gods," he said. "Nothing changes with fighting."

"That's because you only fight with words," she said. "We'll fight like warriors, like we used to before everything started to change."

* * *

We are ready now, prepared like never before. We will succeed because we cut out our hearts. There was no other way. Without our hearts, we can fight. We knew we couldn't work the way we had worked in the past, because in the past there was always failure. Something went wrong, some part went weak. It was an old Chol woman who had the idea. Take out the part of the heart that stores love and leave the rest behind to do the work that needs to be done.

I remember the night the soldiers stood in line in the forest camp. I stood with them, but my mother saw me. "Chan Nah K'in, you're too young. You need every bit of heart you have." She pushed me towards the edge of the clearing. I stood and watched the others from there.

The moon rose high and the clouds came low. The ceiba, the tree that unites underworld to sky, spun out the night in layers that covered the earth like blankets. The air warmed. The big animals were quiet, like they always get in that kind of darkness, but I could hear my friends scraping and chewing behind me. I didn't have to go looking for them anymore. I knew them. I called them *payasos* because they lived *disfrazados*, in costumes. Looking like one thing, they were really another. You had to watch closely to see that the bits of leaves, some new and green, others brown and dried, had feelers coming out of one end, like thin, long strands of weaving thread blowing in the wind. They were forest grasshoppers and they looked like the leaves they fed on, and as long as they were still, they could sit on the tops of leaves and no one would see them. Hidden in plain sight.

The old man told the soldiers to shut their eyes, but I kept mine open a little. I wanted to watch. The old man and my mother walked up to the first soldier. With a knife the old man made a small slit in the skin. I could see the soldier grimace in pain, but he did not cry. The old man had to be careful to only cut out the love part. He had to leave enough so that the heart could work like always. It takes an expert to know which part is which. Everyone is a little different. There was blood, but I couldn't see how they were getting the heart-piece out. It didn't seem like the cut was deep enough. I saw my mother take something from the old man and wrap it in soft banana leaves, folding it into a little package that she tied shut with the stem of another plant. I couldn't understand how that little piece could be all the difference, how that little piece of flesh could change our history. I guess love doesn't take up too much room. My mother went into the forest to store the heart-piece. When she returned she picked up a fresh banana leaf from her pile and readied it for the next heart. Like that they went down the line of soldiers, taking the love-part from each heart and storing it away so the men could fight better. Since that night the love-pieces have been in the forest, pumping quietly in the banana leaves. They are waiting. After the new year, they can return home.

* * *

Today we marched from the forest up through the steep, rocky canyons, and now we sit at the outskirts of Ocosingo and listen. We wait for time. Soon we'll take Ocosingo, Altamirano, Las Margaritas and San Cristóbal de las Casas. We'll take Huixtán, Chanal and Oxchuc. We'll take the cities when everyone is drunk and asleep, after they've been celebrating, when they're not expecting us. We'll have to fight but we are trained. We have weapons, and we have anger.

When we've succeeded, we'll go back to the forest to our camp hidden deep in the wet leaves. I will beat a hand against my chest to shake the anger loose. I'll cough it up and spit it out. We will celebrate and the soldiers will take their heart-pieces back. One by one they'll swallow the red flesh. They'll pop them into their mouths like pieces of ripe papaya. The love-pieces will slide down their throats and back into place, and then the soldiers will be whole again. After the love-pieces are home, we can all begin to live the future.

CHAPTER TWO
Amy

Christen slowed the green Subaru to a stop in front of the airport terminal. He got out of the car, but Amy waited a second more. The car was finally warm and she'd just stopped shivering. She considered what she should say to him, and wondered if it would be better to say nothing. She'd expected him to park the car and help her in, and was surprised when he'd stopped at the curb, but given his lack of enthusiasm for her trip, perhaps it'd be easier if they didn't prolong the departure. She got out of the car and braced herself against the raw, sub-zero air. The muscles in her face felt frozen. She decided she would say nothing; it was too cold for discussion. She joined Christen at the back of the car, and together they pulled the two large, unwieldy duffel bags from the trunk and set them on the curb.

"Jesus! Do you have bodies in these bags, Amy?"

"I didn't know what I'd need." She contemplated the bulky bags lying on the curb. "I don't know how I'm going to manage these alone."

He tried to take her in his arms, but their bulky down parkas kept them from getting too close. "I'm sure some nice Latino guy will jump at the chance to help you. You know how they like to prove themselves, especially to pretty American blonds." He kissed her briefly. "Be careful, okay?"

"Right, to a woman who towers over them? I'm always careful," she smiled. He kissed her once more.

"Don't have too much fun," he said as he walked around to the driver's side of the car.

"Wait," she said, not wanting him to go, suddenly feeling apprehensive about the trip, and their separation.

"What?"

He looked up at her and she could see that he was annoyed. She hesitated, wanting to say more, but instead, she unzipped her parka. "I doubt I'll be needing this and it's too bulky to carry around."

He came back around the car and she handed him her parka.

"*Hasta la vista*," he said as he got into the car.

She could tell by his clipped kiss and sarcastic Spanish that he was still hurt she'd cut their Christmas vacation short, opting to spend New Year's Eve doing research instead of with him. And it wasn't only the trip. There had been tension between them for three months now. She waved as he pulled away and stood in the freezing air for a second after he was out of sight. The muscles in her back tightened and her shoulders rose higher up on her neck. She reached down for her bags and dragged them inside.

The check-in line was long and it moved slowly, as if everyone had eaten too much during the Christmas vacation. She pushed the two bags forward with her feet, a few inches at a time, shifted her weight and looked around. Her body was warming again after the exposure to the outside air, and only her fingers felt cold now. She blew into her palms, rubbed them together and looked around. The crowded airport hummed. Airports were like living creatures, she thought. They reminded her of ant colonies with thousands of workers going every which way, performing their specialized duties, while soldiers patrolled back and forth. This morning there were the usual business men in dark suits, briefcases in hand, as well as the post-Christmas group. Children sprinted back and forth, carrying new stuffed animals and driving remote control cars between the feet of people standing in line, while their parents tried to keep them in order. Grandparents headed home, moving slowly underneath heavy baggage.

For the hundredth time, she went through a mental checklist. She hadn't wanted to forget anything, and so she'd brought most of the collecting equipment she owned. She had four white cloth insect nets, two with light-weight extendable poles that could be used with a branch cutter to sample the tops of small trees. She brought Winkler Funnels to sieve insects from the leaves on the ground, and three malaise traps to collect flying ones. She had five rolls of duct tape, forceps, an aspirator, thousands of vials, a pinning block, hundreds of small plastic bags, notebooks, pencils and her new Zeiss binoculars.

This was the first time she was traveling abroad; she hadn't even owned a passport until a few months ago. In fact, she was the first in her family to ever go to a foreign country. The closest her parents had come to foreign travel was going to Hawaii for an anniversary, but they hadn't stayed long because her mother didn't like it. But her family had traveled a lot within the country; they'd lived in six separate states at eight different Air Force bases. Moving was as much a part of her life as insects, so why not move around the world? And this was her first tropical collecting trip! As she inched forward in line, she thought about insects. She could hardly wait to see what creatures came out of the nets. For weeks now she had been dreaming of discovering a species new to science. She thought about what she knew about Mexico. Spicy food, mariachi music, drugs, migrant workers, Maya ruins. Not much. But for that matter, what did she know about any country? Despite the fact that she now lived within hours of the Canadian border, she'd never been across. All she knew about Canada was that Canadians seemed just like Americans, only they didn't like it if you said that. She knew they were supposed to have a good health care system, but obviously there were no jobs for scientists; half of the post-docs she knew were from Canada. Still, Mexico was more exotic than Canada—in every way she could imagine: people, food and most importantly, insects.

She was thankful that Parker Holt would be meeting her at the airport in Mexico City; they would take a plane to

Tuxtla Gutiérrez together. At least she wouldn't have to navigate within the country alone. She hadn't admitted it to her family or Christen, but she'd felt conflicted about this trip to Mexico—both apprehensive and excited. When she was fourteen and they lived at Fort Huachuca in southern Arizona, her father didn't allow the family to go into the border town of Nogales without him, and there really wasn't any reason to go there. They had everything they needed on the Air Force base: a grocery store, school, church, movies, an Olympic-size pool, even bowling alleys. A world unto itself; there was no reason to venture outside the base.

She remembered the first time she accompanied her father to town. She felt afraid and stayed close to his side. The town gave off a dry heat. Empty cola bottles rolled up and down the streets and plastic trash bags floated in the wind. Many of the storefronts had broken windows, the cracks sealed with duct tape. Skinny dogs trotted along the sidewalks and loud music announced every beat-up car as it passed. It didn't seem like the United States. On the Air Force base, men standing at attention looked serious and tough, but they were controlled, part of the whole organization. Here the boys and women had unsympathetic faces and there didn't seem to be any orderliness to their clothes, or the free way they walked, or how they crossed the street any old place instead of at the corners like you were supposed to. They stared at her, her father and their car with its military insignia, and they didn't look friendly. But then, shortly after that day, she'd found her prize saturnid specimen, one that she still counted in her top ten possessions. It was a Mexican moth species whose range only occasionally reached far enough north in the Sonoran Desert to enter Arizona. She knew that South meant more amazing insects, and despite the fear that Nogales had instilled in her about Mexico, she'd always wanted to go.

Finally, she checked in at the ticket counter, and when she got to the gate they were already calling her row. She sat next to a man and his son, a boy of perhaps seven or eight. The boy fidgeted back and forth.

"Don't kick the seat, Sam," the father said. He looked at Amy, "It's his first flight."

She smiled. She didn't mind because she felt nervous too.

"How do planes fly?" the boy asked his father.

She was tired of staring at the silly emergency card and so she put it away and listened for the father's answer.

"The engine is big and pushes us up."

Amy knew this wasn't quite right.

"But how come we don't fall out of the sky? The plane is so heavy."

"I'm not sure, Sam. We can look it up when we get to grandma's house," the father said.

"I can tell you," she finally said. She didn't like people misunderstanding simple scientific principals, and explaining flight was much better than "sitting back."

"You know?" the boy asked her.

"Yes," she said.

"How come you know that?"

"Well, first, my dad is in the Air Force and he taught me about planes, and second, I study insects, so I have to understand how they move around."

"Wow. Your dad's a soldier *and* a pilot?"

"Yes, he is. Here, I'll draw it for you." On the back of the white emergency sick bag, she drew a sketch of an airplane. "There are two main forces to flying," she told him. "Lift and thrust. A plane gets thrust from the engines and once it's going fast enough, when the air going over the wings is moving faster than the air going under the wings a lift gets set up, which is what pushes the plane off the ground and keeps it up." She drew arrows so that he could imagine air going over the wings. "It's all about the way the wings attack the air. The wind under the wings actually holds the plane up."

"So is this how birds and insects fly too?

"Not exactly."

"Because birds don't have engines," he said.

"Well, not gasoline engines, but their wings are like little engines. Flight in birds and insects is way more complicated than in planes. They get the thrust from the power of beating their wings, but they have to beat them really fast. Some insects, like honeybees, beat their wings two hundred seventy times a second!"

"Wow. That's fast. Thanks."

Only she didn't tell Sam about the real difference between animals and machines. Animals had will. They could control their flight in a split second and they had reasons to fly: getting from one food patch to another, escaping a predator, finding a mate, but a machine was just a machine. No will, no desire, no need to fly. A machine could malfunction in ways an animal never could.

She closed her eyes and thought about the Sunday she found the saturnid moth. The rain had continued all night and into the morning. She sat in church during the sermon and watched huge raindrops roll down the windows thinking that the collecting wouldn't be good, but then in the middle of the sermon the sun came out and after that, she knew she'd find something if she could only escape the others during the bible school walk. They were going to Sycamore Canyon "to walk in God's creation," an expedition to try to find the tiny tarahumare frog that lived there. Usually she was good at slipping to the side of the group or staying back so that she could hunt insects, and that was her plan for this day.

August monsoons were the only relief to daytime heat. Inside the canyon, they walked along a dirt road next to the creek. Rugged canyon walls, red, orange, brown, rose steeply on each side. Despite the rain, the creek was shallow. There was little precipitation and every kind of plant life, from mesquite to cacti, had evolved to keep in water with waxy cuticles and small leathery leaves or spines. It was mayfly season and the lightweight flies had just emerged. The poor flyers, tossed about by wind, stuck to the girls' long hair and T-shirts. The girls shrieked and complained about the see-through insects that wouldn't fly away when they shooed them off.

Amy walked at the back of the group, purposefully slow, both to better see what was stirring and also to let them gain distance. They were going to the picnic site ahead and the sooner they got there and away from her, the better. Grasshoppers shot up and out of foot's way, right and left, their wings an instant of red or yellow in the brown canyon. The buzzing of cicadas was loud and incessant, and not easy to ignore.

She knew it as soon as she caught it. She'd pored over enough Sonoran Desert field guides and entomology texts to know exactly what it was. *Eascles oslari.* Family Saturniidae. Order Lepidoptera. Rare in the United States. The Eascles moth, as big as her hand, had been resting on the low branch of a tree, but was disturbed when a boy tossed up a rock. She saw it flutter up and then land again. Quick, quick, she'd caught it in her net. Once the moth was pinned she studied it closely, recording notes about it. She measured it and saw that it was almost six inches across, a normal size specimen. Its upper side was yellow with purple-brown lines and cell spots. Underneath it was brown with dark brown bands. Later, she learned that females moths lay eggs on only three species of trees, the Mexican blue oak, Emory oak, or Western soapberry. The caterpillars, bright green with long stinging hairs, feed on the leaves and then pupate underground before coming up as moths. The adults never eat. As with all her important and rare insects, she only had to think of the experience and she could relive the emotion of first seeing the insect and then catching it.

* * *

She deplaned in Mexico City and was immediately engulfed by a quick-moving group of noisy, people. Her ears were plugged so she held her nose and blew, trying unsuccessfully to equalize the pressure. Ears ringing, she was squeezed between a group of business men and herded through immigration and then customs. The men were short with dark hair and dark eyes. At home she was tall, but here she towered over the men, her blond hair, blue eyes and pale winter skin announcing her foreignness, but they didn't notice, and leaned around her to talk to each other as if she were a pillar or not even there.

She pushed her cart through the main corridor passing a café, chic European shops and a book store displaying newspapers in every language. In the waiting area she saw Parker Holt in a corner chair, hunched over a laptop computer, his frizzy, light hair illuminated from behind by green, white and red letters, a duty free shop halo. As his fingers typed, she could see the muscles working around the bones in his wrists, his elbows sticking out. She smiled when she saw him. Until that moment, she hadn't realized how much she'd been looking forward to seeing him again. A praying mantid, maybe? Time would tell. She wasn't sure he had the slow predatory movements of a mantid, and his eyes weren't quite bulgy enough, but they did have a particular intensity about them. She remembered that he had attracted her in an odd sort of way when she met him at the conference the year before. He'd followed her after her talk, calling her Dr. Bug Girl.

"Can I ask you a few questions about your talk?" he asked.

She was surprised by his informality and of course, she hated it when people referred to all insects as 'bugs.' "I'm not a hemipteran," she told him. "In fact, if you had paid attention to my talk, you'd know that I work on caterpillars—Order Lepidoptera."

He had laughed. "Want to catch a bite to eat?"

She accepted, intrigued, but hesitant too.

Parker was easy-going, perhaps too easy-going, and

maybe even arrogant. She couldn't tell, but she remembered wondering at the time whether he was so thin because he simply forgot to eat or if his hunger was muted by science. She both envied and resented his comfort with strangers, the way he had approached her. She could never have been so forward. Would he have called a man Dr. Bug Boy? She doubted it. During their dinner, she felt studied by him, and charmed. When she asked about his migratory bird research, he became animated, his expression changing from intensity to joy. His arms flew as he described the migratory patterns, as if he were trying to simulate bird-life, and the changes to their habitat in Mexico.

"So, how'd you fare in an Entomology Department with all of those nerdy males?"

Good. The question meant he was aware of gender issues, at least. "They left me alone, mostly, and I was willing to take on the freak-cases."

"What's a freak case?"

"Oh, you know, Entomology Departments are always being called about creepy-crawly stuff. People bring in spiders and insects that they've found in their houses for you to identify. Mostly they want to know if something poisonous is living close to them, but sometimes you get calls from wackos. There was an older woman who claimed there were spiders living under her favorite sitting chair and whenever she sat down, they'd run out and crawl all over her. They sent me to her house to inspect."

"Were there really spiders in her chair?"

"None that I could find, but I sprinkled talcum powder around, telling her it was pyrethrum, and she was happy with that. Sometimes, though," she continued, "there are real cases—the undergraduate with a botfly larva in her labia, a woman with maggots in her nose cavity, a guy with screw worms in his testicles."

"Ouch! And I suppose you got them all out?"

"Actually, yes."

"I was kidding! Are you serious?"

"Unfortunately, yes, not exactly pleasant work, but I couldn't *not* help. Most American doctors don't know how to deal with larvae because people don't get them often enough like in tropical countries."

"So how did you learn?"

"My major professor did tropical research. He had lots of papers and stories about tropical parasites that infest humans. I was interested and so he taught me. Besides, the extraction work gained me some respect with the other entomologists."

Later, she knew he had paid attention to her science because she received an email from him, detailing how he thought her expertise and dissertation work could be applied to the system in Mexico, and then he invited her to come on this trip. He would pay for her expenses and she could survey the insects, and from that they'd start to understand what the migratory birds were eating while they were on their winter grounds in Mexico. She'd accepted right away: the project sounded interesting and she knew she could use some of the field time there to begin to begin to collect data for her indicator hypothesis.

"Hello Parker," she said when she had approached him.

"Oh, Amy. Here you are." He fumbled the computer off of his lap and stood. She remembered now that he was a bit taller than she. He extended his hand toward her.

"How are you?"

"Fine, thanks. I'm looking forward to this trip." The loudspeaker announced their flight from Mexico City to Tuxtla and they stood in line to board the plane. "I'm excited to see what insects I find. You know, the area hasn't been explored entomologically very well.

"Is this your first time to Mexico?"

"First time anywhere foreign."

"Where are you from?

"All over the States, really. My father is in the service, but I did my graduate work in California, at Davis, and now, Minnesota."

"Right, at Macalester, so you're teaching double time and still you're expected to do research?

"Right."

"Ever been to the deep south, Mississippi or Alabama?"

"No."

He looked at her seriously and raised his eyebrows. She couldn't help but notice that his eyes got bigger as he did this and that at this moment, they bordered on a bulge. "Well, then you'll probably see something new."

* * *

From Mexico City they flew to Tuxtla Gutiérrez, and as the plane descended into the foggy valley, she sensed she'd gone back in time.

"This is the military airport," Parker told her. "The domestic one isn't used anymore. I guess there aren't enough people coming here."

The structure looked more like a large garage than an airport. For the first time in her life, she exited a plane directly onto the tarmac, and as she did so, she was overcome with a sweet, sweaty smell, reminiscent of a women's locker room. The air was heavy, viscous and palpable. It was still early morning and she knew they were in a valley, but the clouds were low and thick. The air and light were bright white, the water drops of fog, a billion mirrors reflecting the sun. It was cool, but in the light she could almost feel the sun's strength, the heat struggling its way down through the humid air to her skin. Two gigantic palm bushes, like lady's fans, beckoned them inside to collect their baggage.

Once outside the small airport, a horde of cab drivers surrounded them, shouting in unison up at Parker, fighting with each other at the same time. They emphasized what they were saying, which she could not understand, by jabbing their hands into the air and each other. Parker arranged a taxi to the bus station. Inside she looked around for a seat belt, but didn't find one.

Parker glanced back at her rummaging around. "No one uses them."

She stayed close to Parker at the dirty, crowded bus station while he bought the tickets. Inside the bus, most of the seats were taken, but they found two places toward the back. The bus rocked out of Tuxtla slowing often for enormous pot holes in the road. Bright turquoise, green and pink walls decorated the fronts of houses and buildings, their roofs were of red tile or corrugated tin with tilted water tanks like Dr. Seuss top hats above. Chunky block letters spelled Pepsi and Coke on white cement walls. The houses and businesses looked half-built, rebar sticking above the roofs for a future level to be added, or abandoned houses with no roofs at all, as if the people had given up in the middle and just quit.

The bus ground to a low gear and they began to climb a winding mountain road. She looked outside. She was in the tropics! Like a covered bridge, tree canopies shaded the road, and the Pepsi and Coca-Cola colors—red, blue and white— were replaced by green. Vines climbed up blades of grass onto the lowest branches of any tree and wound up around electrical wires. Minnesota and the cold of winter had faded. Mexico City was left behind. Now there was just green, the pant of the diesel bus and Parker next to her.

Mostly, she saw corn tassels, yellow and burnt red. Glossy oversized leaves hung in the mist, an arm's length away. The bus followed the road, curving sharply left, then right and then left again. Small cars sped into the oncoming lane to pass, their drivers ignoring the fact that they couldn't see around the tight bends. The bus pressed on between rock outcroppings blasted away to make the road, the grunt of the engine echoing off the rocks. The bus climbed higher and the road narrowed; green closed in on them. Curves left and right. More corn and mist. The road was a moving green snake. Amy was hungry and slightly nauseated, exhausted with the non-stop travel from Minnesota to Mexico, now to Chiapas, and the bombardment of new sights. Her ears popped and pressurized. Parker reached across her and slid open a window. She smelled wood fires. The soil banks of the road were the color of wet cinnamon and everywhere she looked, she saw corn. Stalks scattered along the roadside, interspersed with grasses and bushes, stalks planted on extraordinarily steep slopes. The fields were haphazardly shaped, squeezed between pine trees, a patchwork of dark green where forest still stood, light green where they were cultivated. A complicated, irregular landscape, without pattern. She glimpsed a bright green bird, but the bus passed too quickly for her to really see. Maybe a parrot or a trogon. How she'd love to see a trogon!

"Mexico has the highest diversity of pines in the world," Parker told her. He pointed to one after the other. "That one is *Pinus oocarpa*, and the one behind is *Pinus pseudostrobus*. *Pinus tenufolia* has the long needles that hang down in clumps. Oh and see those? Those are *Pinus chipanesis*. And then there are the other evergreens—junipers and cypress."

From the window, she looked onto the tops of pines growing on the steep slopes below, but it was impossible to make out one from the other as Parker had. Why was it that biologists all slipped so easily into lecture mode? Parker couldn't help himself from telling her about the landscape, just as she knew that she would be doing the same thing, telling him little stories if they were looking at insects. Even if they were quirky, she loved being around biologists; their passion and interest in the natural world, which struck most people as bizarre, seemed natural to her.

Turkey vultures soared just above the bus. The hills touched the clouds, their tops blurred by the mist. There was a softness to the land that resembled a Monet landscape. It was foreign, but she felt comfortable.

17

"This world is so green," she told him. "I can almost taste it."

He turned to her, their eyes met and he held her gaze. She looked away.

"After you've been here a while," he said "it gets down into you so that you start to crave it. Like a lover," he added.

She felt embarrassed, unsure of his intended meaning, and turned to look out the window again. The landscape dominated her vision, mountains pulling her eyes up, green bringing her back down. Human-made structures appeared as mere afterthoughts. She was used to subtlety and constraint, but here her emotions welled up and spilled out uncontrollably so that she said silly things. And she wasn't sure what to think about Parker. What was he implying with that "place like a lover" comment, and why had he *really* invited her along? His Spanish flowed easily and he knew a lot about Mexico. He seemed perfectly comfortable here, and she liked that. Christen would never be comfortable in another culture. He was one hundred percent Minnesota American, complete with "Fargo" accent and all. She had thought it was an exaggerated stereotype when she'd seen the movie, but that was how Christen talked. Lately, it had begun to bug her, how wholesome and earnest he sounded, how well-meaning in everything he did and said. And well, what was she if not a white-bread, bubble gum American too? But she wanted to get out, travel, collect insects and work in other parts of the world. She had played it safe during her Ph.D., opting for a clean, scripted project funded by her major professor, but really, the work was so predictable it had bored her. Still, she had finished in less than four years and now she was on her way to the more exciting stuff. She felt it. This trip was going to be the first of many. The bus continued to climb up the mountain, into the mist. Clouds separated, letting in blue and white and a blinding sun. Leaves glistened as the wetness dried.

"How much time do you spend here?" she asked Parker.

She could smell him next to her, the hours of travel and heat in the bus making him sweat. There was something pleasant about his smell. She felt dirty and resisted moving her arms too much, wondering if she was giving off a bad odor.

"Not as much as I'd like, not as much as I did during my dissertation research," he said. "Now it's two or three months per year, but it's strung out, so I don't feel like I ever get the rhythm of the place inside me anymore. I come down, maximize data collection and fly home."

"This is the dry season, right?"

"Yep. It doesn't rain every day, and usually just in the afternoon when it does."

The bus panted and pushed upwards for almost two hours before they arrived at San Cristóbal de las Casas. They entered the bus station and waited for another bus.

"San Cristóbal used to be called Ciudad Real, Royal City," Parker told her. "If we had more time, we could drop in on my orchid-saver friend. He rescues orchids from logged trees, and he's got a stunning representation of the six hundred species found in Chiapas. The most exotic, delicate, fleshy flowers you can imagine, only normally we never get to see them because they grow up in the trees. When the companies start to log, branches fall and my friend picks up those that have fallen and brings them back, branches and all, to his house. When certain species are flowering, you can smell his garden from a block away. And San Cristóbal is a fun old colonial city, but it's over seven thousand feet, too high for the birds I'm interested in."

They boarded the bus for Ocosingo. As they left the city, they climbed again into a thicker mist, the mountains coated with an ethereal green hue from top to bottom.

"We're up in cloud forest," Parker announced. "The plants bathe in moisture most of the time. I'll give you the whirlwind ecology tour when we get down to the Ocosingo Valley."

The bus groaned and spouted black smoke as it traversed

one hill after another. The road was narrower than the last road. They followed an oil truck, and their progress was slow enough for her to absorb more of the scene around her. Women and children walked along the red dirt shoulder carrying machetes or hoes. Some women carried huge loads of wood across their backs, propped in place with a rope running across their foreheads. They wore embroidered blouses with red or blue shawls over their backs and headscarves, but no one had shoes on. Small people, their narrow eyes made them look almost Asian, but their skin was the color of nutmeg. The women walked steadily, heads down, swaying back and forth under the heavy loads, uninterested in the passing bus. Small, thin girls walked next to the wood haulers. On their backs they carried even smaller children strapped in place with faded material. Boys with broad, brown faces and large eyes that slanted at their edges stared at the bus. She waved to one boy who stood selling apples, but he didn't wave back. Amy felt as if she had stepped into the pages of *National Geographic*. What a juxtaposition from the airport in Mexico City just a few hours before. She didn't think Mexico would look like this either; this was more like Africa than Mexico. People were much poorer than she'd imagined.

"How can they manage to carry so much wood?" she said aloud.

"World over, women are the human pack animals, except for precious metals, which are carted by young boys."

She wondered what he really felt behind the sarcasm, but she was too tired to ask. She looked outside again. The houses were nothing more than wood plank shacks surrounded by hard, red dirt. Chickens scratched and skinny dogs dozed. Mules grazed in the ditch. She saw a pig on a thick rope leash. She had never seen a place like this, people living in shacks on narrow plots of land along the shoulder of the road, lives balanced at the edge of a mountain. Everywhere she looked she saw corn tassels, the yellow, green and brown of different stages of maturity. The magnitude of the poverty upset her. Shacks instead of houses, bare feet, a precariousness beyond anything she could believe.

"Look here," Parker said. "the peasants farm the hills since they were pushed out of the valleys in the 1950s."

"Who pushed them out?"

"Ranchers. The valleys are prime cattle land. Most of the poor farmers have moved up the hills, like these plots of land we're passing."

She looked at the corn plots just off the road, tiny parcels of land on steep slopes. Women were in many of them, bent over at the waist, working the soil between corn stalks, tassels swaying in the wind above them.

"The rest of the peasants, mostly Tzeltales, Tzotziles and Choles ..."

"Who?" she interrupted him. She'd never heard these names before, only Mayan and Aztec, and she had no idea who he was talking about.

"In this part of Chiapas, there are four main language or ethnic groups: Tzeltal, Tzotzil, Chol and Tojolabal. The people that didn't move up into the hills went southeast toward the Lacandón Rainforest to apply for *ejido* land. According to laws passed after the 1917 revolution, indigenous peasants can apply for land from the government. The parcels, if and when finally given out, are called *ejidos* and the peasants own them communally. They can give them to their children, but they can't sell them. We're doing some surveys on Tzeltal *ejidos* east of Ocosingo, seeing how the birds use shade coffee versus sun coffee. Traditionally, coffee was grown under a mix of canopy trees, and then the farmers started using just *Inga* as the overstory tree, and there are some coffee varieties that are grown in full-sun. I'm testing whether the traditional coffee plantations, called *cafetales*, are better habitat for migratory birds. The canopy trees above shade coffee are usually pretty diverse, so we expect to find more bird species there as well."

"My boyfriend owns a coffee shop and he's been buying shade coffee," she told him.

"Is he a biologist too?"

"No, more of a coffee-shop philosopher."

"It will never last."

"What?"

"The relationship. Biologists don't mix well with other types. You won't last long together."

"That is so arrogant. How can you have any idea?…You don't even know me!"

"I know you're a biologist."

"So?"

"And a little while ago you said you could taste green." He was smiling now.

"Almost. I said I could *almost* taste it."

She turned away from him and looked out the window. She didn't want him to see that she was smiling as well. She didn't want to be smiling. His certainty annoyed her.

Eight hours and she had already seen so much that was new. She was far from Minnesota, the airport and Christen. He would be happy to know she would be involved with a shade coffee project. He would approve of the trip now, and maybe in the future, they could come down together. He could buy coffee directly from the farmers, but even as she had this thought, she knew he would never come with her. He hated to leave the coffee shop, always saying there was no one he could trust to run it.

She was flustered by Parker's confidence, his blanket statements about her relationship, but there was some truth to what he said. Lately, she'd begun to think of Christen as a spider that couldn't leave its web. Ever since she'd been a child, whenever she met someone new, she tried to guess which arthropod fit them best. Some people were easier than others. After a while she'd know if her initial guess was close, and then she'd try to get it down to a specific species. Christen was a spider. She didn't know which species yet, but for most spiders, once a web was spun, the spider could never leave. Female spiders worked diligently and continuously on their webs, catching little flies here and there, having babies, bound always to that one, sticky space they had created.

She felt her ears pop as the bus dropped in elevation and she noticed that the vegetation changed from pines to oaks. She read the signs as they passed through small towns: Huixtán, Oxchuc and Cuxulja. The names didn't look Spanish and she realized she would have no idea how to pronounce them if she were trying to give directions. Some of the towns they passed had the letters PRI white-washed onto the rocks and buildings, while others had the letters PRD.

"What do those letters PRI and PRD stand for?"

"Those are the two main political parties in Mexico. The third is PAN. PRI holds all the real power and has controlled the presidency since the revolution in 1917. Essentially a dictatorship. PRD came out after 1968, made up of the left and a dissatisfied faction of the PRI. They're a sort of decaffeinated left, but still stronger than anything we have in the States. PAN is the old, rich white oligarchy."

Three hours later they arrived at a hill above the Ocosingo Valley and Parker directed her attention to the valley.

"Here's my favorite valley. Look down there. The grass is scattered with just those trees because they're the only plant the cows won't eat."

"Why not?"

"They're ant-protected *Acacias*. They've got thorns with wide bases that house ant colonies. If the cows try to munch the leaves, the ants run out of the thorns, up their noses and sting them hard. At least that's the story. I don't know if anyone has tested it for this species, but Janzen showed it for another *Acacia* in Costa Rica."

23

"I know his work."

"Ah, so you didn't need the story."

"No." She smiled. He had paid attention.

"The vegetation in this valley has changed over the last forty years since the cattle farmers moved in. Before there was a high diversity of tree species. Now we basically have grass and *Acacia* trees. I'm trying to figure out how this change affects the birds' use of the landscape. I'd like a full insect survey from the *Acacia* trees."

"Sure." And then she couldn't resist. "So, Parker, why did you *really* pick me for this trip? There are lots of entomologist-ecologists who have experience in the tropics, who know the insects here much better than I do."

He laughed. "That's true, but I liked the way you talked about science at the dinner we had—big, but still practical, and your mysterious indicator hypothesis. And like you said, you haven't been to the tropics, so you're fresh. The first time you notice things that you automatically will ignore later. I think it's important to be with people who can see more than you."

She looked at the small town that sat above the expansive valley of pasture land. Parker waved his hand to the east and south, "If you continue that way, you go down through canyons and end up in the Lacandón Rainforest. It's a real nightmare."

"Why?"

"The people are poor, malnourished."

"I thought *these* people looked pretty poor."

"You can't imagine then. Rainforest is not a good place for humans to live. On top of that, the forest has been about sixty percent deforested in the last forty or fifty years. Add to that the fact that we're about as far south as you can get without being in Guatemala, and so there are a lot of Guatemalan refugees from the war there."

She wasn't sure which war he was talking about, but felt too tired to ask. She was surprised when she had looked at a map of Mexico before she left to see that Mexico City was much further from the American border than she'd thought, and that Chiapas was at the bottom like a tail. It had been the first time she'd ever really looked at a map of Mexico, the whole country at once. Usually, she only thought of the northern part, the Mexican pieces of Sonoran and Chihuahuan Deserts that were included in North American insect guides to show the complete distribution of some Arizonan and New Mexican species. She conjured the image of Chiapas on that map and tried to situate the cities, forest and mountains in her mind, but failed. She was disoriented, her body exhausted by the perpetual motion of travelling, her brain in overdrive trying to assimilate the images she was seeing and the information Parker was giving her. The whole place, the mountainous road, the misty green mountains, the women carrying the wood, the lush cattle farms below, and the unfamiliar political parties, seemed unreal, like the set from some child's game where one could move the people, animals and trees at will.

* * *

Using his personal car as a taxi, a man squeezed her large bags and Parker's luggage into the tiny trunk and backseat and drove them less than a mile from Ocosingo, back up the road they had come in on. They ascended a gravel driveway to a small, white cement house surrounded by weedy vegetation and four or five tall palm trees in the front yard. From the driveway she saw the small town of Ocosingo and the valley stretching southeast.

Two men came out of the house and each embraced Parker briefly. Parker turned to Amy.

"Pablo, César, this is *la doctora en-to-mo-lo-ga.*" He sounded out and exaggerated each syllable.

"Hello. Nice to meet you." She moved forward, uncomfortable with being introduced as a doctor—even if

Parker was just being silly, and extended her hand to each in turn.

"Did you have a nice trip?" César asked.

"Yes, thank you. It was uneventful."

"Excuse me?" César asked. She realized that he hadn't understood her last sentence. "It was a fine trip," she clarified.

"Sorry, my English is not good," César explained.

"No, no, please, it's me who should apologize for not speaking Spanish."

"You'll have plenty of time to learn Spanish here," Parker interjected. "Besides, these guys need to practice their English, especially if they're ever going to do graduate work in the States, huh Pablo?" He nudged Pablo's arm. "So how are the surveys going?"

"Good. We've finished point counts at Hacienda Rodriquez, Hacienda de los Milagros and on two parcels of *ejido* land," Pablo answered.

"Have you had any more problems with the Tzeltales?"

"No, since we explained our work to them at the last community meeting, they have welcomed us."

"Good. Let's go to Milagro tomorrow. I want to show Amy that ranch and then she can start on the surveys."

They ate a late lunch of rice and black beans in the kitchen. Parker, Pablo and César spoke in Spanish. She knew they were discussing the project because every so often she picked up the name of a bird species. She studied Pablo and César as they talked. Pablo didn't look very Mexican, certainly not like the people she had seen on the bus trip. His curly light-brown hair and green eyes suggested German heritage. He sat with his legs crossed like she had seen European men do in the movies. He was taller than César, but not muscular like Christen. His legs crossed each other easily. He ate in the European way too, with a fork in the left hand and a knife in the right. Maybe a Mesoveliidae, a water treader? César was stocky, like an Italian, but his features

26

were indigenous. His black hair, straight and long, was pulled back in a pony tail. She guessed he would turn out to be a *Xylocopa*, a carpenter bee, or a tachinid fly. She sensed an edge about him, reminiscent of a sting.

She was used to being the only woman, as entomology was still a male-dominated field, but not understanding Spanish made her feel uncomfortable and out of place. She looked around the house. Red tile floors, white stucco walls that were flaking off, very little furniture. From the kitchen table there were two steps down to the living room and the windows there had a view of the bucolic valley below. She didn't look into the two bedrooms where Pablo, César and Parker slept, but imagined they were like the rest of the house. She would roll her sleeping bag out on the floor in the living room. The house could use some attention, but it had potential. Rugs and furniture could give it a warm feeling, and a coat of paint would make it seem clean.

After lunch Pablo, César and Amy got into the car and drove to town to buy chicken, beer, bread and cheese for a New Year's Eve dinner that night and some alcohol to preserve her insects. Ocosingo was small, made up of perhaps three dozen white-washed buildings, all in need of a new wash, and clusters of red roofed houses built against each other, sharing walls. The main streets were paved, but not the side roads. The buildings, covered in a film of dust, looked cheerless in contrast to the surrounding fields of green. They parked next to the market, a roofed pavilion, open on all sides, and got out. The air smelled like a mix of burning wood and diesel fuel. At first the market seemed like a disorganized mess of people milling within the pavilion, but once they began to walk between the women she saw the rows. Women sat with their legs tucked underneath their black skirts: only their bare hardened feet stuck out. All wore variations of the same outfit: brightly embroidered flowers on white scooped neck shirts, black glossy hair in two long braids down their backs.

"This is a production market," César told her. "People can sell only what they produce themselves."

The women sat next to cups of dry beans or small piles of ground coffee, heaped like a child's volcano in a sandbox. There were avocados of all sizes, tamales, and produce she couldn't identify. She couldn't tell if they were fruits or vegetables. She recognized chayote and some of the peppers, but there were many kinds she had never seen before.

From the market they walked up a street to the plaza. The stores were like booths at a fair, with propped-up windows for serving customers. Plucked chickens hung by their feet collecting dust. Plastic bottles and scraps of paper were scattered about. A white fronted church stood at one end of the rectangular red brick plaza, a colonial-style yellow municipal building at the other end. There were only a few people in the plaza, all men. Pablo and César seemed to know everyone, stopping to shake hands and share a few words with most people they passed. These people were different from the ones she saw from the bus. They looked like the Mexicans she had seen working in Californian fields during the summer: short men in worn jeans, dusty boots, straw cowboy hats drawn low across their dark brows; leathery, wrinkled faces, well-trimmed thin mustaches on their upper lips. They spoke softly with Pablo and César, stealing glances at her, but looking quickly away when her eyes caught theirs.

"I'm going to the church," she whispered to Pablo.

She walked across the street and up the steps and entered the coolness imparted by thick walls. A few songbirds fluttered up and the sound echoed off the high ceiling. They perched on one of the wood beams and their sounds quieted to a whisper. She moved slowly past the few people sitting in pews, heads and hands in prayer to the altar. To the right of the altar, a twenty foot Jesus on the Cross had been patterned into the rock façade with black, gray and white stones. On another wall, yellow and red stones had been used to make corn stalks and two large peppers. She felt reverent and safe and the feeling always surprised her because she had given up any belief in God when she was twelve or thirteen. The sermons at church were boring and Sunday school afterwards didn't make any sense. In later years, her parents allowed her to forego Bible school, but she still had to attend sermons. Afterwards, while the others were reading Bible stories, she tromped in the weeds, crawled through the grass and dug up insects. She liked finding out where they lived, sneaking up on them and watching what they were doing. She had no trouble believing the stories the insects told her. Years later, in college, she discovered the religion of science. It was easy to believe in because it made perfect sense, and yet there was still a spiritual part to the endeavor, a sense of constant exploration, of never fully knowing. There were always new questions to ask, layers of subtlety to unfold. Still, if no one was preaching, she felt a reverence in churches. It didn't matter which religion it was, or if the buildings were large or small, she felt the same quiet resonance that filled her with calm.

When she came out of the church, Pablo and César were no longer there. She crossed the street to the red brick plaza and sat on an iron bench underneath a ficus tree to wait. She watched the people. The church and the municipality building sat on the short sides of the plaza; across the street on the long sides were a series of two-storied buildings, shops and restaurants. The sidewalk in front of the shops was covered by an arched walkway, colonial arches much like those on the municipality building. The plaza served every purpose, a meeting place, a place to rest, a shortcut across from one street to another. Two policemen strolled on the far end in front of the municipality. These were not impatient people. Their slow rhythm suggested they were conserving energy. She imagined the policemen were bored in this sleepy town where nothing ever happened. Her eyes captured by movement, she turned her head to watch white butterflies work a series of red hibiscus flowers. Both ficus and hibiscus were ornamentals planted all over southern California. She felt at home with them.

* * *

In the evening, she and Parker discussed the plan for the next day. She would begin by sampling the upper branches of the *Acacia* trees. She prepared her nets, screwing the collapsible pieces together to form long poles and then attaching the nets to the end. She filled vials with alcohol and began to carefully print the location labels she would later insert into each vial.

César spent the rest of the afternoon and evening cooking. He lit the charcoal grill outside and seared the chicken over the flames and then he cut it into large chunks and added it to the bubbling dark sauce on the stove. While it was cooking, he made tortillas and when everything was ready, he called her to eat.

"It's a treat tonight," Pablo told her. "Señor César cooked his famous Oaxacan mole!"

"Great. Do you like to cook?" she asked César.

"Not really, but Pablo can't cook a mole to save his life. In fact, he can't even make coffee, and Parker, over there, we don't trust him with food."

"Yeah, yeah," Parker said. He handed Amy a cold beer.

"César's right," Pablo said. "He's a good cook, but if I left the daily cooking up to him, we'd both starve. He's too lazy to make food."

César handed her a plate full of chicken in black mole sauce, more of the rice and beans from lunch and a fresh tortilla. The mole was rich and spicy, and tasted delicious after so many hours of travel. The chicken was tough and impossible to chew, but she ate as much as she could. She felt too tired to wait for midnight and so they toasted the New Year of 1994 early. She washed her face in the sink, the only place with running water, and used the stained toilet in the cramped bathroom. It didn't look as if they ever cleaned it. She didn't bother lowering the seat. She braced her thigh muscles and held herself above the bowl trying to orient her pee inside. Afterwards, she flushed with a bucket of water from the kitchen. She wondered where and how she would manage to keep clean without any shower or privacy. She spread out her sleeping bag on the tile floor of the living room and nestled in, happy to be in bed, happy to be away from the tension of Minnesota and Christen, happy to be with people who talked biology. She fell asleep quickly, but was awakened hours later by the noise of fireworks celebrating the new year.

CHAPTER THREE
Pablo

"*Salieron los guerrilleros de verdad*," Pablo said.

"*Parece que sí*," César responded.

Pablo flicked on the windshield wipers to clear the fog that was condensing on the window. He wanted a clearer view of the men on the road.

"Are there five or six?" he asked César.

"Six," César said.

He caught César's eye in the rearview mirror; a glance was enough to know that César was calmer than he was. The mirror also caught Amy's reflection and Pablo remembered that she didn't understand Spanish. He hoped Parker would explain the indigenous men on the road to her. His English wasn't good enough to explain it quickly and he needed to pay attention. Pablo nodded to a man on the hill, the look-out, and then slowed the car to a stop at the soccer ball-sized rocks that had been positioned across the road.

"Who are these people?" Amy asked.

Pablo, César, and Parker responded almost in unison, "*los guerrilleros*."

"Rebels," Parker translated.

"Rebels?" she asked.

Pablo nodded. He heard her inhale loudly. Through the wipers, Pablo saw the men, red bandanas covered their noses and mouths, moving toward the car. They weren't in a hurry. What could they be doing at the outskirts of town?

"I knew there were guerrillas in Nicaragua a few years back," Amy said, "but I didn't know there were any here, in Mexico."

Her voice quivered and Pablo thought she sounded like she was going to cry.

32

"That's partly because you've been focusing on insects," Parker said, "and partly because the newspapers don't report much about subversive movements in Mexico. It's bad press for free trade, you know, NAFTA, and all of that."

Pablo felt a rush of adrenaline. He rolled down the window and the foggy morning, dense and lugubrious, seeped in. He felt nervous, too, but perhaps not for the same reasons as Amy. The wipers were still going, but now they had cleared the water and were making a squeaking noise against the glass. He sensed an annoyance, but he was so focused on the men coming toward him, that he didn't connect the noise to the wipers. Parker leaned over and turned them off. Two of the six men approached his side of the car. They had hardened their looks, trying to intimidate, but Pablo could see the fear in their young eyes. One man had a large black mole above his right eyebrow. He looked very young, maybe fifteen or sixteen. One had a machine gun, four held rifles. The young one with the mole held a piece of wood carved into the shape of a rifle.

"*¿Adonde van?*" the one with the machine-gun asked Pablo.

"We're going to Hacienda del Milagro to study birds," Pablo answered in Spanish. He was sure it must sound suspicious to these boys, but it was the truth.

"Come out of the car," the taller one said. Pablo shut off the engine and got out. César got out of the back seat and joined him. The men frisked Pablo and César up and down, hands on calves, thighs, hips, feeling for weapons.

"What's happening?" Pablo heard Amy ask, but he couldn't hear whether or not Parker answered her.

Only one of the boys spoke. "Give us your bags. We're looking for weapons," he told Pablo by way of an explanation. His Spanish was heavily accented and awkward. The others seemed nervous, shifting their weight back and forth, turning their heads to look down the deserted foggy road.

César reached into the car for the backpacks.

Amy hesitated, "I don't want to give them my bag. My binoculars, they're new."

"They're only looking for weapons. It's okay," Parker told her.

She handed over her backpack.

"*Compañero*, what's going on here?" César asked.

"We have begun the revolution," the tall one answered. "We want liberty and land and sanitation." He recited it as if it were a well-practiced phrase. "You can't go on. We've taken Ocosingo and all the cities around here. Go back to your house."

Pablo and César got back into the car and Pablo started up the engine. He spoke to the men through the window. "*Compañeros, suerte.*" Good luck. He turned the car around and headed back toward the house.

"What's going on?" Amy asked.

"They are making a demonstration," Pablo told her. "We'll have to wait."

"A demonstration with a M16 machine gun, three hunting rifles and a shot gun?" she asked.

Parker turned to look at her in the back seat. He was smiling and Pablo could tell that he was interested in what she'd just said. "How do you know it was a shot gun?"

Amy didn't answer him, but instead asked, "Demonstration against what, Pablo?"

Pablo was considering how to answer her, but Parker did it for him. "Against the government. These people have been screwed forever."

"Damn," César said. "Too young. They don't have a chance."

"Yeah," Pablo replied. "Did you see the guns they had? They looked old, like from the 1950s."

"They weren't from the 1950s," Amy said.

Parker turned to look at her again.

"I know guns," she said.

"Obviously." Parker said. "And?" He wanted an explanation.

"And nothing," she said.

Pablo saw that Parker was smiling. He was surprised and Pablo knew that Parker liked surprises. Pablo glanced in the rearview mirror. Amy was looking out the window and she looked afraid. He wondered where she had learned about guns; it was unusual that a woman would know anything about guns, but then again, almost all the Americans he'd ever met were a curious mix of knowledge and innocence.

"Hopefully they'll come to their senses before they're blown away," Parker said. "We've lost today, but it will all be over by tomorrow and we can continue the surveys. These things never last long."

Usually Parker would be right, but this time Pablo thought it could be different. He and César had walked down to Ocosingo the night before, after Amy and Parker had gone to bed. People were everywhere. It was New Year's Eve, and the streets and the plaza were alive. Small children ran down sidewalks across from the plaza and jumped out through the arches of the colonnade, fizzling sticks of sparklers in hand. Older boys lit firecrackers in the street, their bare feet scrambling away before the loud snap exploded. Young couples cuddled on wrought iron benches in the shadows, and older women hung onto the arms of their men, stumbling together through the crowd. The sharp odor of spicy peppers mingled with the burnt smell of grilled ears of corn, tamales and sugar-roasted peanuts. There were guitars and singing at the kiosk-restaurant in front of the municipal building, and plenty of sweet wine. People responded to the smells, the wine, the music. They danced. The odd thing was that there were many Tzotziles, Tzeltales and Tojolabales—each with their own type of poncho, hanging around as well, and they weren't drunk. They just stood against the church wall on the far side of the plaza looking, watching. Normally, they might have made the town's people nervous, so many of them here at night, but it was New Year's Eve. They were part of the crowd.

This wasn't the first time Pablo and César had met *guerrilleros*. A few years ago when they started the bird surveys, they hardly ever saw them, but lately, they'd been running into them often when they crossed over into the indigenous *ejido* land to sample birds. People rumored that they were buying weapons, getting ready for something, and Pablo had told Parker about it, but neither of them thought it would interfere with the research. The *guerrilleros* weren't bad or violent people. They just wanted to exercise what little power they had. Pablo couldn't blame them, and he knew that he and César looked suspicious. Two guys from the city with binoculars, a big spotting scope, and notebooks. Their story sounded preposterous too. Every time they crossed paths with the *guerrilleros*, Pablo would pull out the permit to show them they were allowed on the land, knowing they probably couldn't read. They'd look at him and then look to César for explanation, as if his indigenous features would explain everything.

César would explain in simple Spanish, "We're biologists. We've come to count the number of birds in the trees and the number flying over. Some of these birds fly from here to the United States to lay eggs. They spend the winter here...We don't know a lot about them We want to know more."

The *guerrilleros* would stare without any look of recognition or understanding on their faces. Pablo didn't know whether they were pondering what César had told them or whether they couldn't understand the Spanish. They would glance at Pablo, then back to César, not sure what to think. Sometimes, even Pablo thought it was absurd. To think that gringos gave so much money for birds, when there was none for the people here; all of the groups—Tzotziles, Tzeltales, Tojolabales or Choles were equally poor. But César would assure them. He had a way of relating to people, especially

36

these people. They trusted him. Pablo was always amazed at how, despite César's pony tail and city clothes, his looks worked so well to his advantage here, but brought him so much suffering in Mexico City. Pablo knew that in Mexico City there were dance clubs César couldn't enter because he wasn't white enough and parties he would never be invited to. César had told him about all of the nights he'd been picked up by the police in Mexico City for no reason other than he passed them on the street.

"You learn that if you look at them too long, or fail to make any eye contact at all, they nail you," César said. "If you ignore them, they don't like that, but you can't pay too much attention because then they suspect something."

"What would they do?"

"Grab me, throw me against the wall, rough me up, act like I was carrying drugs, or was a fag. Mostly, they just wanted to handle me a bit, show me that they had power. I'd just keep quiet, act respectful, but afterwards, I'd go home and no matter how tired I was, I couldn't ever sleep. I'd lie in bed, rabid and seething, fantasizing about all of the things I'd like to do back to them. Horrible things, you can't imagine, Pablo. Even now, it scares me to have had such thoughts, to have played those fantasies out so completely."

"Maybe thinking about it let you go so that you'd never have to do it."

"I don't know. Sometimes I thought I could do it. You know, it actually made me feel better, the thought of them suffering. That's the worst part, and it's part of the reason I came here to Chiapas. Life is less violent down here."

Until today, Pablo thought, and it was only less violent for César, not for the people living here. Only the violence in Chiapas was different than the kind César was talking about—here it was more about hunger and illness than police. Mexico and violence were synonyms. Things had always been this way. This was the country where everything was always the way it shouldn't be and nothing ever changed.

His parents also had a difficult time understanding what he was doing.

"Why can't you study the birds here?" his mother asked. "There are plenty of birds around the city."

His father didn't say much at all, not anymore. He was distant and busy, but Pablo knew he'd disappointed him by choosing biology. He had assumed that Pablo would study business, take a masters degree in the States, and then come home to work with him.

"That's ridiculous!" he exclaimed when Pablo first talked of studying biology.

"Ridiculous to study what I like best?"

"You can't make a living at that. How will you support your family?" his father continued.

"I don't have a family," Pablo answered. His father became angry and left the room.

Lately, Pablo realized that choosing biology, and particularly this job in Chiapas, had both been ways to distance himself from his father. There was no phone at the house, so he only had contact with his parents when he chose it. He called home once a week, and mostly talked with his mother. And he had options his father didn't know about. Parker had put him in touch with a friend of his in the States, a physiologist who studied bird songs, and there was the possibility that he could do a Ph.D. in that laboratory, all expenses paid. Parker had insisted that Pablo fill out an application last time he had been in Mexico.

"I'll mail it from the States," he told Pablo. "Think about it."

Pablo did think about it. He liked the idea of spending the next five or six years doing research, and he especially liked the fact that he wouldn't have to ask his father for money or permission. He wasn't fond, though, of the prospect of living in the States. There was so much about that country he didn't like: the politics and economics, the arrogance and ignorance of the people, their sense of entitlement. Still, he had experienced something unique the last time he was there, a freedom he knew didn't exist for men like him in Mexico. And Americans were a 'can-do' people, not easily stopped. When they saw a problem, they all jumped up to fix it, not like in Mexico where everyone talked about problems, shrugged their shoulders and gave in to the impossibility of the situation. He knew the U.S. had given rise to the concept of grass-root organizations that at first were nothing more than a few people, but little by little got big and became national, and sometimes their effects influenced international policy as well. In the end, though, despite some of the freedoms that existed for him in the States, Pablo was Mexican and Mexico was where he wanted to live.

Pablo liked the indigenous *campesinos* here and the Hach Winik, or Lacandón people, who lived in the forest to the southeast. Even if he didn't speak any of their languages, he knew they shared an appreciation of life, a respect for the mystery around them. They accepted a simplicity that city-people thought was backwards. And they laughed. He couldn't always understand their humor, at times it seemed childish, but they enjoyed life. He had more in common with them than he did with the cattle ranchers, who saw grass as needing only to be churned through the guts of cows before it came out money. Or the timber companies who saw bills hanging from the trees instead of leaves. Cut them down, grind up the wood, get rich on the pulp. It wasn't that the *campesinos* were perfect stewards of the land either, but they were forced into an impossible situation. The forest soil was no good for long-term farming and so they cut and burned more and more trees to eke out a place to grow food. He forgave them. At least when a bird flew over, they saw it. They saw a lot. He had tried to explain it to his mother the last time he was home.

"You see, *mamá*, if my work is successful, if the birds are to be saved, the forest will also have to be saved, and so will the people. There is a connection."

"But how will you ever meet someone there?" she asked.

"I've met plenty of people," he said.

"You know what I mean," she pressed. "A girlfriend, a wife."

He knew she worried about the fact that he'd never had a girlfriend, and she was panicked by the idea that he'd remain a bachelor, or worse yet, end up with an Indian for a wife.

"I just want to do science right now," he told her, and then he quickly changed the subject. It was best to avoid certain conversations.

If he could speak their language, Pablo knew the *campesinos* would marvel as he did at the fact that a ruby-throated hummingbird put two grams of fat on its three-gram frame and then flew thousands of kilometers north, to sing, copulate, build nests and lay eggs, just because they were driven by the instincts of life.

* * *

Back at the house again, they dispersed to separate corners. Amy and Parker settled in the living room to read. Pablo sat at the rickety kitchen table, and César put on water for coffee.

"A matter of time," César said. "We know what's coming."

"When do you think they'll be here?" Pablo asked him.

"Who knows how fast they can get it together? Maybe tonight," César guessed.

"From Tuxtla?"

"Or Villahermosa. There's an airport there too." César's brow was furrowed so that his black eyebrows met at the center above his nose. It was a look of worry Pablo hadn't ever seen before. They waited for the sounds that would announce the army's arrival. There would be machine guns. The planes would fly low and the windows would shake.

Pablo and César had been in Chiapas for three years, since 1991. Parker flew in and out a couple times a year. Every morning they walked through the dark fog to survey birds in the different kinds of coffee plantations and forest types. Pablo, who always rose first, made coffee and then woke César.

"*Chinga*, Pablo, you make the worst coffee ever." He took the entire cup in two or three gulps.

"You could always get up first and make it," Pablo suggested.

"No, without this shit, I'd never be able to wake up at this absurd hour. I'll be glad when the field season is over."

Their schedule—early bed, early rise, day after day of bird surveys—constrained César. He'd studied biology at the university, but his love was film. He stayed up late at night reading about cinema and trying to write a screenplay. Pablo sensed that César needed a world created totally by himself, and the day after day of early rising and bird surveys was not only monotonous but stifling for him.

"What I want is to write a *real* Mexican screenplay," César said.

"And what would that be?"

"A movie that portrays Mexicans as we are—not the European model. Have you ever thought about the fact that European features are ideal here, but no one in Mexico—except maybe you—lives up to that ideal?"

"Thanks."

"Seriously. The people who are closest to the ideal are those who are most foreign—the most recent Spanish immigrants, and the lighter-skinned the better."

"And so what's the screenplay about?"

"I can tell you what it *won't* be about. There will be no magical realism shit, no ghosts of dead relatives drifting around old houses, no Maya or Aztec ruins, no Frida and no tequila. It's about a big family mess—and about everything that isn't said. The space between words."

"I can't wait to read the dialogue," Pablo told him. They both laughed.

"Yeh, that's the easy part to write!"

Unlike César, Pablo loved the steady routine of the surveys, which bordered on ritual. He enjoyed the small variations, of how one day was slightly different from the next, how the seasons—wet and dry—folded into each other. He and César made a good team, he thought, and this fall had been the best year yet. In October and November the songbirds began to return from the north, so that by December, mornings were filled with boisterous calls. Pablo had re-conditioned his ear to recognize the calls of White-eyed vireos, Indigo buntings, orioles and ovenbirds and the warblers: Black-throated greens, Orange-crowned, Yellows, Nashvilles. Catbirds returned from the north, sometimes re-learning songs from the resident tropical birds. There were bluebirds, thrushes, woodcreepers and hummingbirds. So far, they'd noted one hundred twenty-six different birds species. The rustic *cafetales*, with an overstory of diverse rainforest trees, were more interesting than the modern coffee plantations with a monoculture overstory of *Inga*. Bird species either liked or didn't like the *Inga,* so there weren't many surprises to be found in those plantations.

Every morning, they left the house at dawn and walked through Ocosingo to one of the farms on the other side. They found a place to survey and then they stood back to back and synchronized their watches. They stood quietly and did a ten minute survey together—noting each bird species they heard and counting the number and kind that flew over. They never used the data they collected from the first survey.

"I can't be trusted this early," César said. "Let me wake up a bit."

César would head north and Pablo would walk south for two hundred meters where they'd begin the point counts. For ten minutes they would listen, watch and record every call they heard and every bird that flew over. They took notes on habitat type, tree species, canopy height and plantation size. After ten minutes, they walked two hundred meters more and repeated the process. When they had each completed a kilometer transect, they returned to their original point, and headed out east and west. Usually they finished the surveys by mid-day, when the fog had lifted and the clouds were still blue and purple-gray. By the time they returned to the house, the day would be hot and the blue-gray clouds would have turned black. It was important to enter the data into the computers before the thunder and rain started, before the power began to wane and surge, before the computer could be damaged.

Occasionally, they took a day off from the surveys. Just last week, they had walked to Toniná, a Maya ruin from the classical period just eight kilometers outside of Ocosingo. Pablo thought about the early anthropologists who came to study ruins in Mexico and Guatemala. Initially, they thought the Mayas had disappeared. Even today, tourists who swarm over Palenque wonder at the sophisticated people who are no more. In reality, though, they had just changed. Like a butterfly, they had morphed into something new.

The Toniná site, still undiscovered by tourists, was being excavated by Tzeltales laborers. The men, some in bare feet, others in rubber boots, dug shovel after shovel full of water-soaked clay soil into wheelbarrows and then pushed them up the hill away from the canals. Other men placed excavated rocks into the canal banks, re-establishing the elaborate canal system that had once run next to the Maya terraces. The ruins themselves rose from black soil and grass. He could see how the whole thing must have looked before excavation, a group of enormous, symmetrical hills in the rain forest. Buried underneath decades of soil, trees, weeds and flowers were temples, pyramids with flat tops, their sides decorated with etched reliefs. Toniná had seven pyramid terraces and two ball courts where the Mayas played their games. Except for César, himself, and the Tzeltales excavating, the site was empty.

They climbed the sandstone, *laja,* steps. The *lajas,* thousands of flat, light tan rocks stacked upon each other, were cemented in place by earth and roots. They climbed slowly to the top of the tallest temple, *El Templo del Espejo Humeante*, The Temple of the Humid Mirror. The sun burned through the fog and Pablo began to sweat; the breeze at the top cooled him. César went to one side of the temple and Pablo sat at the opposite side. They spent the day together, but alone, sitting, walking over the ruins, discovering, not talking.

Pablo looked out over the valley and named the shades of green: avocado green, chayote green, yellow green, banana green, emerald green. Everything—the mountains, the different trees, the grass—had its own color, but how you saw it depended on perspective and time of day. In the mornings, all the greens were paled by the mist. By noon, the shades were bright and vibrant, and when the clouds rolled over in the afternoon, everything turned darker, almost black. From the vantage point of the temple, the colors merged into one another, like an enormous seamless weaving, and from up here he couldn't hear cattle or people; the only sounds came from birds and words in Tzeltal drifting up from the men excavating below. Butterflies fluttered up toward him. The tops of trees were at eye level. He was close to the sun. Vultures soared at his fingertips.

Later he walked around and sat at the back of the temple, next to where the red roots of a palo mulatto tree grew over the *lajas*. He sat in the shade and watched a colony of leaf cutter ants work a trail up and down the tree and then back along the stones where they disappeared into a hole between two *lajas*, to their nest inside the pyramid. The trail was like a busy freeway. Ants laden with leaves, the pieces wobbling above their heads, descended past their unburdened sisters on their way up the trunk to cut more leaves. Pablo knew that down in the colony, they'd pass the leaves over to another caste of ant, which would then chew the leaves and plant them in tiny ant gardens. The chewed-up leaves were used to grow fungi, and the fungi were fed to the larvae. He wondered what the inhabitants of Toniná thought of the leaf-cutters a thousand years ago. Were the ants as much of a pest to their agricultural crops as they were today? Did the slaves who carried the stones for the *lajas* see themselves in the tiny ants?

He heard César whistling for him and made his way back around to the front of the temple. César motioned for him to come down to a lower temple. When Pablo arrived, he saw why César had called him. Underneath a corrugated metal overhang, a man was working on a statue, cleaning the sculpture with a small brush. The sculpture was of a decapitated male, three feet high. In his hands he held his own head, an offering or a sacrifice. Behind the statue, etched into the wall, was a depiction of four ceibas, trees sacred to the Maya people. One giant tree inhabited each direction of the world.

* * *

Even if they didn't understand everything that happened, Pablo and César had been in the Ocosingo Valley long enough to feel the timbre of the place. They had watched the changes, seen the signs, felt it coming. It was like a storm, moving steadily across the valley. At first, the bright white clouds collected moisture, a droplet at a time. The drops crowded together, pushing up against one another, vying for space. From the ground, it didn't look like much was happening. The clouds were a little bigger, perhaps a touch darker. These were the kind of clouds that held on for as long as possible, stretching and expanding their shapes, trying to make room for every drop that had been forced at them. But for every drop they took, two more were pushed in. In the end, they were overburdened, saturated, and heavy. When clouds get heavy, rain falls.

It had been like that. The people were getting pushed back and pushed back, the good land taken by the cattle farmers, their cows eating better than any Tzotzil could.

45

Pushed and pushed up into the mountains. They cut the forest down and grew their corn and yams for a few years until the soil stopped giving enough for a growing family. And then they'd push back some more, always further up the hills, and then later, down into the forest. They were down there in the Lacandón Forest, without good water, little food, no schools, nothing. The cattle ranchers didn't seem to get it. Anyone who looked could see the inevitable, but most of them lived in San Cristóbal de las Casas and probably didn't see it at all. They just knew that they didn't want to give up an inch. "Give them a little bit, and they'll be up here begging for more," he had heard them say. "They never work. You ever notice how most of them can't even speak Spanish? They don't know what's good for them."

Pablo had seen the demonstration in April 1992, shortly after he started working on the bird surveys. A thousand indigenous *campesinos* descended from the hills and came up from the forest. They marched down Avenida Central to converge on the municipality building of Ocosingo. The women with shoes shuffled along; those without walked with wide, flat arches, splayed toes grasping cement, their movement and approach hushed, virtually soundless. They were dressed in embroidered blouses, long braids tied in ribbons down their backs. The men had put on their best shirts, but even the good clothes could not mask their faces, etched with lines by the sun, by age. Such silence! If the women hadn't been ornately dressed he would have thought they were a funeral parade.

The *campesinos* arrived at the plaza and proceeded up the steps and stood in front of the municipal building. The president of the municipality, who didn't know what was happening, became afraid, escaped out the back door and rode off on a small motorcycle. The people played music and danced in front of a huge bobbing image of Emiliano Zapata. There was poetry in four languages and translators for each into Spanish. Then a man read a speech denouncing the changes that President Salinas had made to Article 27, the changes that essentially took the hope of land grants and new *ejidos* away from the indigenous people. The people cheered and hollered and danced. They made their declarations and spoke their poetry, and then they left as calmly and quietly as they had come.

* * *

After coffee, Pablo turned on the short-wave radio and moved the dial slowly past crackling noises until he found the station out of San Cristóbal de las Casas. The *guerrilleros* were broadcasting, but he couldn't understand the man's speech because it was in Tzeltal, or maybe Tzotzil. He listened anyway. When the speech was done, another man came on the radio and spoke in Spanish. Pablo adjusted the dial for better reception and he and César listened. The man said they were the Zapatista National Liberation Army, the EZLN.

"*Somos producto de 500 años de luchas: primero contra la esclavitud, en la guerra de Independencia contra España encabezada por los insurgentes, después por evitar ser absorvidos por el expansionismo norteamericano, ... surgieron Villa y Zapata, ..., sin paz ni justicia para nosotros y nuestros hijos.*

Pero nosotros HOY DECIMOS ¡BASTA!... "

The reception became fuzzy and so Pablo turned the dial to locate the international stations. He found the BBC and listened to their report of the rebellion. Again, he heard the voice of the same man speaking a poetic Spanish, with a British reporter translating the words.

"Our war cries opened the deaf ears of the almighty government and its accomplices. Before, for years and years, our voice of dignified peace could not come down from the mountains; the governments built tall strong walls to hide themselves from our death and our misery. Our strength had to break down those walls in order to enter our history again, the history they had snatched away from us, along with the dignity and reason of our peoples.

"In that first blow to the deaf walls of those who have everything, the blood of our people, our blood, ran generously to wash away injustice. To live, we die. Our dead once again walked the way of truth. Our hope was fertilized with mud and blood.

"But the word of the oldest of the old of our peoples didn't stop. It spoke the truth, saying that our feet couldn't walk alone, that our history of pain and shame was repeated and multiplied in the flesh and blood of the brothers and sisters of other lands and skies.

"Take your voice to other dispossessed ears, take your struggle to other struggles. There is another roof of injustice over the one that covers our pain. So said the oldest of the old of our peoples. We saw in these words that if our struggle was alone again, once again it would be useless. So we directed our blood and the path of our dead to the road that other feet walked in truth. We are nothing if we walk alone; we are everything when we walk together in step with other dignified feet...."*

"Are you listening to this, César?" Pablo asked. "This man is something."

"An imposter, most likely," César said.

"What do you mean by that?"

"You're so romantic, Pablo! He's all rhetoric. Listen to him. You can tell he's not indigenous. He's co-opted their language, their poems, their cause. He's probably one of those Marxists who studied at the university and then ran away after the 1968 massacre when he realized his studies and rhetoric got him nowhere with city people. Only these people, who are so naïve and poor, will grasp onto anyone's arm who promises help."

"I don't know."

"He's manipulating them, taking advantage of their

---

* "We are Nothing if We Walk Alone," *Shadows of Tender Fury: The letters and Communiqués of Subcomandante Marcos and the Zapatista Army of National Liberation*; *Monthly Review Press*, Feb. 1994.

poverty. Wait and see who ends up dead. God, Pablo, sometimes it's so damn obvious that you come from money. You're exactly the type of person this guy is going for. Boom. Right in the upper-class progressive heart."

"I think he could be different," Pablo said.

"It can't be different," Parker said in English from the living room. "The problem is that there are too many people. These people need to think more and reproduce less. They're having too many damn kids."

"What did the radio say? Can we leave soon?" Amy asked Parker.

"No, but don't worry," Parker told her. "They're talking about the injustices suffered by Indians, but believe me, they'll go home tomorrow and we can get on with the research."

"You're so crass," she said. She was upset and disgusted by Parker.

From the kitchen Pablo asked, "What does crass mean?"

"Insensitive," Parker told him, and then to Amy, "I'm not crass. It's just that racism in Mexico is much better developed than ours. In the States, we just obsess about black and white, but here it's more sophisticated, subtle gradations of color, class, heritage. And except for occasional uprisings like this, people get along much better across racial and class lines."

"I don't call armed uprisings getting along," she said.

"It's true, isn't it César? Pablo?"

"It's true," César said. "We've got white, black, mulatto, criollo, mestizo, indigeno, and many more."

"This is why I like Latin Americans," he said. "They admit more about human nature. Life is *out* here."

Amy ignored him.

Still at the kitchen table, César asked Pablo quietly in Spanish, "Why do North Americans seem like they woke up yesterday?"

"It's different up there," Pablo told him. "You watch

television and they mostly talk about the weather on the news. They do the entire world news in one minute."

"One minute?"

"Yes, that's actually the name of one program, 'world in a minute'."

"I hate that country. I don't ever want to go there, and I don't know why you do. At least we're not like a bunch of newborns."

"They live differently," Pablo told him. "You see it in the way they drive. There are big, four-lane highways filled with cars. What you notice first is that the cars stay perfectly in their lanes. The drivers look only forward, and sometimes in their rear-view mirror, but they don't have to pay attention like we do because they know that everyone else will stay in their lanes too. So, they only end up seeing what's in the front and back. It's easier than here where we have to be constantly looking for people passing around curves, on hills, at what's on your right and left."

"But how can she have a Ph.D. and be this hot-shot young entomologist like Parker said she is, and know nothing about anything else?"

"That's what a Ph.D. is all about, focus," Pablo said.

César shook his head in disgust. "Another reason why I want to make film. I want to study all of life, not esoteric pieces of it." He turned to the living room. "Well, Parker, I bet five of these kids don't waste as many resources as one of yours up there!"

"Ah, but César, *mi amigo.* You forget. I don't have any up there," Parker answered him.

"Well, you better be careful, man, pretty soon you'll have some down here!" César laughed. "Seriously, I'm wondering if we should leave, go up to Cristóbal for a few days."

"No way," Parker told him. "I've got three weeks of work, and I plan to do it as soon as this is over. If conservation is deterred every time there is a human problem, we'll never go forward."

"Anyway," Pablo said, "I'm not sure it would be a good idea to leave. There was a lot of tension out there this morning. The rebels might get confused and shoot."

"They wouldn't shoot us," César said. "The most they'd do is stop us and ask for money. They're not stupid, just undereducated."

When the BBC broadcast was over, Pablo turned the dial a little further to the right and found the French station. They were also offering translations of the Zapatistas' declarations. Again he heard the same man's lyrical voice, this time behind the French translator. The world had taken interest, but the national radio from Mexico City hinted at nothing. The newscasters talked about Christmas, their presents, and gossip.

"*Hijos de la chingada,*" César said and turned off the radio.

Pablo was pissed off too. People in Mexico City tried hard to seem sophisticated, as if they weren't part of this at all, like they had more in common with gringos instead of Mexicans. It was bullshit, but he didn't think Parker was right, either. Even though Parker had been coming to Mexico for a while, and he knew Mexican history and spoke Spanish well, he didn't have a deep understanding of the nuances of Chiapas. He came, did his research, and flew home. Once he'd had a short romance in town, although Pablo wasn't sure what a Mexican woman would see in him. It certainly couldn't be his frizzy hair that always looked like he'd just been struck by lightning, or his thin, lanky body. Perhaps it was his light skin, his height, his foreignness, or more likely, she was dreaming of him as a rich American husband. Pablo knew he didn't exactly understand the nuances of the local cultures either, but he had a sense of them and he knew enough to know that everything was exceedingly complicated.

Pablo was happy here, working with César. They were comfortable with one another, and close—even if Pablo hadn't told César everything about himself. He had wanted to, especially the night César had shared his fantasies for torturing the police, but Pablo couldn't bring himself to risk the comfort between them. He was afraid that if he told César about the last time he'd been in the States and about David, everything would change. When he first came back from the States, Pablo told another friend, Carlos. He didn't like Carlos like that, but they'd been friends since childhood and Pablo thought they were close, but after he told Carlos about David, the party in San Francisco and that he was gay, it was never the same. Carlos couldn't relax because he thought Pablo was going to try to get close; his caution was so intense, it bordered on repulsion and fear, until finally, it became too painful to spend time together.

Pablo didn't like the States that much, but in San Francisco he had felt free for the first time. Up there he wasn't the only one. He didn't have to hide. In some parts of the country, it was natural to be with other men, to flirt, kiss and go home with someone. There was the possibility of meeting not only someone like David and having sex, but of meeting someone he could talk with as well, like César. A gay César. The idea made him smile.

During the last few years, Pablo had come to wonder whether he'd ever be comfortable in Mexico. While all of his friends at the university had been going from girl to girl, experimenting with sex and love, he was isolated and celibate. "Hey, Pablo," they said, "that one, Mariana, she's hot and she likes you. You should go with her." Pablo laughed and feigned interest. The same story over and over, and he knew that many of the women did like him. He was attractive to them and they made little advances with their eyes or they touched him under the tables at the bars. Sometimes they even kissed him and he kissed them back. It wasn't bad to kiss, but it got uncomfortable quickly because he never wanted to feel their breasts or get much closer; he could never tell them that he didn't desire them.

Chiapas was a relief not only for César but for him as well. Everyone who wasn't born in Chiapas, he thought, had his own reason for being here, a way to avoid something else: César to escape the violence of the city; Parker to escape the U.S.A. and save birds; and himself to escape his father and the constant knowledge that his being gay would be the ultimate disappointment to his parents. It was an impossible situation that he only knew how to avoid. Until now. Until hearing this man on the radio. Maybe now things would change in Mexico. César was wrong, he thought. There was something about this man. Past the rhetoric, there was organization and great emotion. "*...our hope was fertilized by mud and blood....*and, "*we are nothing if we walk alone...*" The words impressed him, inspired him, and Pablo felt drawn in, hopeful and excited about the future.

CHAPTER FOUR
Mario

"This is like being given our last rights," Javier whispered as he knelt down on the wooden pew.

"Don't say that, Javier." I knelt down beside him.

"Why not? I mean we've never gotten orders to go to church before. They must think that some of us aren't going to make it."

"But it could be bad luck to talk about it," I told him. Javier was right, though. When they came with the bus and brought us to the cathedral for a special mass, we all knew it was weird. Still, I felt safer in church than anywhere. I bowed my head and tried to listen to the priest, but my mind kept going to my own thoughts, my own prayers, thinking about the past three years.

"Who would have thought we'd be mobilized?" Javier whispered.

"Shh." I told him. I wanted my mind to be with God and not Javier. Javier talks a lot and usually I don't care, but not in church. It's not right.

Why did they have to go and start this right now when I was so close? I was planning on just one three-year term in the army when I signed up. It was the only way I could figure to help my mother feed my brothers and sisters. There aren't any jobs in Guerrero, and after my dad died two years ago, there was nothing else to do. There was no way my mother was going to let me go north, over the border to *el otro lado* like my father had. There are eleven of us alive and I'm the oldest. The army was the best option. Regular food. Steady money. At first it was even good because I was learning stuff, things I could maybe use later. They taught us to build furniture. I learned how to read patterns for making tables and chairs. I learned how to work electric saws and planers and to sand and nail, and I made some really nice stuff. They even let us keep one piece so I sent my mom a little table for her bedroom. I sanded the wood until it was smooth as flour and then I stained it with a pretty chestnut color. I packed it up and sent it home. I'm sure she put it in her room. We learned some mechanics, too. I was pretty good at that, and I liked it even more than the woodwork. At first, I did simple things like take apart motorcycle gears, one piece at a time, and then put them back together again. Then I started in on the engines—pumps, generators and motorcycles. I'd disconnect a wire to see what happened to the motor. Did it make the same sound? Did it stop altogether? I'd tinker and fool with all the pieces until I was sure I knew what every one did, and then I started trying to fix the broken stuff around the station, and I guess I figured it out pretty good, because I was able to fix most everything that was broken. I liked figuring out how things worked, how they didn't work.

And my Spanish got a lot better. Not many of us guys grew up speaking Spanish. Of course, we spoke it, but not every day, not at home or on the street, just in school when we went to school. When we got to the army, we had no choice but to speak Spanish, otherwise we couldn't talk to each other, and of course, the sergeants made sure we all learned pretty fast. It wasn't okay *not* to understand, so we helped each other out and pretty soon we were all speaking just fine.

"At least we're not sweating in here," Javier said, his head still bowed.

"And we're not doing push-ups," I whispered back, but then I noticed he was ready to say more, so I just said, "Shh" again. The church, with its thick walls, was a lot cooler than the barracks. He was right about that. It was dark and quiet, too.

We got the orders this morning. They woke us up and told us to get ready, so we started pulling our equipment together, lacing up our boots, cleaning the guns. Most days, we just sit around sweating in this thick air. You'd think they would have figured out a better place to put the capital of Chiapas, not in some stinking hot valley where the air heats up and can't get out. The buildings at the barracks are made out of wood and just a thin coat of cement, so they get really hot. At night, when we're lying in our bunk beds, you can hardly sleep because there's no air, just stinky sweat from other men.

Most days we work cleaning the barracks, making tables or on mechanics, but today they made us do push-ups, as if you could get strong in a day. What a joke. Half the time there's nothing for us to do, so they make up stuff. Like the time they made us go out to some captain's farm, "for exercises" they said. There weren't any exercises, at least not the military kind. We worked for two whole days, a hundred of us, cleaning up the guy's cattle farm. We cut trees and brush, moved rocks and shoveled shit sun-up to sun-down, and then they brought us back here. On the way back, we figured out how much money the guy saved by taking us out there. A hundred guys for ten hours over two days would have cost him.

"None of this *pinche* Zapatista shit was supposed to happen," I told Javier as we left church. "I was supposed to go home in March."

"Good luck." he said. "I heard that all of you who were supposed to get out will be kept on, because the army might be needing more guys. It all depends on how long it takes us to get the *indios*."

"Do these *indios* really think they can take the Mexican military?" I said. "We're thousands and we have guns. They can't be more than a couple hundred guys with some cheap rifles."

"Well, they can't be too smart," Javier said.

"Shit. They must be really stupid. Zapata died about a hundred years ago. Everyone knows that."

Javier laughed. "They sure are far behind down here!"

"It's not funny, Javier."

"Well, it may not be funny, but it's for real. You heard the orders. They're going to send us out tomorrow," he said.

"Goes to show you that it's no good planning the future," I told him. "It never comes out the way you thought. I was thinking I might finally go north when I got out, cross the border like my cousins did, like my father used to do. They're all up there. My mother won't want me to go because of what happened to my father."

"What happened to him?"

"He didn't come back."

"Must of found a *gringa* woman, eh?"

"No!"

"Shit, man, take it easy. What happened?" he said.

"I don't want to talk about it, and I don't think I *want* to go north, but who knows? Maybe it's better than this."

"Maybe," Javier said, "but I like Mexico. I don't know anyone who really likes it up there. You've got to learn another language and *gringos* don't like Mexicans."

"My cousin, Domingo, does. He told me all about it. He's been going for years now, working odd jobs. There's even some rich woman who gives him easy work whenever he wants it. He just shows up at her house, and she asks him to weed the garden or wash the car, and she pays him double what he makes doing anything else. He says that she controls everything and the husband doesn't even care. The husband just brings home the money and the wife spends it anyway she wants. Can you believe that?"

"*Gringas*. Another reason to stay in Mexico."

"Domingo said he'd help me so that I don't screw up like he did. The first time he crossed and went to California, he paid a *coyote*, but the guy took his money and left him. He got across anyway. It was March and later he found out that the border patrol didn't really mind about people coming in March and April, but if you try later, in August or December, they stop you. Domingo said they need us in the spring and summer—that's why they don't care if you come over in March—because we work for half of what an American would charge; so when the crops are getting ready, they don't mind letting us in to do the picking."

"How much does a *coyote* cost?"

"A thousand dollars, so I guess I'll be crossing whenever I can and I'll be picking vegetables in California. Only Domingo said that California's no paradise. He said there are tons of Mexicans there already, Mexicans who never come home, and they have all the good jobs—cleaning hotels and apartments and factories and cooking in restaurants, and so the only jobs left for newcomers are picking the crops: fruit, beets, lettuce, and that work is hard. You have to keep moving all the time from south to north, following the crops, following the hot sun, and it doesn't pay shit.

"Sounds no better than here."

"Now he's making out good, though. He goes to a different state. I can't remember which one, but I think it's more up north because it gets cold. He told me that in winter flakes of white snow come out of the sky and cover everything. He complains about the cold, but I'd sure like to see that snow. He says that except for the snow and the cold, life is good there."

"I don't know," Javier said. "Sounds fucked up. If I'm going to be fucked by people, I'd rather it be Mexican people."

"Not me," I told him. "I'd like to be fucked by somebody new!" That made Javier laugh and we didn't say more, but I didn't think Javier knew much about life up there. Domingo talked to me a lot about it. "If you find the right people, you make out," he told me. "Lots of gringos speak Spanish and they give you little jobs weeding, painting, digging holes. Or, you can always get work in restaurants—either washing dishes or cooking. American women don't cook; they just go out to eat, and it's really funny because they like to eat food from different countries. I've cooked in restaurants with food from Thailand, Lebanon, Italy, you name it. All the waiters are from those countries, but back in the kitchen, we're all from Mexico and you only hear Spanish. The owners try to keep us a secret. They tell us to come to work through the back door so that the customers don't see us. It's really funny the way they try to hide us, but I don't care. You work, and they pay cash when you're done."

Sometimes Domingo gets longer stints, six or eight months of work. Last year he worked on a chicken farm. "The gringos have huge farms just for chickens," he told me. We laughed hard at that. Everyone knows that the guys who travel across the border are called *pollos,* chickens. "*Los pollos* killing *los pollos,*" we said.

"I hated wringing and plucking and cutting up chickens from morning to night," he told me. "You couldn't breathe with the heat and all the feathers flying around. We were supposed to wear white masks over our noses and mouths, but it was so hot we couldn't bear them. We breathed feathers and chicken shit all day long, but I made out good, good enough to buy real papers, good enough to get a real job."

I guess he was right because this year he's working construction, putting roofs on houses and he's making a lot of money. Ten times what I make in the army. Last time he was home, he showed me a picture of his white car. A sweet machine. It was all shined up with big, fancy tires and chrome hubcaps and it was sparkling in the sunlight. He says that up there everyone has one, and gasoline is cheap so you can drive around as much as you want. He said he'd help me, show me the way. I could work and send money home every month. It'd be nice to have a car.

But now this mess. I watch Javier run his fingers over his weapon.

"Hey, Mario, we're finally going to see some action."

I just look at him and nod my head.

"I'm glad to be going somewhere. I'm sick of staring at

these white walls full of mold," he said. "Ever notice how that one over there looks like a chick with big breasts? Look at the way the green mold is shaped in circles."

"You're the only person who could get hard looking at mold," I told him.

"Hey, I didn't say I was hard."

I looked at him, but didn't say anything, so he continued.

"Action, man! Aren't you sick of staying around here with your head buried in an engine? We'll take these *indios* and show them who's in charge."

"And you think *you're* in charge?" I asked him.

"I've got this machine, don't I?"

"We're just for show. The real guys will go down in helicopters," I said. "Besides, I don't look forward to fighting on their turf."

"Don't worry, man."

"I'm not worried," I told him.

"You look worried. Anyway, good thing you've got a uniform," he said. "Otherwise, the army might mistake you for one of them *indio* boys."

"Me? What about you? You look more Indian than one of Montezuma's little house boys."

"Watch it man."

I could tell I'd pissed him off. Everyone knew Montezuma kept young boys around for sex. I didn't say anything else. Just let him think about that before he calls me *indio* again.

"Fuck you," he said.

I looked at him again, but I didn't say anything. It wasn't worth talking about. I knew Javier was just sick of being here, like we all were. There wasn't anything more to say. Javier and I made a good team that way because we forgave each other really fast, even after talks like that. Most of the time, he talked and talked and didn't care that I didn't say much back. He knew I wasn't slow, just quiet. Most people think if you're not talking all the time, then you're stupid, but Javier knows I'm not stupid. My silence didn't bother him. Just cause I don't rattle at the mouth all the time doesn't mean I don't think about stuff. I watch and think. If you're talking, you can't be thinking. Silence means I'm busy thinking, which is why I'm good at the mechanics. I pay attention and I think.

Truth is I'm really mad at these *indios*. I was going to get the last of my money and go home, but now the army tells us to get ready because we'll be leaving tomorrow. What do they think, starting up some kind of revolution? Like they're the only ones who suffer, like they're something special we should bow down to? Idiots who think they can make Zapata come back to life. Nothing good will come of it and they'll be as poor as before, and I'll still be stuck here. After more troops fly in from Mexico City, we'll leave these barracks in Tuxtla and head south to Villahermosa and from there to the jungle to fight the guys who call themselves Zapatistas, guys who might as well already be dead.

CHAPTER FIVE
Amy

Silence. Cold. Indian men with guns. Faces hidden behind red bandanas. Quiet talk from the kitchen and then more silence. The fog sank deeper into the valley. The house was clammy and the sweating from fear made her cold. She wished she hadn't left her parka with Christen, but she'd never imagined southern Mexico would be cold. Obviously, she'd been completely unprepared about lots of things; she'd never imagined she'd be stopped by rebels and stuck in this house, either.

Just a few hours earlier, Parker had bent down and woken her before sunrise with a light touch on her arm.

"*Buenos dias, entomologa.*"

"You look like you've been up a while," she said. He was fresh and totally awake despite the early hour.

"I can't sleep much. I like to sit a bit in the mornings."

"Meditation?"

"I guess so."

Definitely a praying mantid, she thought. She liked the fact that she was getting good at pegging people. She stood and stretched. The world was quiet. Outside the sky was just beginning to lighten, but she couldn't see more than twenty feet because her vision was obstructed by fog and the silence thick, as if not even sounds could penetrate. The vibrancy of the day before was gone. No more heat, and the complex, fleshy colors were veiled. There was no more green with shades of black, blue with shades of green, the white-blue-gray of clouds. A dreary, dark morning. She shivered and jumped a few times to warm herself in the cold, heavy air. The place felt different, as if the world had fallen into a heavy sleep and could not wake.

"We'll have coffee when we get back," Parker told her.

Pablo and César helped her load the equipment— insect nets, killing jars, vials and a spotting scope for birds—into the car. They'd driven no more than a hundred meters when she saw dark shapes in the road. Men with guns. Pablo stopped the car. The men approached, spoke, searched them. She couldn't understand what was being said, but the heat started deep within her body and rushed outward and her sweat smelled unfamiliar, the sugary, slightly burnt scent of fear. More words were passed in Spanish. César got back into the car with the bags. It happened quickly, and then as if nothing out of the ordinary were going on, Pablo turned the car around and they returned to the house.

Pablo said, "*Los guerrilleros* have taken over Ocosingo. They told us to come back here and stay. They won't bother us if we don't interfere."

"What are they doing? What do they want?" she asked.

No one answered at first and then Pablo responded. "These are people who don't have anything. They used to have more land, but they've been pushed off by the large cattle farmers. They just want basic stuff to live: running water, electricity, a plot of fertile land."

Back at the house, César and Pablo went to the kitchen and spoke quietly in Spanish over their coffee. Parker nestled into the one chair in the living room to read a scientific article. Everyone seemed relaxed but her. Wanting to be a good scientist, she pulled out her folder of reprints to read about the twenty year decline of North American migratory songbirds, but she couldn't concentrate. Pablo, César and Parker seemed oddly calm despite their having been stopped that morning by rebels with guns. She tried not to let them see her shivers and shakes, but it was hard to control her body. The T-shirt underneath her sweater was damp and so she went to the filthy bathroom to dry off and change.

Now, four hours since they'd been stopped, the fog remained over the valley like a heavy, wet blanket. Parker was still absorbed in his books. César sat at the kitchen table and wrote in a notebook, while Pablo listened to the radio. The world was overcast with silence.

From the kitchen, Pablo said, "I've heard the BBC and the French radio. Both are reporting the Zapatista uprising."

"Parker," she asked quietly, "what are we going to do?" He looked up from the scientific paper.

"Nothing. We sit and we wait for a few poor Tzeltales to die, and then the rest of them will go home and we can work again."

"Tzeltales?" She tried to mimic his pronunciation of the word.

"One of the larger indigenous groups here."

"...be killed?" her voice rose.

"Probably." His eyes met hers. He was serious.

"That's disgusting. How can you talk so casually about it?" she asked him. Now she felt more angry than afraid and the change in emotion made her feel better.

"Because there is nothing I can do about it." When she didn't respond he continued. "Humans are animals. I see it in the sense of competition." He put on a professor voice. "What do you get when you have two species competing for the same resources?"

"Gause's Exclusion Principal, but..."

"Exactly!"

"I don't need a lecture and besides, these are humans! You can be infuriating, do you know that?"

"And humans are animals," he said. "This conflict, every conflict is inevitable with so many people. What else do we expect to happen when we've all crammed ourselves into the same tiny place?"

His reply shocked her. How could he be so callous? She didn't reply and so he continued. "In the last five years, since I've been working in the third world—Central America and Africa..."

"I hate that term," she said. "Third world. There is only one world."

"What would you rather? Developing nations? That's more offensive because it's a euphemism. They're not developing, they're barely surviving, and worse all of the time."

She'd never thought about it that way.

"Pablo," she asked. "What do you call it?"

"Latin America."

"I actually *like* 'third world'," César said. "Our poverty means we're less touched by the greed and decadence of the U.S. and Europe. Third world is otherworldly, reminds me of Tolkin, a seamy underworld. No one can predict us." He laughed and his laugh sounded sordid.

"Anyway," Parker continued, "since I've been spending time in these countries—whatever we call them, I've formed a simple vision of human nature. If you travel and observe, you'll see that in most of the world—Central and South America, Africa, Asia, perhaps seventy percent of all people, spend their days searching for something to eat. From morning to night, they are planting crops, hunting, gathering in forests or city dumps, or trying to find small jobs to make enough money to buy something to eat. When you comprehend the sheer number of people on this earth, who on a daily basis can endeavor to do nothing more than fill their stomachs, a lot of things that happen make more sense."

He might be right, but his relaxed nature made Amy feel like it was the most normal thing in the world to have these Zapatista people with guns outside the house, as if it were normal to imagine people dying. He never mentioned any of this to her in the States when he'd talked about the project.

"Did you have any idea this could happen here? On this trip?"

"No, well, yes. This is Mexico. Anything can happen in Mexico. That's what I mean, and that's why it's such a great place."

His answer didn't reassure her. She felt vulnerable not knowing what was going on, who these people were, what they wanted and how they thought they would get it with guns. She stood and went out the front door to sit on the cement porch. It was damp, but at least she was separated from the men inside. She wanted to be alone. This place wasn't safe. She was confused by Parker. She liked him, was attracted to his energy and his interest in conservation biology, but some of the things he said were obnoxious, and it was infuriating because she didn't really think he believed everything that came out of his mouth. Maybe he was playing devil's advocate, or maybe it was a defense. Either way, she didn't like it.

The trip had been a mistake. Once again, she'd disappointed Christen. She knew that, but felt unable to fix things. The night before she left, her mother worried over the phone.

"Honey, are you sure you need to go?" she'd asked. "I've just never had good vibes about that country."

"Of course she *needs* to go, Carol," her father interrupted on the other extension. "She's a scientist. This is what she's trained to do."

And her father was right. She didn't have a choice. In ambition, she matched him stride for stride. "It's a matter of how you do things: plan and follow through," he had always said.

Christen didn't understand. "For three weeks? There goes New Year's Eve and the semester break."

"Look Christen, I'm not happy about the idea of missing New Year's together, but I have no choice. Don't you see how important this is for me? If I can get this research going, publish my dissertation papers, I'll be in a great position to come up for tenure early."

"I wonder."

"What do you mean by that?"

"I mean you're fixated on this idea of coming up for tenure early and you use it as an excuse for everything."

"What do you mean by that?" she asked him. But she didn't need him to answer. She knew what he was talking about. The abortion. She'd gotten pregnant and when she hadn't even considered keeping the baby, he'd been upset and hurt. She still felt somewhat guilty, but mostly angry.

"You can't understand the need for this trip because you're anti-career," she said.

"And what's career besides societal validation?"

The conversation had ended there, but he *was* anti-career. He was anti-anything that he didn't figure out for himself, and he truly had no need for approval. He worked his coffee shop in the city, could match the philosophy intellectuals word for word, but he didn't feel compelled to do anything with what he knew. It was enough to serve good coffee, read and talk.

* * *

They'd met the year before in his coffee shop, a month after she'd moved to St. Paul. She happened upon the place and entered, attracted by the smell of fresh coffee seeping into the cool air outside. The cafe was dim and empty of customers so she didn't know if it was open for business. There were wood tables and chairs, a sofa and an over-filled bookshelf along one wall. Burlap bags of coffee were stacked on each side of a brass roasting machine in the corner. She saw a tall man with a flop of blond curly hair hanging over his eyes. He was standing behind the counter slowly pouring steaming water through two odd-looking filter contraptions. He heard her steps and looked up over cobalt-blue framed glasses that had slid down his nose, his eyes partly obscured by the flop of his hair. "An experimental subject!"

She approached the counter and he held out two espresso cups to her. "Try a sip of each of these and rate their tastes on a scale of one to five, but take a piece of this bread between sips to clean your palate."

"I thought you only did that with wine." She sipped one coffee, thought for a moment. "A two." She chewed the bread and sipped the other. "Since we're doing the wine thing, I'd say this is more full-bodied. Three point five."

He recorded her answer in a notebook.

"I'm working on producing the perfect cup of coffee. What can I get for you?" he asked.

"How about more number three point five?"

"You're new to the city."

"Do you know every customer?"

"Most," he shrugged. "Why St. Paul?"

"I've got a job at Macalester, teaching biology."

"Aha! You must know statistics then."

"Some. Why?"

"I'm having trouble analyzing these data. I'm trying to figure out which brewing system works best among these four—the single filter, the double filter, the press and the drip. Customers taste and rank them as you did, but I have no idea how to analyze the results."

"I'd have to think about it," she told him. She was impressed. She'd never met anyone who used statistics outside of science.

"So, what kind of biology?"

"Ecology and entomology."

"Cool. I've been reading a lot of biology lately."

"Really! About what?" she asked.

"Here, let's have a coffee." He poured one for her and one for himself and walked them over to a wood table. He reached into his pocket, pulled out a lighter and lit the votive candle. She'd never seen a man do anything so intimate. He was tall, taller than she, and muscular, probably from hauling around bags of coffee beans.

"Actually, the philosophy of biology. The idea of how we define life. What is alive, what is not. I'm reading Schroedinger, Jacques Monod and Schopenhauer."

"I don't know any of those guys," she laughed. "I study the corporeal side of biology, stuff I can see and touch."

"If you're ever interested, a group of us gets together every Thursday night to talk."

She'd spent the next two evenings poring over statistics text books, neglecting lecture preparation, before she figured out the answer to his problem. Three days later she was back at the coffee shop with an answer.

"There is no simple way to analyze those data. You need to collect data on all four techniques at once and have people rank them one through four, with one being the best. Then, you can do a non-parametric test called a Friedman Two-Way Analysis of Variance by Rank, and that will tell you whether one technique consistently results in a better tasting coffee. Does that make sense?"

"No," he said. "Are you saying that all of the data I already collected are useless?

"Essentially. They're too hard to analyze."

"Geez." He looked dejected.

"Welcome to the world of science. Design the experiment and know the statistics *before* you collect data. That's the mantra. I'd be happy to help you do the analysis when you've got data."

A few weeks later, he called her office.

"I've re-done the coffee study," he said. "Are you still willing to help?"

She'd assumed he'd given up trying to compare the different techniques for making the perfect cup of coffee because he hadn't mentioned it anymore when she'd been in the shop. She liked reserve. She liked persistence. She liked him. "Of course."

His computer didn't have the software, so he came to her office at the college and they did the analyses together. After that, she often stopped by mid-afternoon for a cup of "number three point five." He'd serve her, "for my number one scientist." Six months later, they were spending most evenings and nights together.

She doubted her father would like Christen. They were opposites. Christen was smart, intellectual, and a resolute and convincing atheist. He could talk for hours about the contribution of organized religion to human suffering, and he referred to believers as people with "religious issues."

"Doesn't the name Christen mean Christ?" she asked him jokingly.

"Yes. It's a common Swedish name." She saw his body stiffen and could tell questions about his name bothered him.

"So why not call yourself Chris?"

"Because my name is Christen." He hated short-hand. "You cut corners to be practical and things start to deteriorate. That goes for everything—names included."

With coffee, he was fastidious.

"There is a science to a good cup of coffee. I've been experimenting with every step. The type of bean, where it's grown, how it's roasted and ground and the type of machine used to brew. Lately, I've been getting some interesting beans from rustic shade coffee."

"Rustic shade coffee?"

"It's the latest technique. You should know—it's related to conservation. Instead of deforesting the rainforest to grow coffee in pure sun, these trees are planted underneath a canopy of native trees."

"Sounds like an old technique."

"Exactly. They're just starting to use it again. Most of it is grown by cooperative farmers."

* * *

He was right when he said, "You prefer insects to people." Insects excited her in a way people couldn't, and they were more dependable too. They called her to look closely at them and their lives, and their worlds were radical compared to any she knew. Sometimes at night, after a stressful day at work, she'd go to the storage cupboard in her laboratory and pull out a box, choosing among her favorite orders: Phásmida, Mantódea, the praying mantid order, Coleoptera, Hemiptera, and of course, Lepidoptera, the butterflies. She had them arranged by order, family, genus, species. Every family had a separate wooden box and she liked the way they stacked up neatly on the shelves. She would run her fingers over the soft wood before undoing the dainty latch, and then peer inside. She always felt the same sense of wonder. All of those creatures, each one a specimen of a separate species with a separate way of life. Each represented a different alternative, another way to make a living. Specialized mouth parts: jagged mandibles for chewing, sword-like stylets for piercing plant material, or the palps and lapping tongues of flies. The probosces of butterflies and moths coiled up and out like yoyos. In some insect species, life cycles were split between water and land and the two phases looked nothing alike. Exoskeletons, made of waxy, scleritic plates, were such a thin layer, but enough to protect them from the outside world. And insects had evolved flight, the ability to lift off the earth and travel through the air on their own energy. Their cellophane wings were unimaginably intricate, the venation beautiful, and they were better at flying than most birds, save the hummingbirds, but people didn't notice them, their agility, or their complexity. How many more there were supposed to be, out there, in the tropics, undiscovered, unnamed!

Amy loved collecting them, going out into the field and scooping them up with her muslin net from their hideaways in the vegetation. From the net she transferred them to a killing jar and when they were dead, she pinned them into her insect box. Good pinning was critical. She did it as soon as the insects were dead, having learned that if she waited too long, they became brittle, and the hardened exoskeleton would split and crack under the pin. With fresh insects, the exoskeleton resisted, like thin egg shell. Once through the shell, the innards felt like Jell-O. She liked the precision of the process. Hemiptera were pinned through the upper scutellum. Ants were mounted on paper points, and Orthoptera were pinned through the posterior part of the pronotum, just to the right of midline.

* * *

Parker stuck his head out the front door. "Hey, Amy, I'm going crazy cooped up here. We're going to take a walk. Do you want to come?"

"Sure." She liked the idea of a walk. She was tired of sitting, anxious to get out and stretch her legs, and maybe she would see some insects. She went into the house. Parker, César and Pablo were looping binoculars over their necks. She gathered her collecting supplies, and they left from the backdoor of the house, walking away from the road up a small hill. Pablo and César led; Parker was at her side. The world was quiet, as if humans had simply disappeared. She didn't see any people; there were no car or bus sounds and she heard no voices, only the buzzes and hums of insects. The dry grass reached her knees. The sun was still covered with clouds, but the air was thick and sticky. As they climbed the hill, perspiration quickly wet her shirt. There were so many plants she'd never seen before. She stopped at one with bright pink flowers. Parker noticed what she was looking at.

"That's *Lantana*, a really common tropical plant usually found in disturbed areas."

"I was actually looking at the ants and aphids on these flowers."

"Let's see." He moved closer to her. She felt him near; his body gave off heat. "Are the ants eating the aphids?"

"No, they're farming them. Look here." She pointed to the tiny insects clustered at the base of the pink flower.

"Aphids have stylets, little suction mouths, like straws. They pierce into the plant's phloem and suck up sugar, but phloem isn't super rich in nitrogen, so they need to pass tons of it through their guts to get enough nutrients. What comes out the back, the so-called honeydew, is still pretty sweet and the ants lap it up."

"I'd figure the ants would eat them."

"Sometimes they do. Or, if the aphids aren't producing enough honeydew, the ants move them around to different parts of the plant."

"Life at the mercy of the ants."

"Exactly."

"They're so tiny, almost transparent."

"In some species, you can actually see through the female and see an immature baby inside her and another immature baby inside that one. It's so cool! The grandmother carries not only her daughter, but her granddaughter too, and they're parthenogenic, so babies are exact replicas, and they're born alive."

"Amazing. Better than any science fiction, isn't it? Let's go up to those *Acacias*," Parker said, pointing to the top. "I'll show you the ants that live in the thorns I was telling you about."

She looked to where he was pointing and saw a clump of trees with yellowish bark and a canopy of branches all on the same plane. They climbed the knoll. A large bird soared over and Parker, César and Pablo simultaneously lifted their binoculars to their eyes. It must have been something common, because they made no remark. She kept her eyes focused downward hoping to see something new. She listened to the familiar sounds, the buzz of grasshoppers and cicadas, and the rattle of dragonflies, all insects that didn't mind the heat. She needed to be out early in the morning to look for herbivores—katydids and caterpillars avoided moving during the middle of the day. If Parker was right and this whole thing blew over, she would be able to come out in a few days, and maybe she could even begin to collect data to test her indicator hypothesis.

She looked up when she felt Parker's hand grab her arm.

Twenty feet away stood a small man in calf-length pants and bare feet, just on the other side of the top of the hill. In his hands, he held a rifle. Pablo and César stepped backwards so that the four of them formed a line. The buzz of cicadas was loud and annoying, the air suddenly heavier. The man looked more afraid than angry, and she knew that fear was not a good emotion to have when one held a gun. Just then, a large bird flew into view. Parker's eyes locked onto the bird and he followed it with his head. The man flinched at Parker's sudden movement and raised the gun further, nudging at them symbolically with the gun, gesturing that they should return down the hill. They stepped backwards.

"Don't run," Parker said.

"Brilliant idea," she said

The four of them moved quickly back off the hill and headed for the house. By the time they arrived, she was livid, furious with Parker.

"You could have gotten us shot with that pseudo-epileptic move out there!"

He started to laugh. "Pseudo-what?"

"That thing you do whenever you see a bird that isn't obviously a finch. You lock onto it with your eyes and then roll them until you start to lose it in your vision, and then you jerk your neck back and your head follows the bird before anything else on your body moves. It looks like you're having a seizure." She was laughing now, a nervous laugh. Parker laughed harder and they laughed together, unable to stop. Pablo and César stared at them, not sure of the joke, or what they found so funny, especially since Amy had been yelling at Parker a second before.

"Well, it doesn't matter anyway," she told him. "He probably couldn't have shot us with that gun. It's an old make and rusted on the barrel. That model was known to jam a lot, and I'm sure it hasn't been cleaned in while."

"And how do you come by all of this advanced knowledge of guns?"

He was interested, but at that moment, she had no desire to share anything about herself with him. "I'll tell you some other time time. Not that I ever plan to follow you again."

"I didn't know you were following," he said.

"Ugh." An exasperating man. She turned away from him and quickly went out the front door to sit on the stoop again. She wanted to be alone. She was angry at herself. She should have known enough to stay inside, to respect guns, no matter how old they were. Even old, neglected guns could go off, and they usually killed the person holding them. Her father would have been disappointed in her having gone out to walk in this situation, and Parker was so annoying, sometimes, making her laugh at things that weren't funny.

She stood and stepped off the stoop, crossed the gravel driveway and walked under the palm trees. Their trunks were smooth, thickening slightly at their middles, narrowing toward the tops. The leaves all rose from the same place, like an enormous, floppy mop. She imagined the valley she had seen the day before, green and endless, but today she saw nothing but the white of clouds. She looked down and watched for movement in the grass as she strolled toward a sweet-smelling bush with red fruits. When she was almost to the bush, she looked up, froze, turned and rushed back into the house, returning with her net and killing jar.

She readied the light net. The enormous *Morpho,* anticipating danger, beat its wings once and took off. She swung the net. The butterfly's wings beat two more times and it floated out of her reach. She watched it fly, the beauty of its elegant movement canceling out her frustration at having missed. Iridescent blue, a gem under light, the metallic color reflecting off the upper surface of its wings was like a child playing with a magnifying glass in the sunlight. The ventral surface was drab brown, almost invisible in the sky. A flash and it was gone. She hadn't expected it to be so acutely sensitive to changes in air flow, her subtle movements enough to warn it away. How it had moved! Floating rather than flying, like a colored leaf sailing down from a tree, or the undulating flight of a woodpecker, but so much more graceful and controlled, ballerina-like, as if it could hang endlessly, defying gravity, held up by the humid air. She saw another flicker. Could it be, or was it a sunspot on her eye? Yes, the butterfly was turning back and floating down toward her. She readied the net first and then stood motionless, waiting while the creature drifted down and landed on the fruits, closing its wings, becoming brown again. Swoosh. One clean sweep. This time she was deft. She felt the familiar giddy rush of having succeeded, of having caught something so beautiful. There was no comparison to the happiness that came after such a collection, the complete relaxation of every muscle and nerve that had been on edge. She tightened the net so that the butterfly could not move, and then opened it enough to allow her hand inside where she found a light hold on the wings with two fingers. She transferred the butterfly to a large glycine envelope and then to the killing jar. Insects, especially butterflies and moths, needed to be immobilized quickly; otherwise, they flayed themselves against the glass trying desperately to escape captivity, the container, the toxic fumes. Eventually, the thrashing spoiled them and damaged specimens were less valuable, less useful. While the *Morpho* died, she returned to the house for her pinning equipment and insect box.

With two fingers of her left hand, she held the freshly dead and pliable butterfly over the Styrofoam pinning block and exerted pressure on the soft brown body with the pin in her right hand. There was something intensely intimate, almost sensual to the process: the thin pin rolling between her thumb and index finger; the warmth of the butterfly's thorax; the resistance and then acceptance by the dead insect. When the body was properly pinned and positioned at the standard height on the pin, she placed it on the spreading board, pushing the pin into the cork until the base of each wing was even with the upper surface of the top of the board.

She spread the iridescent blue wings over the board. She was careful not to over-extend the wings; she liked to position butterflies so that they looked as if they were flying. She oriented the slender, black antennae to a symmetrical position and studied her work. A magnificent creature, and ow he was hers to care for. A six-inch wingspan of blue sparkling scales. The outer edges of the wings were lined with brown and spotted with a few white circles. Its body, also brown, seemed too small to work such enormous wings. She held out the pinning block and watched how the sunlight, muted by fog, shimmered and reflected off its wings, and she couldn't believe her luck. A species of *Morpho*. She'd seen numerous specimens before, but colors fade in museums, and she never could have imagined how delicately and gracefully they flew. She knew that this one was young because its wings were untattered and every scale shone brightly. Life beat up the older insects so that you could often tell something about their age and experience by looking at them. Sometimes the wings had perfect bird-shaped beak pieces missing, a close encounter with death, or they were tattered from wind and trees. This *Morpho* was young and perfect. At home she would key it out and type a formal label with its scientific name, another with the location, the latitude and longitude of Ocosingo, the date and then finally, her name.

When she began her collection as a child, she only collected insects that were already dead. She hadn't liked the killing part, forcing the unwilling animals into the glass bottle with ethyl acetate, but later she'd become accustomed to it, diverting her eyes while they squirmed. Accepting had been a necessity. The dead specimens she found were often cracked or half-eaten and they had to be relaxed in humid jars before pinning. They never looked quite right. If she killed them herself, she could pin them immediately and manipulate their body parts so that they were life-like and in good positions for identification. Collections were critical for accurate identifications, cross-referencing and for teaching students. And her collection was beautiful. Some of the beetles, the Chrysomelids, shined green; others were purple or iridescent black. The butterflies were like works of art, painted with tiny, exacting brush strokes. If you were not careful and touched the wings, the colors flaked off in scales. She liked the katydids and grasshoppers too. To properly preserve grasshoppers, you pulled out a wing and pinned it open. Many species had brightly colored wings, but you had to open them up to know. Most of the time they just looked like bits and pieces of green hopping in the grass.

She knew the scientific names of all the insects in her collection, even before she looked at the labels. She knew them personally, each representing a separate story. She could remember where and when she'd collected each one. She had collected a beetle in the Passalidae Family, shiny and black with a robust horn pointing forward, from the Air Force base in southern Texas. She'd hunted for years for a Mantispid in the Order Neuroptera, and then found one hiding under a leaf on Fort Huachuca, its raptorial forelegs making most amateurs think it was a Mantodae, a completely unrelated order. The long-horned Cerambycid beetle had red legs, yellow and black wings and antennae that curved back and looped around. Stretched out they were twice as long as the beetle's body. She'd collected a stocky orange and black Chrysomelid in Arizona as well. Insects were her steadfast friends that she could take as her family moved from Air Force base to Air Force base when her father was transferred. Old friends were easier than making new friends. After they moved to Indiana from Fort Huachuca, she could look at her saturnid and immediately she was back in southern Arizona, remembering the day she'd found the moth in Sycamore Canyon. She began to see each move as an opportunity to explore a new habitat and add to her collection.

* * *

She jumped when she felt a hand on her shoulder.

"Amy, are you okay?" It was Pablo. "I was talking to you, but you didn't hear."

"Sorry. I was looking at this *Morpho* butterfly."

"I cooked. Are you hungry?"

"Look at it. It's in the Family Nymphalidae, Subfamily Morphinae, and they're only found in rainforest of tropical Central and South America. There are more than sixty species in the genus *Morpho*. I'm not sure which species this is, but I'll find out when I get home. This one was gorging itself on exudates from that over-ripe fruit on that bush over there, getting drunk on the juices. Do you know that some butterflies and moths never eat as adults? They fatten up on leaves as caterpillars and then make the cocoon. That's what I studied, the caterpillar part, what they eat, what they don't eat, how they escape their predators in that relatively immobile stage, how they deal with all of the nasty plant chemical compounds. Really, though, everything that happens after that is so much more interesting to study. After they leave the chrysalis, life is all about finding a mate and laying more eggs. Of course, many of them do eat, like this one. They've got an extraordinary proboscis that allows them to lap up nectar from the deepest flowers, sort of like *Xylocopid* bees, but even better. Almost like hummingbirds. And look at the way the scales on this butterfly's wings reflect the sun. The integument is put down in a series of layers that refract and interfere with light. This is a male, and it's all to attract a female. I'd always thought that the bright blue wings would make them more vulnerable to predation, all that shimmering must catch the eye of hungry birds. Then when I saw it fly, the iridescence made it almost invisible in the sky, and I thought the reflective blue could be camouflage as well, but aren't these mostly forest species? In the forest, the iridescent blue could never be invisible against all that green. What do you think?"

"Yes, possibly," he said. "Dinner. I have dinner ready. Do you feel okay, Amy?"

"Oh, yes, thank you. I'm coming," she said. She put the *Morpho* away and carried her supplies back into the house. Parker, César and Pablo spoke mostly in Spanish during the meal, but she didn't mind. She was still delighted at having caught the *Morpho*. She relived the sight of it flying, the blue glimmer of its wings against the sky, the incredible luck she'd had to catch it when it returned.

After eating, they watched the news from Mexico City on the fuzzy black and white television. When it was done, Pablo turned off the television, and no one spoke or offered to translate for her.

"What did they say?" she asked.

Pablo glanced her way and seemed embarrassed. "They say nothing about the uprising."

"But you said earlier that it was reported on the BBC," she said.

"In Mexico, the government controls much of the news, especially television," Parker explained.

"But what about the reporters? The newspapers? I don't understand," she said. "You mean they know about this in Europe, but not in Mexico City?"

"They know in Mexico City, just not the general population," Pablo said. "It will probably be in the papers tomorrow. They're less controlled, but since lots of people don't read, the government buys some time by not putting it on the television. This kind of thing happens a lot in Mexico."

"You mean armed rebellions?" she asked.

"No, he means censorship," Parker answered.

"I mean there isn't *any* country where all of the news is reported every day," Pablo said looking at Parker. He placed his hand on her shoulder. "It's okay."

She wanted to call home, but there was no phone at the house. She missed Christen and hoped he wasn't too worried about her. If the world press was reporting the uprising as Pablo said, then Christen would have heard about it, but she couldn't remember if she'd given him the exact location of where she was going. She hoped that he didn't know she was in Ocosingo, in the middle of this rebellion. She went to bed, and despite her fear, she slept deeply, her last thought of the blue butterfly.

* * *

In the morning they gave her thick black coffee, but no food or news. The paucity of sounds, of bird songs, of insects, of people talking was horribly disconcerting.

"Sorry," César told her. "We don't have anything to offer for breakfast."

"It's okay. What is happening?" she asked him, but he only replied with shrugged shoulders.

"Is this common?" she asked.

"Not knowing the future is common in Mexico. The uprising is new, but there has been talk of this group of *guerrilleros* for a while," he told her.

She went to the window and stared into the fog, repressing the urge to cry. There was an intense silence, not a bird song or the buzz of an insect or even the call of a rooster. She hated not knowing what would happen. She saw the *guerrilleros* in olive-green shirts walking along the road. Red bandanas covered their faces, held in place by green baseball caps. She didn't know if she should feel afraid or not, but she did feel afraid. She hated being kept here by people she didn't know, her fate controlled by others. Hours ticked by. She was beginning to hate this country and the Indians and she resented her companions for their unalarmed, almost cynical attitudes. If César and Pablo knew something was going on, then Parker must have also known. He should have told her. Suddenly, she despised her job, which brought her to this wretched place where there were men outside with guns, where she understood nothing.

When she arrived two days ago, her mood had matched the landscape. In her excitement, she felt connected to the richness of greens and blues, the glossy broad leaves, the freshness of misty air mixing with smells of burning wood and the complicated texture of a landscape created from corn stalks in every stage of development. And even yesterday, when she caught the *Morpho*, she knew it was not all in vain. Now, though, she couldn't stand the landscape, the absolute calm and quiet clashed with her emotions, and the opaque fog felt like a giant sponge collecting every insecure and turbulent feeling. The difference between her internal state and the external calm was so stark it felt like an affront, and the endless ability of the fog to absorb and exacerbate her tension was ominous. In just two days she'd gone from professor in Minnesota to neophyte in Chiapas to hostage in this house. She was tired and she wanted to go home. She felt closest to Pablo, and so she asked him.

"Pablo, how can you be so calm? Are we safe?"

"We're safe," he told her.

"How do you know?"

"Because they don't usually harm anyone."

"You mean, they've set up armed roadblocks and taken over the town like this before?"

"No, not exactly like this," he said. "But, you shouldn't worry."

For the first time, she felt a small regret about having had the abortion. She hadn't even considered having the baby.

"Why not?" Christen asked. He wanted children and he wanted this child.

"I'm too young. I need to be set in my career first," she said.

"Ugh."

"Christen, there is time. I'm only twenty-seven."

"My days are flexible. I can do a lot of the care. I should have some say too."

"Do you really believe that?" She was annoyed. He had no right to this decision. It was her body.

"No," he conceded, "but I don't feel like you're even considering what I want."

"That's not true," she said. "I'm not saying no, I'm just saying no for right now."

He didn't understand, or refused to understand. Maybe, she thought, he had sensed it was more than that. She didn't want a baby now, that part was honest, but there was something more. She wasn't sure about him, about them together, but now, in Chiapas in the middle of this mess, she wondered if she'd made the right decision. If she were four months pregnant, as she would have been, she wouldn't have come. She'd be at home working, living with Christen, planning a future. His arms would be around her; he'd be happy; they'd be excited about the baby; she'd be safe.

She felt cold, so she slipped her legs into her sleeping bag in the living room, rested her back against the wall and tried to believe Pablo. She picked up the only book she had been able to find in English, something called *Jubiabá* by a Brazilian writer. The first pages were about a boxing match. Big, sweaty men screamed and yelled while a huge, muscled black man knocked down a large white man. Blood sprayed out in all directions. She pushed the book away from her and closed her eyes tightly. What good could possibly come after an opening like that? She had no desire to read more. She was acutely aware that she must sit and wait without any control over what would happen, as if she were at the mercy of someone else's story, as if she were reading a book and she just had to keep on turning pages to see what came next.

CHAPTER SIX
Chan Nah K'in

I never planned on being a soldier in this war or any other. Circumstances arise. We make choices. The news of this war arrived at the forest years ago—long before other people took note. My mother was not like other Hach Winik people. She wouldn't stay in her father's home. She joined the movement and prepared me to join. We walked away from our forest village years ago. We've been fighting with this group ever since. A woman fighter among men, I am tolerated because people are desperate. We go back sometimes to visit our village, to remind ourselves of our home and to be in the part of the forest we know best, but every time, it's less like home because our people shun us. They don't understand what we are doing.

In the beginning, we went from town to town with Subcomandante Marcos. He told us we could stop the bad changes from coming. We learned we didn't have to run away. We could say no. My mother's father couldn't understand why she wanted to join.

"To keep the forest the way it is," she told him. "To stop the changes."

"Everything always is changing. You know that," he said. "It's best to let the white people fight for us. They have the words. They came here, they learned our language. They wrote books about me, about you. They fought with their white words to get us the forest preserve."

"Father, those white people. They got famous off of your story, set up a little museum about themselves and us in San Cristóbal de las Casas and then they died. It's over."

"They were good people, and they got land for us. Why are you making trouble?" he asked her.

To me she said, "Chan Nah K'in, your grandfather's gods and stories don't work in this new world."

"But, he's right that things do change," I said.

"Of course things change, but not all changes are right for every place; the forest cannot survive the same changes as the highlands."

Our people said she was silly for joining with Tzeltales, who are not smart. She shook her head.

"We walk with two legs, work with two arms and get hungry a lot," she answered. "So do they."

They said she was risking her life by going to meetings with Choles because everyone knows they have bad moods, especially when they drink. She didn't listen to those warnings either.

"Thinking about what is different has kept us apart; now we need to look at what is the same."

My mother became a leader of this new movement made up of a few people from communities around the forest. Tzeltales. Tojolobales. Choles. Tzotziles. She went from village to village and organized meetings. Her passion and words charmed everyone, convincing them of the value of the forest and our rights. People followed her, and I followed her like everyone else. In those days the movement didn't do much. People met in the evenings, got to know one another, learned each other's languages and customs. They talked in quiet voices. They told their stories like secrets.

The Tzeltales said: This is the story of our community. We have lived like slaves, without land, without hope of land. We pooled our money, a little bit from each family, and sent someone to Tuxtla to apply for an *ejido*. We asked the government for our own land to plant corn, beans, squash, but we got no answer. "The forms you filed," they said, "were the wrong ones. You'll have to file again." Then later, "*El Señor* isn't here today. Come back later and he'll hear your case." We waited and waited for an answer. After many years, the answer came. We were told no. No, we could not have land to grow our crops.

At first it was only a few of us who walked from hut to hut in the village, but soon everyone walked with us. Yes, you're right, they said. We work here like slaves. We have rights to land of our own, and so we went to Don José, the owner of the *finca*, and said we claim this land, five hundred hectares for us, the rest is for you. We will no longer live as landless slaves. We felt good and powerful and sure of our success. We walked back to the village to tell the others. The women cooked, the children played and we drank glasses of *aguardiente* to celebrate. For the first time in a long time we felt like men.

The next morning, Don José came with his guards. Big pale men. They didn't say anything. They had guns. They burned our houses, and then they took some of us as prisoners. They shut the local school, turned it into a jail, and kept us there for a month. Day after day we sat on the cold floor like cobs of corn being stored for later. After they let us out, we were silent. We have been silent for a long time, planting our thoughts in the soil.

The Tzotziles said: Our messengers run back and forth. No one sleeps. We are always on guard. When they come, we can only run. What else can we do? They have guns; we do not. The last time we took a new piece of land, they came after us fast, faster than we had expected. There were many of them, nine landowners, some from the state police and maybe forty private guards. We sent someone over to the next village to get help, but it wasn't enough. They too had heard about the arrival of the guns and had already fled into the hills. The guards shot us. The police did nothing. Just like that. Five men died. Five women were left without husbands. Seventeen children fatherless. After that we stayed quiet. Since that day, we have been resting our tongues.

The Choles said: They called us radicals, communists. We didn't know what those fancy words meant. We didn't even care what they meant. We just wanted land to plant our corn. We wanted doctors, too. Our children die, hungry and cold. When one gets sick, we try not to hope. We know the running nose turns into the hot fever and the hot fever turns into the runny *caca* and the runny *caca* kills the child. Death comes quick and often. To lose a child is the fate of every mother, of every father.

One day we made a big protest. We started in one village and marched to town. There were many of us in front of the town hall in Ocosingo. We demanded land and doctors. We threatened them. They said nothing. A few days later, the police came and murdered everyone. Women and children and men shot down like flocks of birds. Since then we have been quiet.

The Tojolabales said: We, too, have asked for land. We have asked for doctors. Nothing ever happens. We live on a tiny scrap of land at the edge of their *finca*. We pick the coffee. We work the cattle. We harvest corn until our hands bleed. We buy what we need in the local store. We know it is more expensive, but town is too far away. They pay us, we pay them, and after that, we are in debt. We work and work, and we always end up owing.

One time we said stop, enough. We went to the owner, and we demanded an increase in our wage. We went on strike. For ten days, we did not work his fields. For ten days, we waited for him to agree. Then they came. The owner and two other men. What could we do? They had guns. The owner watched, his face calm as his men grabbed our women. One man raped while the other stood watching, his gun pointed at our chests. And then it was his turn. The screams of the women were like knives into our souls. We stood helpless and quiet, feeling blood flood our hearts.

My mother, the Hach Winik, listened to the others talk and then she said: Promises. Threats. Promises. Those are your stories. Our story is different. Our ancestors lived in this place, the Lacandón Forest, separated from them since the time that they came, and we have lived separated from you. We always lived here. It was a hard life, but we were used to it. We understood how to live *with* the forest. And then you started coming, pushing into our land. We hated you. You seemed stupid. You didn't know how to use the forest. You cut down too many trees. You planted beans when you should have been planting cassava, corn in the time of tobacco. You worked for the loggers who cut our mahogany and cedar and gave us no money. You planted grass for the cattle farmers who followed the loggers. You moved fast, and the forest shrank. Peccaries disappeared. Deer, agouti, paca, turkey, and monkeys; they all ran away. They're gone. Yes, we hated you. It was only when we came out of the forest, climbed up the canyons to the towns that we could see what was happening. Everyone was being pushed. You people had been pushed out of the valleys up into the hills. You were pushed from the tired land of the hills down into the canyons. From the canyons, you were pushed down again into the forest, into our land. We were all there, squeezing in on each other. After the forest, there is no place else to push and when it is gone, we will die. We see that there is no more room. So now, she told them, we have become like a new baby, big and ready to be born.

After we told our stories we huddled over a map of the world and we saw that Chiapas was like a scorpion's tail at the bottom of Mexico. We understood that we had the power to whip around and sting those who had been stepping on us for so long. We could protect ourselves and fight back. We could make them let go, make them give us what was ours. Realizing that made us angry and the anger gave us the strength to come together, to buy guns and to learn to fight. Anger gave us courage. Yes, first we would free ourselves of them and their hold on us. After that, we knew we must be careful and free ourselves of the anger. If we held onto the anger, it would choke us. We knew we must cough it up. Then we would fill the empty spaces with the parts of our hearts that we cut out before.

* * *

I was little, but I still remember the first time we visited Marcos in his camp. He spoke of a great place called Mexico.

"Where is Mexico?" I asked him.

"Mexico City? It's a long way north of here."

"What is it like?"

"Noisy and filled with bad odors."

"Then why do you say it's a great place?" I asked him.

"I'm talking about the country Mexico, not the capital."

"How far away is that country?"

He didn't answer right away. His face looked like he was remembering something sad, and then he said, "You are Mexico. That country is right here." He tapped my head with his fingers.

"Listen." He pulled me onto his lap. "I'll tell you about someone who wasn't Mexico, even though he lived in the biggest, most important house in the country and for thirty years he told the people what to do. He sold a lot of our land to American businesses and he became very rich. His name was Porfirio Díaz, and he looked a little bit like you." Marcos ran his fingers lightly over my eyes. "His eyes were oval and dark, with long lashes that looked purple in the sunlight. Like yours. His skin was brown, very brown. He thought it made him look indigenous, Indian. He was so unhappy with his brown skin that he hid it. He wore loose white shirts with long sleeves that closed with bright gold buttons around his wrists, and long pants and boots, even in the summer when it was hot. He got very sweaty and smelly." Marcos held the tip of his nose with his fingers, and we laughed. "He wore white gloves to hide his hands, and a scarf around his neck, but there was still a big problem."

"What?"

"His face! What could he do?"

"He could put a piece of cloth over his face to hide it!" I told him.

"*Pues*, that probably would have been the best idea. He was more or less blind anyway, but he didn't do that. No, he decided that he would make it white."

"Make his face white?"

"Yes. From an Indian woman, he bought cream made from special, strong plants. She told him to rub a little bit on his face every night, but he didn't listen. He wasn't patient. The first night he smeared on every bit of that cream until his face was completely covered with it. Only his brown eyes and two holes for his nose peeked out of the white cream. He had to sleep on his back so that it wouldn't rub off. The cream burned like fire, but he was strong and suffered the pain, knowing the worth of being white. In the morning, he ran to wash his face, imagining how soft and white his skin would look, but when he rinsed the cream off, his face was red and burned. Within a couple of days, his cheeks and nose were covered with blisters. He looked terrible! He was so embarrassed, he wouldn't leave his big house, or go to any meetings. After more days, the blisters dried and his skin started to fall off in pieces, like when a snake changes its skin and leaves the old one behind. Underneath his skin was lighter, which made him very happy, you see, because he thought that meant he wasn't an Indian anymore. Really it only meant that he was too scared to be Mexican."

Marcos told me about life in the big city. He said that people there were too tired to change anything. He said that he studied and was a teacher, but then one year, the government killed a lot of students and teachers in a square by the university. After that, everyone was too afraid to work for a better life. He said he realized that things would only come to change if they changed in the rest of Mexico first, so he came here to Chiapas and went to live in the forest with a few others like himself. They told the people they were here to help, that they would live and learn and wait until they were needed. Only most of the city people he came with got tired of waiting. When the women had babies they wanted to raise them in a safer place—the forest gives little food and the rainy season brings illness. The men got to feeling like they were playing a game. Only Marcos stayed. He stayed and was here when we needed him, when we wanted him. Soon after that, he met my mother and she joined with him. Together with other people, they formed a movement. He taught them about the city and Mexico's history, to speak Spanish and how to fight with guns; they taught him how to live in the forest, how to hunt and walk.

My mother was impressed with how fast Marcos learned to speak Tzeltal and Tzotzil. She liked that he listened and thought about everything, and his patience, but she told me that he would never be part of the forest. "He has learned how to walk in the forest and how to survive here, but he does not love the trees. He is not made of the trees. Still, he can help us move people out of the forest and back onto the land they came from. And he speaks well; we need someone who can speak all the languages."

Marcos taught my mother to speak Spanish and then he told her she should go to Ocosingo to learn how to be a nurse. He said they would need someone who knew about medicine. She thought that was a good idea and so we went to live in Ocosingo for three seasons. My mother found a job in a rich woman's house and we lived in a little room off the kitchen. My mother worked six days a week cleaning and cooking. I helped her. The people in the movement had given her a little money and she used that to go to school three nights a week. She studied how to make bandages to stop bleeding, to clean cuts and sew them shut. She studied about all of the things that make us sick and what to do to help people get better.

I went to school too, but she taught me that I must not be noticed. I was not allowed to play with other children and I could not tell people who I was. She said I must keep secret the place that we came from. She said I must prepare myself for the future. She made me practice going for a half day without food, then a whole day and finally two or three days. She taught me to only need to drink a little water, and how to know if my body was getting too thirsty. I learned how to put myself in a costume when I went to school and how to take it off when I came home.

After three rainy seasons, when my mother had finished her medicine course, we returned to camp to live with Marcos. Soon after that, I began to bleed. I was a woman. During the day my mother sent me out to train with the men, mostly Tzeltales and Tzotziles, some Choles, a few Tojolobales. At night she told me stories of my past, her past and her parents' pasts. We are the Hach Winik. The true people.

She said, "Do not forget. The forest must be kept alive. Nothing is more important."

She said, "We have lived in this forest for a long time, before the Tzeltales came here, before the Tzotziles, Tojolabales and Choles, long before the *ladinos* too. We collected cacao, palms, sapodillas and honey. We planted corn, beans, chayote and squash in small gardens. We hunted monkeys and peccaries and ate good meat, and we carved canoes from mahogany trees and fished in the lakes. But now, they have come. They are poor, like us, but they burn through the forest faster than we ever could. There are too many of them. Loggers cut down the mahogany, which is dear to us. Ranchers and cattle push back the farmers and the farmers push us deeper into the forest. The roads have grown big and the forest is now small. We have to help them stop."

She said, "You see, the land they come from is different. It's the kind of land you can be sure of. They live on it a long time without moving around because the soil is deep. The land gives and gives, from grandparents to grandchildren, always the same piece. Only they got pushed off that good land and now they are here, and they don't know that our land is different. In the forest, the soil only goes down a little way. Life is on top and when life leaves an animal, its body is used up right away by something else. Nothing is stored or wasted. Yes, in the forest there are many animals and plants, and they all want the same thing. You must share. You take a little bit at a time, and then move on so that later you can come back. We have to help them learn about coming back."

Those were the stories I grew up on, but now they are stories of the past, not the future. People are understanding that they must pay attention to us because we rose up on the day their agreement, called NAFTA, went into effect. They called it free trade. Marcos said it would not make us freer; it only meant we would be in a smaller prison. He called it the road to death. We didn't care too much about that agreement, but we knew we must act now, before they attacked us again. We couldn't wait any longer.

Just a few months ago we were deep in the forest, practicing to defend ourselves and suddenly the army was there, coming at us through the trees and leaves. They made a lot of noise, otherwise, they might have surprised us. We took up positions and when they shot at us, we shot back. The fighting continued for most of the day while it was light. We retreated deeper into the forest and finally, they stopped following us and left. When we regrouped we realized that we were one less than before. This has always been our fate.

The next day we sent two soldiers back for our *compañero*, and when they found him, they saw something strange. He was lying there, dead on the ground, but at the same time, he was talking to them. He said it was time to do more than defend ourselves. He said if we didn't, we would all end up like him. They were afraid to go near him, but they couldn't leave him either. They told us that when they picked him up, they saw a big scorpion scurry out from underneath his body and run into the brown leaves. They brought him back and told us the story.

My mother said, "The forest has spoken. It is time for us to understand. We must leave the forest and go out to fight.

In the past, like now, they came to us and we died every time. Haven't you noticed? There are no new hoof prints of deer or paca, and all of the old imprints are filled with blood."

My mother said: "The present is a repetition of the past, time cycles, repeats. Back in time, we've been through this war before. To see the future, you must understand the past. We are the Hach Winik and the Hach Winik remember. Our memories go so far back they meet the future. It's hard to explain to those who only live for a short time. It's hard for others to see that time is round like *K'in*, the seasons. You go out, forward into time and for a while it seems straight. It is straight because you can't make out the curves, but if you keep going and keep going in that straight way, you end up back where you started, only it's not exactly the same spot either. You have covered all that ground and the distance changes how you see the first spot. Still, the first time it happens you can hardly believe it. It's only after you've struck out straight many, many times, and ended up in the future at a point in the past that you come to believe that this is how it works. Of course, that is just the way we explain it," she said. "What really happens is you stay in the same spot and time moves through you."

We buried José and then we went to talk to people in the communities. We told them the army had come to us, that we had fought and we told them what had happened to José, his body, and about the scorpion. We told them that they must decide, and that we would wait for their decision. After a few months, when they had discussed it over and over, they told us it was time.

CHAPTER SEVEN
Amy

Like a Fourth of July fireworks show, the noise was organized and intentional. She heard the crackles and sputtering of approaching machine guns. She jumped from her chair in the kitchen and joined Pablo, César and Parker at the living room window, only she couldn't see anything but the palm trees in front of the house and then more green on the hill that dipped down to the road in front of the house.

César said the obvious, *"Compañeros*, the army has arrived."

"You were right," Pablo told him. "They're coming from Villahermosa."

"Oh, thank God!" she uttered, feeling the muscles in her back and shoulders relax. Pablo, César and Parker turned from the window and stared blankly at her. She saw Parker roll his eyes at César. She'd obviously said the wrong thing, but she didn't know why. She was confused by the fact that they didn't seem relieved, as she was reassured by the army's presence because this meant that she could leave this place and return home. She thought of her father, and for the first time in two days, felt some comfort. The gunfire came closer and soon there were three young men running in a crouched position, holding their guns in front of their waists, running up the hill, moving towards the house.

"Don't thank the almighty yet," Parker said. His tone was curt and sarcastic.

She noticed César flinch and shy away from the window, and wondered why he seemed afraid, but there was no time to ask because the soldiers were almost at the front door. She saw that they were dressed in army fatigues, combat helmets strapped below their chins and clips of ammunition decorated

95

their chests. The soldiers approached the front door and she followed Pablo when he went to speak to them. The taller soldier gave orders to the two short men. She couldn't understand what he said, but he sounded confident and in control. The short ones looked hesitant and unsure of themselves. She smiled at them, trying to relate her relief and friendliness, but they didn't smile back. They were working. The tall one took a quick look in the house and then spoke with Pablo for a few minutes.

When they finished speaking, Pablo told her, "Collect your passport. They want us to follow them."

"They suspect we are involved in the uprising because we are American and arrived just before it happened," Parker said.

"That's absurd! I'm sure they will escort us away from here," she answered him.

"My experience," Parker said, "has been that in Latin America whatever you assume will happen is usually closest to the opposite of what will happen."

Parker was being his usual cynical self, she thought. She gathered her money belt with passport and cash from her luggage and followed the others outside. The sun was burning off the morning fog, and the day was heating up. For the first time since the rebellion started, the air felt warm and there was a hint of clearness in the sky.

The gravel driveway gave out to the paved road in front of the house and as soon as she stepped onto the pavement she saw a at least a hundred young privates, each with an M16 assault rifle standing at attention lining the road, on the gasoline station's roof, along the length of the military bus they had ridden in on. The soldiers were small, stocky men. Their faces were dark and young with identical crew cuts hidden under their camouflaged berets. They stood stiff at attention with hard faces, but their eyes moved as she and the others walked by. Pablo made eye contact with them, and nodded hello, but she didn't like the way they looked at her—

two hundred eyes following her—and so she looked away. Waiting for them down the road was a jeep equipped with a heavy-duty machine gun, probably an M60, a belt of blunt head bullets snaked through the gun. In fifth grade a boy, who made fun of her and her insects, told her that those kinds of bullets looked just like his erect penis. He had pictures of a man putting one into a woman, and he told Amy that he might do it someday to her. He didn't scare her, though; he was too stupid to be intimidating, never able to answer the simplest question in class. As long as she kept a cockroach or beetle in her pocket, she was safe. She'd pull it out, shake it in his face and he'd leave her alone. If she chased him with it, he would run. Still, after he told her about his penis, she always thought of the belt of large blunt bullets as penises that had been cut off and loaded. The four men inside the armored jeep stared at her, one was resting his hand over the top of the gun. It was pointed at her.

She knew their artillery at a glance. Her father had taken measures to prepare her. Every Saturday for most of her life, they practiced shooting. At first, she just got to shoot the .22 rifle from a sitting position, but as she grew, she was allowed to shoot everything: M16 assault rifles, Russian AK 47s, heavy duty team fired machine guns, even a M79 grenade launcher once.

"You should know how well this country is defended," her father said. "And I want you to know how to shoot."

They spent the first hour after Saturday breakfast reviewing whatever weapon he had chosen, and then he would quiz her.

"What's this?" he asked.

"M-16 A1 Assault Rifle.

"Operation?"

"Gas operated. Air cooled, hand held, shoulder fired."

"Weight?"

"7.75 pounds."

"Ammunition?

"High velocity 5.56 mm."

"Loading?"

"Magazine fed."

"Clip capacity?"

"20 rounds per clip."

"Right," he said. "The old ones carried 30. Range?"

"500 meters."

"Excellent," he told her.

After the tutorial, they went to the range, taking the M16 he had just explained and his rifles, shotguns, and handguns with them. If the military weapons were too heavy for her, she just watched while he shot.

"Get a sense of the power of the machine," he told her. "Look how it kicks me back. Watch the target." The human form was obliterated, the black body shadow blasted clean through. "I did that on semi-automatic because the gun is more effective at long distances on semi."

"So why even bother to have full automatic?"

"Full automatic is great when you're up close. These new versions can only fire three round bursts on full. With the old models you could fire the whole clip in one burst. It didn't work well because when novice soldiers got scared, they went through their entire clip in one round and then ended up dead while trying to re-load."

They practiced with the .22. She put small, clean bullet-holes into the upper right chest of the target.

"You're good, Amy," her father said.

He was pleased, and so was she. Sometimes they watched popular action movies together and laughed at how the actors got it wrong.

"Look at the way that guy is jerking around," her father said. "The recoil is completely wrong for that weapon!"

And he taught her to respect the gun over the person. "Never try to disarm someone like the heroes do in movies. A trained person shoots on reflex, faster than he can think, and you'll end up dead."

* * *

The soldiers were all looking at her, at her face, her boots, her body, and this, not the guns, made her nervous. They were supposed to be standing at attention, but they didn't seem particularly serious about it. They shouldn't be so relaxed, she thought, letting their heads turn to follow her. They stared at her, moving their eyes up and down her body. She focused lower, not wanting to meet their eyes, and then she became afraid. Her eyes rested on the hands of a soldier who was moving his index finger on and off the trigger on his gun, caressing it, smirking at her all the while.

"You put your finger on the trigger when and *only* when you are absolutely ready to shoot. Not a split second before," she heard her father say.

She looked away. Now she knew something was wrong. These men weren't professional. Playing games with guns was the same thing as playing games with life and death. She heard Parker's comment again about the opposite thing happening and realized he wasn't just being cynical. He was much more experienced in this part of the world, and he was right; things certainly did seem flipped south of the border. Nothing worked as she presumed it would. She had no idea what was happening and felt the heat in her body again. Adrenaline, she thought. Keep watching, she reminded herself. Stay alert. Be ready. But for what?

As they neared the Pemex gasoline station where the army had set up, they walked right next to two soldiers standing on the grassy shoulder of the road above a man in a blue shirt, brown pants and rubber boots. César hesitated and stopped walking, and they all stopped with him. The man was face-down on the ground, neck twisted to one side, cheek in the grass and his hands tied behind his back. There was a bloody cut on his forehead and the skin around the cut was starting to bruise. One soldier held the barrel of his rifle at the man's back. The other had his in the man's face. She couldn't see what their trigger fingers were doing. She looked at César. His jaw muscles were flexed and his right hand was fisted. He was obviously worried about this man. Did he know him? Pablo put a hand on César's shoulder and said something she couldn't understand, and then César reluctantly began to walk down the road again.

They had almost reached the Pemex station when she heard it, the low staccato pound of a helicopter, growling as it approached. It rose over the hillside, as if straight from the earth itself and came toward them at the station. Huge, dark and unstoppable. As the machine hovered, Amy was overcome by the menacing sound. She felt a need to cover her head, to try to protect herself, but all she did was focus on the tremendous noise, wishing it would go away. The helicopter landed briefly and then took off again; men hung out of the open doors like GI Joes in a little boy's play set. As the machine rose, the staccato sounds gave way to one constant hostile noise that shook the air and slammed into the earth, echoing off the ground and the gas station.

A light-skinned middle-aged man came out of the building and walked over to talk to them. His short legs and fat stomach made speed impossible, challenging any attempted image of authority. "No matter what rank," her father said, complaining about one of his fellow upper rank colleagues, "a soldier should be fit. How can you expect novices to aspire to anything if you yourself are slovenly and incapable?" Close up she saw the acne scars covering the man's bulbous face. If the stripes were the same as in the States, he was a sergeant and in charge. He spoke gruffly to Pablo and asked a number of questions. He took their passports and stared for a long time at Parker's and hers, studying each page before he flipped to the next. Pablo showed him some papers. César and Parker said nothing. There seemed to be a problem, but finally it must have been cleared up because Pablo, César and Parker turned to walk back up the paved road to the house. She didn't understand what was said, and they didn't bother to explain anything to her. She followed them. The soldiers stood at attention and stared, but now, the two soldiers at the shoulder of the road and the man on the ground were gone. Pablo, César and Parker walked in silence and so she didn't talk, but when they arrived back to the house, and began to enter the front door, she could no longer resist.

"What happened?" she asked

"They told us to stay in the house and that we are not permitted to leave, " Pablo said.

"Why not?" Their short answers annoyed her. They were rude. Why didn't anyone explain what the sergeant had said? Why didn't they tell her exactly what was going on?

"Because we are not important to them," he told her.

"They made me nervous, the way they looked at me. Soldiers at home don't stare like that."

"They were probably only looking at your boots," Pablo said. "They're good quality. Those guys could never afford them." He seemed angry at her as he said this.

"Are you afraid?" she asked Pablo.

"Yes, now I am," he said. "The military makes lots of mistakes."

She realized she had been wrong. She assumed the military would escort them away and deal with the rebels. She had been afraid of the rebels, but Pablo and César had not been; now they were afraid of the military. Everything *was* backwards.

"What will they do now?" she asked.

"They are looking for local people who might be involved in the uprising," he told her.

"Like that man on the ground?" Suddenly, his being there on the ground, the cut head, made sense. "He was a rebel!"

César, who had been headed toward the kitchen, reared around and all at once he was coming at her, his face twisted with anger. He was on top of her faster than she could think.

He clutched her by the shoulders, pressing his fingers into her skin and bones.

"You are such an idiot!" he yelled. His face was inches from hers and she felt his spit spraying across her face. "That man will be dead soon!"

She flinched, stepped back and tried to get away, but she was pinned by his grasp.

"César!" Parker shouted. He and Pablo rushed toward her. Together they coaxed César's grip off of her.

"César?" Pablo said.

"Sorry," César said. "Shit." And then he went into the bedroom.

"Amy," Pablo said. "Are you okay?"

She nodded.

"I'm sorry," he said. "He didn't mean it. César has had trouble in Mexico City and all of this has gotten to him."

"Trouble?"

"His looks. They're indigenous. The police sometimes pick him up."

"Oh."

"Really, it had nothing to do with you. He was wrong. Are you okay?"

"Oh," she said and excused herself to the bathroom.

In the filthy, tiny bathroom she sat on the toilet without a seat and as soon as she rested her weight, she began to sob. She wrapped her arms around herself and tried to quiet her shaking body. Her lips trembled and the crying came out hard in loud sobs. She stuffed the sleeve of her shirt in her mouth and bit down; she didn't want them to hear her. She realized she had no idea what was happening around her. Tears wet her shirt and even when she tried to stop crying, she didn't succeed. She gained bits of control over herself, only to lose them to a new bout of tears. She felt scared and angry. Instead of fighting César off when he attacked her, she'd reacted like a pill bug, simply rolled in on herself. Why hadn't she defended herself? She wasn't accustomed to being afraid of men, but she'd never been so close to someone as angry as César; no man had ever been mad at her. His anger and force had taken her by surprise and she'd crumpled under the stress. Men on the military bases were tough, but good. They were respectful, never staring at her body or saying anything inappropriate, and no one had ever attacked her.

She was angry with Parker. He must have known more about this situation than he let on. He should have told her, at least given her enough information to decide whether or not she wanted to come. Even if it was a defense mechanism, his cynicism and callous attitude disappointed her. And now César. His assault confused her. She didn't understand what happened, why he reacted like that. She had never been called stupid. She was angry, and her arms and shoulders hurt where he had pressed his fingers into her skin. She kept seeing the image of him coming at her, his face a mask of rage, his body overtaken with furious energy.

She was frustrated and embarrassed that she hadn't fought back; instead she'd acted just like women were expected to act: weak and passive. A pill bug, but she didn't want to be a pill bug, didn't see herself that way. She was tired of them and their macho behavior. She stood, straightened her clothes and wiped her eyes. A pill bug wasn't even an insect; it was a land crustacean. She left the bathroom. César and Pablo were in the kitchen; Parker was reading again in the living room. She spoke from the landing.

"Listen, you guys think *I'm* an idiot, well I'd just like to tell you that you three are the most sexist, pseudo-macho borderline idiots *I've* ever met!"

"What?" Parker said. "Amy..."

She cut him off. "No, you listen. Number one, you invite me to participate in a research project where there are known rebels without ever telling me about them. Two, even though the three of you know I don't speak Spanish, you don't bother to explain a goddamn thing to me so that I have to make guesses and figure it out myself and watch you all smirk at me when I get it wrong. And three, I get attacked by some crazed rebel-supporting ornithologist who happens to also be anti-military and anti-American!"

"I'm sorry, Amy," Parker said. "It was wrong. César didn't mean to....shouldn't have....but we're not sexist."

"Not sexist? What do you call it then?"

"Insensitive. I agree...."

"It's definitely sexist. You guys should look at yourselves strutting around the countryside with binoculars like they were guns, when you know nothing about guns or how to use them. Do you realize how many reams of bullets we just saw? Do you realize how quickly we could be killed by one of those unprofessional kids playing with his trigger finger?"

No one said anything. In that second, she recognized that her real fear was having seen that soldier tease her with his gun and the trigger; her *real* fear came from the realization that the army would not save them.

"I know one thing, if any of you were in *my* world, on a military base or trying to identify insects in a lab, I certainly wouldn't play macho and keep all the important information to myself. I'd fill you in, and not only because I'm sensitive, but because I'm a woman and women don't believe in withholding information for the single purpose of upping their own sense of power, especially not in these kinds of situations. We share, something you're too sexist and insecure, and okay, insensitive to do!"

They stayed quiet, which was just as well. There was nothing they could say to make anything better at this point. She hadn't articulated well why she thought they were sexist; in fact, she'd surprised herself when she'd shouted the word at them. She hadn't thought about it in those terms, it'd just come out that way. Still, in her gut, their behavior did seem sexist even if she couldn't explain why.

For the rest of the day she stationed herself at the window and watched in disbelief as the American-made planes flew over, each with two gray bombs strapped underneath. These weren't jets, just old-makes of bombers, the kind they used when they weren't really afraid of being shot down. The planes circled low over the house, down to the valley, across, and back again, rattling the windows every time they passed. She stood and listened, feeling like a fly in a house buzzing uselessly at a window.

In late afternoon, César made food, and Pablo invited her to eat. "There isn't much, but we won't starve."

"I'm not hungry."

"You need to eat. Look at your arms. There's nothing on them. You'll disappear!"

She tried to be polite, somewhat embarrassed by her outburst, but mostly still angry. She sat at the table and ate a little rice. She avoided looking at César, and he seemed to be avoiding her as well. The atmosphere was like the fog outside. Although it had begun to lift when the military arrived that morning, it had settled back down into the valley.

After dinner, César returned to his room, and Parker to his reading. Pablo stretched out a map of the Americas on the kitchen table and invited her over. His hand rested for a moment on her shoulder.

"Are you okay?"

She nodded.

"Look. The battalion came south from Villahermosa," he moved his finger along a thin red line on the map. "Past Palenque and Agua Azul."

"And where did the Zapatistas come from?" she asked.

"I'm not exactly sure. There are indigenous communities all around here, but from the radio broadcast, it sounds as if they've come from southeast of Ocosingo, up through the canyons from the rainforest."

She looked on the other side of the map and then flipped it over to see the western U.S. and Central America. She glanced at Fort Huachuca in Arizona just north of the border and then let her eyes move down toward Chiapas, to Tuxtla Gutiérrez, San Cristóbal de las Casas, and Ocosingo. To the east were Guatemala, Honduras, Belize. She placed her finger over Ocosingo. This was where she was. Now the U.S. was up instead of Mexico being down. To be here in the world, to have the United States above her was a different feeling. From the vantage point of these people, she thought, the U.S. must seem enormous, powerful, lurking.

* * *

She went to her sleeping bag, unrolled it and climbed in. She was too tired to think of washing her face or brushing her teeth. She closed her eyes, but despite her exhaustion, she couldn't fall asleep. She was lying on her side, facing the wall, when she felt someone next to her. She rolled over and saw that Parker was sitting next to her, his back propped against the wall, his headlamp strapped around his head, his eyes focused on his book. He looked at her briefly and then returned to his book. She turned back to facing the wall. After a few more minutes, he placed his hand on her back, removing it only when he turned a page. She listened to the sound of the pages turning, felt the weight of his arm and fell asleep.

Late into the night, she was awakened by gun shots. They were deliberate, single shots from a pistol or a rifle. One, two, three and then there was silence. Again. And again. Seventeen shots in all. She noticed that Parker was still beside her; he had made a bed next to her and was sleeping on his side, facing away from her. She wondered if he was awake, if he heard the shots. She thought of the airport in Mexico City, of waiting safely for a plane to take her away. She thought of getting off the plane and phoning Christen, until finally, she succumbed to a dreamless sleep.

CHAPTER EIGHT
Pablo

Pablo was the first to rise the next morning. As he rolled from bed, his teeth hurt and he felt an aching in his jaw that reminded him of going to the dentist when he was younger, the throbbing after each tightening of the metal braces in his mouth. His mother had insisted on braces so that his teeth would always be straight, and within months, braces had become part of the school uniform. Practically every boy in his private French school got them that year.

In the kitchen he put the water on for coffee, and rubbed his fingers over his jaw muscles, coaxing them to relax. He opened a window. The air was dense, damp and cool. The world was still asleep, the silence limpid. Except for some isolated shots, the night had also been quiet, without the constant machine gun battering of the other nights. Usually by this time of morning, he'd be hearing roosters calling out the morning, dogs barking for food, tropical kingbirds cawing in the backyard, and cars with mariachi music spilling from their radios as they passed by on the road below. Today there was only silence, this eerie emptiness. As a rule, did silence mean peace or war? Were there rules? The night had done nothing to refresh him. His eyes burned. He was tired.

* * *

Yesterday morning at this time, it had been just as quiet, but then the day had been shattered by helicopters and cracks of gunfire from the east. He was exhausted by it all: the arrival of the military, their march to the PEMEX station, César's attack on Amy and then later, Amy's outburst.

Pablo had been the first to see the black helicopters rise over the small hill to the north and east of the house. One after another, they landed in a pasture below. He stood in the doorway and watched two soldiers, dressed in army green with shiny black boots laced half way up their calves, prowling in the neighbor's yard. They moved quickly and confidently. He heard boots above him and realized there were also men on the roof. His heart picked up speed when the soldiers found a green shirt hanging on the clothes line near the neighbor's house. They looked in the windows of the house, and when no one answered their knocks, they shoved the door open. The house was empty. The soldier with the shirt in his hand came out, saw Pablo and walked toward him.

"Who lives in this house?" He shook the limp and faded shirt at Pablo.

"I don't know," Pablo lied. "We haven't seen anyone there for a long time." Pablo knew the couple had gone to hide, not because they were Zapatistas, but because they were Tzeltal and they knew that looking indigenous was dangerous right now.

The soldiers stared out hard from under their combat helmets. "Who are you? What are you doing here?"

"We are biologists studying birds in this area," Pablo responded.

"Birds?" the soldier asked. With a lift of his head, he pointed at Amy, Parker and César, "Who are those people?"

"Biologists, two Americans, here to study birds," Pablo told him.

"Birds?"

"Yes, birds," Pablo said.

The soldier's eyes lingered on César, moved to Amy and Parker and then he turned his gaze back to Pablo, as if he needed time to assimilate their story and decide what to do. "Come with us. You need to talk to the sergeant. Bring identification."

Down at the station, Pablo explained their research to the sergeant. He showed the sergeant their permits and told him which cattle ranchers they'd been working with.

"I would like permission to leave," Pablo said, "to take the Americans to San Cristóbal, to a safer place."

"Impossible," the sergeant said. "Wait." He took the passports, identifications and permits to another man with a black radio strapped to his back and an enormous antennae wobbling above his head. He left that man and entered the Pemex station. Twenty minutes later, he returned to the group. "You must stay put in the house."

They walked back up the road to the house, without words, each in his own world, but then when Amy started asking questions, César attacked her. César's reaction scared Pablo. He'd never seen César explode like that, didn't think he was capable of losing control so quickly, and Amy's outburst afterwards made Pablo feel guilty. He hadn't given any thought to the fact that she couldn't understand what was going on. Not the language or the military. He knew that in the United States the military wasn't seen or heard. People never had much chance to interact with them and certainly no need to fear them. The military was there to protect them, not kill them. He thought about how it must be for her. He'd never been anywhere where he couldn't understand the language and make himself understood—Europe, the United States, South America, he could always communicate. After the outburst, even though César stayed in his room until dinner, the tension inside the house was palpable, only adding to the distress Pablo already felt with the military outside.

Shooting continued in spurts for the rest of the day in loud crackling noises, some across the valley in the direction of the town of Altamirano, others closer. There were rifle shots, single pistol shots, machine gun shots, and then there was silence. Planes arrived. Pablo was not surprised to see that they were American-made, their old technology still useful here. The planes flew low and mean, swooping over the land. Helicopter blades ripped the air as they landed on the pavement below the house and more soldiers spilled out. Their guns were huge black semi-automatic weapons. Each man carried belts of ammunition across his chest and packs of supplies around his waist. Their eyes were hard, the kind that could take in brutality with ease. Pablo wondered what it was like to run with all of that weight strung over your shoulders, but maybe with one of those guns, you didn't have to run, you just stood and shot.

The noise came and went through the day and continued into the night. Silence and stillness were broken by occasional blasts of machine guns, planes or helicopters and then there was silence again. The transition between the two extremes was abrupt and jarring. At dusk they watched the news on the television from Mexico City. For the first time, the national channels reported the uprising.

"A small faction of radical Indians, calling themselves the National Zapatista Liberation Army has taken over the towns of Ocosingo, Altamirano, Las Margaritas and Los Altos. So far, the uprising has resulted in the death of fifty-five people, mostly armed Zapatistas whose activities have caused a state of terror for the Chiapan people."

That was enough for Pablo. He couldn't bear to listen more because he knew that they wouldn't say anything of substance. There would be no analysis of the situation on the television—that would only come in a few days when the good reporters and editors wrote. He got up slowly, went into the bedroom and got in bed. César followed him shortly. Pablo wondered how they had decided on the number fifty-five. The real number was probably double. A hundred people who would never hear birds returning from the north, smell garbage, feel hunger, or make love again. Just like that. One minute they were alive and then they were dead. He couldn't sleep and he could tell from the sounds next to him that César wasn't sleeping either. They hadn't spoken since César's outburst.

"Are you okay, César?" Pablo asked him. He knew that César was thinking of the *campesino* who had been face-down in the grass when they walked to the Pemex station. He could have been a Zapatista, but he could just as easily have been a poor man who happened to be walking along the road to his plot of land. Pablo suspected that César hadn't told him the worst of what had happened to him in Mexico City.

"He'll be too frightened to speak, so he won't be able to defend himself, and then his silence will give the military reason to suspect him even more," César said. "He could end up dead."

The thought sent a shiver through Pablo's body. "But he might also be let go."

César sighed. "I know."

It was true that whiteness protected and it blinded. Amy didn't understand much, but César shouldn't have jumped on her. She didn't deserve it. She was from up there. She couldn't really know. Pablo couldn't ignore the heaviness inside him, and his emotions moved from fear to anger to hate to boredom. He was afraid for himself, for all of them because he knew how these things could go. It wasn't likely, but they could be casualties of the military's attempt to rid the country of terrorists.

"I can't get over the soldiers," Pablo said. "Such angry eyes. How can you be that young and angry? The two shouldn't go together."

"I think it's an unconscious defense," César said. "The only way they can do what they do. At some level, they know they're part of the powerless class, too, only for a little while, they're given the power of guns. Did you see them? Most of them looked indigenous. Indigenous killing indigenous. That's what this country has come to. I'm going to use this in my film—not the Zapatistas, but this idea of indigenous people killing other indigenous people to better themselves by ridding the world of themselves. Some sort of sickness, like anorexia."

"You should apologize to Amy," Pablo said.

"I know," César said. "But she's such a typical *gringa*. I'm so sick of them."

"I know, but it's not all her fault."

Pablo thought of all the killing in the world. Every other country seemed to have a war going on, and killing was senseless, a way to solve problems that only created more problems. He detested the powerful men in Mexico City who governed this country for the worse, men like his father. These were men who worked long hours every day and made a lot of money, men who understood business and economics, but never thought about how little money their workers received or about how difficult their lives were. Men like his father must know how most people lived, but they didn't think about it. They worked hard and thought they deserved everything they had.

Pablo missed the daily routine of their research. He wanted to walk in the fields, in the *cafetales* and census birds. He wanted to hear songs of catbirds and wrens and warblers. He wanted to scratch marks into his notebook to record their numbers and feel the morning mist on his face.

* * *

Now, as he lifted the whistling kettle from the stove, he heard a voice drifting toward the house. He poured water over the coffee grounds and went to the living room window to look out. The voice was louder here and he could hear a man yelling orders.

"Faster, faster, you pussies," the man yelled. "What's wrong with you?"

Pablo went out onto the front porch and looked down at the road. There were ten soldiers carrying rocks on their shoulders and placing them in the middle of the road. He watched as they ran to the grassy side of the road and came back with big rocks.

"What kind of rock is that?" yelled the man again. "Are you so weak you can't carry anything heavier? Find a bigger one!"

Pablo walked down the driveway to talk with them,

hoping they would see him before they heard him. Something was happening and he wanted to know what it was. A soldier ran back to the grass and traded his rock for a bigger one, returning more slowly this time. He placed it on the road, and with the other rocks, it formed a roadblock across the tarmac. The man in charge saw Pablo and walked over to him.

"What do you want? Can't you tell it is dangerous to be here? You should go back to your house."

"What is going on?" Pablo asked.

"We've received information. We're expecting a large caravan of them to come through here. There is a bus and some trucks, full of them. We'll stop them at this roadblock and attack. The planes are ready to bomb."

Now Pablo was nervous. "Bomb? Here? Our house is *right* here," he told him. "Why don't you let us leave? We have a car, we could drive out." He was getting mad, but trying not to let his anger show.

"No, that is too dangerous. Didn't you just hear me say that there is a caravan of them coming down the road, the same road you want to drive out? You want to be shot?"

"Well, perhaps you could move us to the other side of town, so that we would be away from the fighting here."

"No, that's impossible. There is no time. Don't you see how fast my men are running just to get the roadblock set before they arrive? Go back to your house. Do you have tape? Tape the windows so that the glass doesn't shatter. Stay low. Stay calm. We'll come for you."

Pablo returned to the house with a sour look on his face. The others were awake.

"What's happening?" Amy asked him.

"The military is setting up a roadblock in front of the house," he said. "Supposedly, the Zapatistas are coming and the army is going to bomb."

"Jesus," said Parker.

"Bomb?" asked Amy.

113

"I asked the man in charge to move us, but he refused. We're supposed to tape the windows so that the jolts and vibrations from the bombs don't shatter the glass."

They stood looking at one another, not sure what to say, and then the silence was broken by the sound of airplanes, which were beginning their daily vigil of flying over the valley. The windows rattled and then hummed as the planes flew over.

"I have tape!" Amy said after the first plane had passed. Her happy face seemed forced, or maybe she was truly pleased that she could offer something. Pablo couldn't tell. She went to her bags and came back with rolls of duct tape. She handed them out, but when she offered one to César, he refused and returned to the bedroom. They started taping the windows. Reality, Pablo thought, had become as fragmented as the strips he pulled out and ripped from the roll of duct tape. He smoothed wide pieces of the gray tape onto the glass, first pressing one strip from corner to corner and then crossing that one with another one, at a diagonal. He wanted to believe their doing this meant something, that somehow the duct tape would shield them. His thoughts moved in slow motion, his vision, patchy and obscured by the gray tape, mirrored his emotions. His body was uneasy, nervous and worried. It seemed clear now that no one knew what was happening. Not the military, and probably not the Zapatistas. Still, he pulled, ripped and pressed gray tape onto glass. Big Xs of gray, shiny tape began to cover the windows around the house. He was on his second window when he peered out over the X he had just made, and in the little triangle he saw a caravan of cars and trucks, maybe twenty in all. The vehicles stopped and men got out, but these were not Zapatistas; they were the press. Pablo dropped his roll of tape.

"César!" he called. "*Llegó la prensa.*"

He went out of the house and the others followed him. Down on the pavement, a small crowd of reporters and photographers flitted around the roadblock. All the major networks were there: CNN, NBC, ABC, BBC, the national channels from every Latin American country. The hyperactive reporters and their cacophony of different languages reminded him of a mixed-species flock of birds whose species-specific calls sounded like a noisy, out-of-tune chorus as they travel together through the forest prying insects out of bark and turning over leaves, looking for food. The reporters spied them and ran toward them.

"Who are you? Have you been here since this started?" they asked in unison, in English.

"We're biologists, here to study birds," Pablo answered.

"Birds?" a reporter asked, repeating the English word and elongating the vowel. "Yes, migratory birds," Pablo answered. "We're studying birds that migrate between Chiapas and the United States."

Another reporter joined the group. "What did he say?" he asked the cameraman on his right in Spanish.

"*Están acá para estudiar pájaros,*" he told him.

"*Pájaros?*"

"*Sí, pájaros.*"

Pablo began to explain the migratory bird project, "... it is a collaboration between Mexican ornithologists and those American biologists over there." The reporter looked in the direction Pablo had pointed and saw Parker and Amy.

"Americans? Those are Americans?"

"Yes. Biologists."

The reporter immediately left Pablo, called his cameraman and raced over to Parker and Amy. Pablo joined them. The cameraman lifted his camera onto his shoulder and dropped the extended microphone into Parker's face. In no time it was joined by a slew of other microphones.

The reporter stationed himself in front of Parker. "I'm with CNN, can you tell us what you've seen here?" In his hands, he juggled a tape recorder, notebook, map and pencil in one hand.

"We really haven't seen anything," Parker answered.

The reporter shifted his microphone so that it was in front of Amy. "You, Ms., what have you seen?"

Pablo saw Amy take a step back, and shake her head. The man turned back to Parker. "What do you think of the Zapatista's demands?" a woman reporter asked.

"I haven't thought much about them, really," Parker told her.

"How does it feel to be in the middle of a revolution? Are you afraid?"

"Not particularly. We haven't been threatened in any way."

Pablo repressed a grin. Parker was purposefully making it seem boring. He didn't want to be the token gringo in the midst of a Mexican uprising. Even before the reporter began to thank Parker for his time, Pablo noticed that the cameraman, who was chewing ferociously on gum, had switched off his camera. The reporters lost interest quickly and moved on. Meanwhile, César had been talking with a Mexican reporter, explaining their situation. He returned to Pablo's side next to Parker and Amy.

"I told them that the military wouldn't let us leave," he told Pablo. "We can leave with them after they've gone down into Ocosingo to take pictures. The military won't stop us with the cameras around."

Pablo let out a deep breath and felt the release of pain in his chest.

* * *

Within an hour they were part of a caravan of cars speeding over the deserted tarmac road. Many of the cars had PRENSA written in large white letters on their rear windshields. Most of them were flying white flags tied to their antennas. Their car flew an almost-white insect net. César worked the steering wheel hard to the right, then left, then right, the car cutting fast through heavy air, tires squealing at each curve. Pablo clenched his stomach against the turns to keep his body from being thrown left and right. Blurry green rushed by. For the first time in days, the clouds had lifted and he could feel sun shine on his face.

"Hey, César," he said. "Slow down. I'm pretty sure I don't want to die in this car."

"I know how to drive."

"You won't be saying that when you lose control at a curve and we run off the road and roll all the way back down to Ocosingo."

"I'm just anxious to get out of here."

"Well, you won't be out if you're dead."

César drove a little slower. They'd driven almost thirty kilometers out of Ocosingo when César slowed to a stop. A pine tree had been cut down and now blocked the road. They got out of their cars to look at the tree. The reporters told Pablo that it hadn't been there just a few hours earlier when they first drove by. It was a big tree and heavy, but they thought if they all cooperated they might be able to push it out of the way. The male reporters all lit cigarettes. The women stood together at the shoulder of the road, holding white flags and smoking. The men spoke Spanish loudly, all at once, and pointed at the tree with their cigarettes as they spoke. When they finished smoking, they lined up along the tree trunk. Pablo stood next to Amy, anchored his heels, and when a man called out, *uno, dos, tres* they pushed and grunted in unison. The trunk moved a few feet. Again and again, they pushed and strained, the tree moving a few feet each time. Sweat rolled down Pablo's face and his red palms hurt from pushing against the hard tree. They took a break, wiping the bark from their hands onto their pants and then the sweat from their faces with the backs of their hands, their palms sticky with sap. A few of the reporters lit cigarettes and smoked. Pablo didn't usually smoke, but he took one when it was offered. As he smoked, he noticed a man and woman go back to their car at the end of the caravan. They started the engine and drove to the trunk. Their red Fiat was just small enough to inch through the space that had been liberated on the road, but no one else's car could fit. Everyone stared in disbelief. A reporter bent his arm at the elbow and yelled, "Fuck you!" at the red car, which was speeding away. The group resumed its effort. This time, with anger fueling their muscles, the tree moved considerably further.

Further on César slowed the car once again. They passed a bus, parked haphazardly on the side of the road, its windows shattered and bullet holes strung along one side. Four bodies lay on the grass, like an abandoned scene from some grotesque movie. Pablo looked at them, the men strewn around in the grass and the bus with a bullet-shattered windshield. He wanted to look away, but he could not. He tasted blood and realized he'd bitten the side of his mouth. The taste of blood running down his throat made his mouth produce more saliva and he felt the nausea begin in his stomach. César continued on, picking up speed again, his aggression finding release in the driving. As they neared San Cristóbal de las Casas and he slowed the car again, Pablo saw that enormous red letters EZLN were scrawled on many of the white-washed buildings. The streets were deserted and quiet here too. Closer to Tuxtla Gutiérrez there were tanks rolling slowly and military jeeps racing everywhere. The press caravan passed by the military checkpoints without problem and soon they arrived safely to Tuxtla.

CHAPTER NINE
Chan Nah K'in

Now I sit back and watch them. Through the night we cut and hacked at the tall pine. It fell slowly at first, but then hit the road hard. I can still hear the sound. Death makes a violent tone. Afterwards, there is thick silence. I never imagined war would be so quiet. I am drained from the work and lack of sleep. My breaths are loud, and I am afraid they will hear me down below. Pacho left at sunrise to scout out another tree for tonight, more roadblocks, more sacrifices.

On this hillside, from the crook of this tree, I have a clear view. There are almost thirty of them, mostly men, a few women. The men light cigarettes and shout at one another, moving their arms in wide circles in front of their bodies as they talk. The women clutch white flags and huddle at the side of the road. The cars have *PRENSA* written on their back windows with big white letters. They are the press caravan, armed only with cameras. I suppose they are deciding how to move the tree so that they can return to the city to write the news. I want to tell them that there is no need to fear us. The blockade wasn't for them. It was meant to slow the invasion of our land. I want to call down to them and ask if they took pictures in Ocosingo. When Pacho and I ran away yesterday some people were still there, lying where they had fallen, arms and legs spread in all directions. Others had been taken away, but you could see the part of them that was left, the place marked by dark red stains on the road.

These roadblocks are hard. As we cut into the pine with our machetes, I could feel it resist death. A mute resistance. The outer bark stood firm. It didn't want to give in to the machete, but when we cut in deep, it just fell over, down the hillside and onto the road. Amber-colored sap ran out and covered my hands, warm and sticky. This tree was solid, alive and old. We chopped it anyway.

I try not to think about Álvaro. We were trained to go on, to keep fighting. "There is nothing more to lose," we told each other, but now without Álvaro, it feels different. We left him in Ocosingo. I close my eyes tight to erase thoughts about the moment we left him, about the moment I lost my gun. We were taught that to lose one's gun would mean death. The men will say it's because I am a woman, and women aren't strong enough to fight. The women will say I've proven we can't do it.

The clouds hang low today, but they're not the black kind we have in the forest, the kind that come down fast and bring rain. These are thin gray clouds. No rain falls, still everything is wet. On the road and in the valley below, they are thicker. My vision is caught up in them. Sound, too, so that the shouting below is hushed. It makes the press people sound further away, and that makes me feel safer. But the clouds aren't staying down. They've woken and separated and are floating toward me on this hill, like *pixan*, souls on a walk. I try not to be afraid of them.

I cannot see the forest, but I know it's there. I feel it reaching out to me, pulling me back. I know that land. At home people are collecting corn from the *milpas* now, twisting and pulling the ears. We work in the early morning when the sun is at the tree tops, just beginning to come over, when spider monkeys stretch and yawn and parrots fly from their roosts to the fruit trees. We fill sacks with heavy corn, heave them onto our backs and head for home before the sun is too hot. We sit together and strip husks so that the kernels can dry, always saving some kernels from the best ears to plant again, to give them new life. We care for the corn; it cares for us. We talk and laugh while we work because we know we will not be hungry for a while.

Still, I think of Álvaro. Cold air pushed at us that first night, but we didn't move. We waited on the hill outside of

Ocosingo until Luís, who was stationed in town, came up to tell us time had come. His face was serious. There was no laughing now. In the forest we had teased him as we planned the attack. We'd said he'd go to town for their New Year's celebration and his pretty brown eyes would capture some young *ladino* girl. Once she saw how his feet could dance, he'd be mesmerized forever, forgetting about the revolution, thinking only of a night sweet as ripe mango.

"Fifteen more minutes," Luis told us, "then go down."

Pacho, the only one with a watch, timed it to the minute and then he, Álvaro and I walked down, tying our handkerchiefs around our faces as we went. As planned, we went straight to the municipality building at the end of the plaza. A few people were still there, but they didn't hear us. They were too busy singing and laughing. We broke open the door, and then locked the other two entrances from the inside. It was easy.

While we took over the municipality, other groups of three and four were busy too. One group took over the tiny airport building, another stationed itself at the entrance to town on top of the Pemex gas station, and the third group broke into the radio station. After Luís made his rounds and knew that each group had been successful, he fired two shots. Then we waited.

Morning came late. Alcohol, parties and fog slowed everyone up. When the policemen finally shuffled into work, they must have thought they were still drunk. We stood in their headquarters with three times as many guns as they. It was easy because they weren't silly enough to fight. They gave up their weapons and came inside. We turned on the radio and listened as the group in San Cristóbal de las Casas read what Marcos had written. The policemen told us we were crazy, but we didn't pay attention to them. Word traveled around town and everyone stayed at home. The plaza looked like siesta time on Sunday, peaceful and quiet. In late afternoon, a single airplane flew over the valley.

The second morning was quiet again, but we were more on guard, knowing that yesterday's airplane was theirs. Still, there was no news of us on national radio, other than our own broadcast, which didn't make it past Tuxtla, but we'd been told they were reporting about us in other places in the world. We knew the military would arrive soon, so now the quiet sounded suspicious.

They came from Palenque and from San Cristóbal de las Casas in a blast of power and noise. Our men at the Pemex station saw them first, hundreds of soldiers running toward town. Airplanes, helicopters, tanks, jeeps, so many men and so many guns. From an upstairs window in the municipality building I saw them coming. I ran downstairs to tell the others. The soldiers shot at everything, even a mangy dog. Her belly was grotesquely huge, pregnant with eight or nine pups, and she was trying to get out of the sun, moving slowly across the plaza to the shade on the other side. She fell as soon as the first bullet hit, but they kept shooting her over and over again. In the end, she looked like a bloody rag. We shot back and hit one or two, but more kept on coming. We had to run. We left through the back door and ran along the south wall of the building to the corner. We were standing at the corner of the municipality building trying to decide which way to go when Álvaro was hit on the leg and he couldn't run anymore. I tried to help, but Pacho grabbed my arm and pulled me away. The last time I saw Álvaro, he was coiled on the ground like a frightened snake.

* * *

Down below, only one of the women stands with the men to move the tree. She is tall and pale with arms like twigs and legs that stick out from her short pants like a bird. It would take nothing to break them. Still, I can see when she moves that she is not so weak. She watches the men and when they move toward the tree, she moves too, placing herself next to them. She's taller than most of them. The muscles in her legs get hard and she pushes. From up here, it looks like she is the one pushing the hardest. The other women don't help. They hold little white flags and watch from the edge of the road. That is how we used to be, at the edges watching, but now we are like this bird woman, working with the men.

* * *

Our meetings were held in the dark, usually outside in the village center underneath the stars in the dry season, or cramped into someone's hut when it rained. Men and women came together slowly after work, the men sitting on benches or stools, their wives on the ground by their feet. The men talked and the women listened, but some women talked a little too. Maria was one of those women. One night she arrived and sat on the ground next to a few other women, but it felt particularly cold. She saw an empty stool across the circle, got up, walked over and sat on it. The man who was speaking stopped talking, and that made everyone else look at what she had done. There was a silence.

"Why do we always sit on the ground when it's so cold?" she asked. Just then another woman, Lucia, got up from the ground, pulled her husband's hand and took his place on the chair. "Yes. We should share." You could tell that her husband was troubled. He didn't know whether to protest or accept, and in the end, he didn't say anything. He took a couple of steps back, but he didn't sit down.

"But the earth is feminine, for women," exclaimed one man, and the other men laughed.

"Ah, then we should be more inclined to want to be near it," said Marcos, as he slid from his stool onto the ground.

A woman who had not been brave enough to stand up, chuckled. Her husband stood, grabbed her hand and pulled her away. The next night, we had the first women's meeting. We invited the men, but told them they were not permitted to speak. None of them came. We spoke of everything that bothered us, drunk men, marriages we didn't want, too many children, no chance for school, always the last to eat. I didn't usually say much, but no one had mentioned fighting.

"I want to fight," I told them.

A couple of women laughed at me, but then Maria and some others agreed. They had been thinking the same thing. "If it comes to that, I'll fight with the men," Maria said. That night we decided to make a list of all the things we wanted to change. Because I knew how to write, I was the one who wrote everything down on a piece of paper, and slowly the paper got more and more filled up, so that in the end we had a long list that we called the Zapatista Women's Laws. We presented them at a big meeting. Marcos held up the paper and said, "Nothing will ever be the same for women, or for men. Our cause is stronger."

My mother told me, "Laws on paper are like corn kernels inside the husk. Without people, they can't grow."

Later, we bought guns and learned to use them. The first day, the gun was heavy for my arms. When I held it out and took aim, my hands shook, and I could only hold it up for a few seconds. The harder I grabbed onto the gun, the more it moved. I'd point where they told me, aim like they told me and then force myself to press the trigger. At first that was hard, too. Sometimes the trigger would stick, and my finger would ache so much as I pulled it back that I wanted to cry. I never hit anything. I did everything like they said, but the bullets disappeared into the forest. Shot after shot. I'd press the trigger, my ears would crack with the noise, I'd open my eyes and see the men trying not to look disappointed. "Hold it gently," they said, "like a baby." My mother laughed when I told her what they'd said. "Men don't know. Babies aren't fragile. We can't afford to let them be. How would we get anything done? We sling them on our backs, hold them with one hand and work with the other. Maybe the gun is more like a hoe. If you hold it too hard when you dig, it hurts and bruises your hand. Think of it like a hoe. That way you won't be afraid of it." I went back the next day and held the gun like a hoe. I shot and hit the target.

Now we are fighting for real. We call ourselves the

Ejercito Zapatista de Liberación Nacional, the Zapatista National Liberation Army, after Emiliano Zapata who Marcos said fought this same cause a long time ago. That was supposed to be enough. After Zapata there were laws that said we would have land, but then the government took those laws away again. I don't know how they could do that. I guess my mother was right about laws. Paper and laws don't last. You have to keep writing them down, over and over, making sure there are lots of copies. Otherwise, they get lost or people forget them.

I know I don't belong here. I belong to the forest. Here I smell only grass and cows and people, and right now, I can only smell this dead pine tree. These scents outside the forest are strange and strong. They move too fast, and I can't get a good fix on them. I can't think right. In the forest, scents move slowly in the air, stopping to rest on leaves. They hover around, and you have time to decide what they are and what they mean. I miss the way sunlight moves through the trees and makes dancing patterns on the forest floor. I miss the rich smells of thousands of lives mixing together. And it's too quiet here. This morning, during the time when the sun warms up the spider monkeys, I didn't even hear a rooster. I'm so far from the forest I can't hear life. Without trees and animals, this is a dead world. I want to go back to where it is alive, where I am happy, but my job is to stay here at this tree and watch what happens below. Wait for Pacho, report back and receive more orders.

Look at my hands. They are sore and bloody. Red with my own blood. After we pushed the tree over, I rubbed my hands on my pants, but the sticky sap wouldn't come off. If my hands weren't already cut and bleeding from scraping across bark, I'd simply rub them in the dirt and work the sap off that way, but with these cuts I'm afraid of infection. My mother said once you get an infection, it is hard to make it go away, so I must remain with cut, burning, sticky hands. Human skin against plant skin. The plant wins. Bark cuts easily into the soft flesh. There is not much resistance. Tear away a few layers and you scratch open what lies below. Blistering, breaking, cutting and healing are a constant part of my life now. There is little between living and not living. It is constant work to protect my body from being ripped to pieces. Today this is more true than ever. The planes break the silence and growl above me and I wonder how something so big can fly. What holds them up? Why don't they fall down like everything else that is heavy? I wonder where they will drop the bombs that hang below the wings. They are bad gods, mad gods, come to destroy the earth. Some days, I fight with myself to believe they are real. It seems incredible that someone could want me dead. I have trouble believing.

* * *

At the far edge of the road, where the top of the pine fell, the trunk is higher off the ground than at its base. The press people have managed to push the upper trunk a few feet and now there is a space below. A man and a woman jump into a tiny red car, drive through the space and speed off. The others yell and motion after them, shaking their heads. They go back to the job of moving the trunk. *"Uno, dos, tres, empuje,"* I hear them call. Finally, the trunk has moved enough for the larger cars to fit. The men and women get into their cars and leave. White flags are held out the windows, blowing in the wind. The pine would still block an armored military jeep. Good. Safety for another day. Two men, *campesinos*, come around the corner. They stop at the tree, look it over, and walk on up the road. It is quiet again.

CHAPTER TEN
Mario

Thirty fucking kilometers. We're supposed to walk all the way back down to Ocosingo because they're too busy to pick us up. You know it when you're the last guy. They say go, and you go. They say come, you come. They brought us up this way yesterday to be look-outs, to watch for the caravan of *guerrilleros* that was supposed to come through on its way to Ocosingo. I don't know how they figured it out. I've been in Chiapas for almost two years now and I can say one thing. I don't understand anything here. Not the way the people speak, not the way they act, not even the weather makes sense. I only know I don't like it.

The day before yesterday, reinforcements came from Mexico City, six planes total. The guys in those Mexico City companies were surprised by this rebellion and even excited by the idea of fighting, but the uprising didn't surprise any of us from Tuxtla. We'd already heard that there were rebels in the forest and that some of the Villahermosa guys had fought them a couple of months ago, but we didn't think the rebels would be so stupid to start something big right now.

From Tuxtla we convoyed with the Mexico City guys up the winding road in jeeps and trucks to San Cristóbal de las Casas and then we split into two groups—half stayed there in Cristóbal and the other half of us took the other road north to Villahermosa. From there we went down into Ocosingo past Palenque and Agua Azul. I think if these *guerrilleros* were anywhere between Cristóbal and Ocosingo we would have gotten them already, but the army said they got news that they're coming. I think the sergeants just want to act like they know more than they do, but really I don't think anyone knows what's going on here.

Yesterday Javier and I climbed up the hillside in the late afternoon and sat in the cold pine trees all night and into the morning, freezing our asses off. The night was dark and foggy, and we couldn't even switch off naps because it was too cold to sleep so we just sat together on the wet, sticky needles, shivering, smoking and staring at the dark road below us. They gave us radios and we were supposed to call in when we saw the *guerrilleros* pass by, but we didn't see a *pinche* thing, not until today. This morning we saw the press motorcade, a bunch of reporters whizzing by in shiny cars, windows shut and little white flags tied to their antennae. They passed in a real big hurry, and wound down the road towards Ocosingo. Let them go, I thought. Let them get an eyeful of the mess down there, let them take their pictures, let them figure it out. There mustn't have been much left to see because they didn't stay long, that's for sure. Just a few hours later, here they come, passing us again, heading back to Cristóbal.

After they went by, we picked ourselves up off the ground.

"No use sitting here," Javier said. "They've been down and back. There aren't any *guerrilleros* on this road."

He stood up and I saw him trying to brush the sticky pine needles off his pants. Big mistake. "Shit," he said. "What is this shit made of?" He was staring at the red sap on his hands.

"It has to wear off with time," I tell him.

I don't know what the sap's made of, but whatever it is sticks pretty good. It gets on your hands and doesn't come off—no matter what. He should have known not to try to brush the needles off, but he's from the city and city people don't know much about plants.

So we start walking the thirty kilometers back to Ocosingo. Javier and I walk in silence. Even he's too hungry and pissed off to talk. We walk down the middle of the road, knowing there won't be any more traffic today. My stomach aches. We haven't eaten a thing since they dropped us off yesterday. I keep looking for a farmer, a garden, a house that looks open, anything that might mean food.

"You ever wonder why your stomach never gets used to being hungry?" I ask him.

"What?" he says.

"Well, all the rest of the body gets used to things. You do push-ups every day and your arms get strong. You dig ditches enough and after a while your back doesn't hurt anymore, but I've been hungry for every day of my life, and my stomach never gets used to it."

"Yeh, I never thought about it," Javier says.

"But haven't you ever wondered why?"

"No, guess not."

"I think it's a warning from God," I say.

"Hell. How come there's always God with you?"

"I think it's God's way of reminded us to stay humble."

"Jesus, Mario. You sure come up with some good shit. "

"It makes sense, doesn't it?"

"No."

"Why not?"

"'Cause if I had enough food to eat all the time, I would be thanking God instead of hating him."

"Javier!"

He laughs and I know he just says that sort of thing about God to piss me off. I know he doesn't hate God. No one can really hate God.

The fog hasn't burned off yet. It's quiet and still cold. The sun is slow to come to these parts. The valley stretches out below us, but it's hard to make out anything in particular through the fog; it's just greenish-white and soft, a nice place to head towards. I know better. Javier stops and pulls two cigarettes out of his shirt pocket. He puts both of them in his mouth, lights them and hands me one.

"*No hay apuro*," he says, and takes a slow drag.

"I do the same, and let the smoke fill my lungs, feeling a

little less hungry. He's right. There's no hurry to get back, so we slow down to a stroll. We both know what it's about down there, and we aren't anxious for it. I'm tired of the orders. "Come here! Run this message out to the sergeant across the field. Stay awake, you pussy. Don't you know you've got to be awake to shoot them before they shoot you?"

"Some kind of action, isn't it?"

I grunt in response.

"It's like we're walking in the clouds. Hey, man, maybe this is heaven, only I never thought it'd be this cold."

"At least it's better than the jungle," I tell him. "That was closer to hell."

The first time we were on night duty they sent us out to the jungle at dusk. It was me and Javier and some others. Damn place, full of huge twisted vines climbing up into the trees, dirt and muck piled up on each other so thick you feel it's alive and closing in on you. The air is heavy and too strong. Sweat rolls down your face, clouding and stinging your eyes, and you feel like you're going to drown. Dusk is the worst time to go into the wet jungle. At least at night, when it's dark, you know you aren't going to see anything so you don't expect to see, but at dusk, the light is pink and gray and it plays tricks on you, tricks you into thinking you can see when you can't. You see a small dark man moving, getting ready to attack, and suddenly you realize he isn't there at all. It's just dark leaves moving in the breeze.

That night we went into the jungle as little as possible. It had rained in the afternoon and everything was still dripping. Wet leaves were touching us all over, rubbing against us, soaking our pant legs, making us jump. I stood with the others and we blasted away at the leaves, at the darkness, and then we stopped to listen. I couldn't tell if I'd gotten any. None of us could. Those bastards are too quiet. They don't make a sound, even when they're shot, but we know they're in there because every so often, they shoot back out at us.

During the day, before night duty, we smoke weed. It

makes you more alert and steady. It makes you ready to deal with what happens in the dark. We were standing there in the quiet after shooting off some rounds, just listening for them, when wham! a bullet comes straight out of the darkness and whistles past my ear. It hits the guy behind me. Ding, right smack in the middle of his helmet. He's knocked down good, out cold, but he isn't dead. It must have ricocheted off of something else, a straight bullet would have gone through his helmet, would have killed him quick. When he comes to he's shaking, but he's okay. I'm okay too. Fuck. We were almost dead. There's something about knowing I was that close, and knowing it's not the last time I'll be out here. Knowing I was that close, but God didn't want me yet. Knowing that fucker's aim is just about as good as mine.

* * *

"Hey, look man, there's a couple of sorry ass boys," Javier says. I look up and see two *indios* walking up the side of the road toward us. Small guys with straight hair hanging over their eyes, skinny and dark like the light at end of day. No wonder you can't ever see them in the forest. They're walking slow, looking down, but then one of them glances up and sees us. He reaches over and touches the arm of the other guy, and he must have said something because the other guy looks up too. Then, at the same second, they duck off and split into the grass. Javier and I race after them, but we're slowed up by high weeds and bushes. Javier screams and at the same time, I feel thorns catch and grab my skin, ripping me up, but we keep after them. We can tell that there's something suspicious about them, the way they looked at us and ran when they saw us. Even with the weeds and thorns, we catch up to them pretty quick. I grab one and Javier the other. And now, the way they won't look us in the eye, and the fact that they don't say anything.

Javier yanks them out onto the road. "*Vengan muchachos.* You're coming with us."

"Walk," I order and they begin walking down the road from where they came. After a few steps, Javier stops, and nudges them to stop. He pulls out some twine from his pack and ties their hands behind their backs. He looks at me.

"You can't trust these *pendejos*," he says.

I nod. They look innocent and weak, but if you let your guard down, then wham, they get you. We'll take them back to Ocosingo and let the sergeant deal with them. We continue walking. The sweat stings when it runs into the scratches on my arm. I'm sick of this shit. Funny how a little plant can hurt so much. Seems like all the plants down here scratch, sting or itch. They say some of them could kill you. Who the hell would want to live here?

We've just turned a sharp curve in the road when Javier asks, "What's this?"

I look up and in front of us there is a huge pine tree that has been cut down and lies across the road. Leaves and branches are spread everywhere, and there's the smell of cut wood. The trunk is more than two meters off the ground. It'd take a big jeep, or maybe a tank, to move.

"What the fuck is this?" Javier repeats as he knocks the end of his gun into the back of one of the *indios*, making him stumble forward a few steps, but he doesn't say anything. They don't bother to answer Javier, like they can't hear him talking to them. They just stand there looking down at the ground, like they can't talk.

We stop at the tree. "What the fuck is this?" I ask. "Who did this?" Still they don't answer. One guy shakes his head, like he doesn't know anything, but I know better than that. They all know what's going on. They all know, but none of them will talk, some sort of *indio* loyalty. Well, we'll see how far this loyalty goes. A little pressure, and they'll break. I'm sure of it. Everybody's got a breaking point.

Wham, I knock down the little guy with the butt of my gun. He goes over easy, like there wasn't much holding him up anyway. Fucking sissy. Javier tells the other one to get down and they're both down on the ground, just lying there, not saying a word.

"Who the hell did this?" I scream. I want them to talk. I want them to say something. I don't even care what it is. "Talk," I scream at them again. Seeing me mad gets Javier more pissed off. He kicks one of the guys with his boot, not really hard, but enough to get him to listen or to cry out, but still there is nothing.

"Didn't you hear what he said? Talk, motherfucker, or I'll shoot you." Javier nudges the guy he just kicked with his foot. Neither of them says anything. Javier's face gets darker and redder as he screams. I can feel the cold drops running down my back underneath my shirt, soaking it clean through. I hate that feeling.

"Talk!" yells Javier, and I echo him, kicking into the guy on the ground by my feet. They just lie there, like mute dummies.

Bam! Bam! Javier pulls around his gun and shoots his guy. One short pull of the automatic, and it explodes. Before I know it, my gun has gone off too and I've shot the other one. We stand above them looking at their bodies, at the blood seeping into their clothes. My heart is pounding hard and loud, my hands are vibrating from the gun, and I'm still pissed. I'm so fucking pissed at these mother fucking mutes.

"Fuck," says Javier and pulls out the cigarettes. He lights two and hands me one. We inhale. "Fuck," says Javier again, just breathing the word softly as he exhales. We turn away from the bodies and look out at the quiet green valley below.

CHAPTER ELEVEN
Chan Nah K'in

Silence. I am not used to the lack of sounds. Nights in the forest are dark, but sounds of my *payaso* friends and owls sing through the darkness. During the day, small parrots screech, howler monkeys roar, spider monkeys fly through the trees, and the insects hum, their songs making music with the wind. Here the sharpness between silence and noise keeps me from sleep. Just as I move into the dream world, I am jarred awake by loud choppy sounds that come on fast and are gone even faster. A scary silence remains. In the forest silence also exists, but it's a different kind of silence. Sometimes, in the very middle of night, I am swallowed up in a quietness and I wake from my sleep. It's not harsh, more like soft leaves brushing my arm. I lie in my hammock and let the silent world touch me. I let it feel me. Then it slowly takes me back to the sleeping world.

I must stay alert, but I am so tired right now. We have been busy every minute since the fighting started. I haven't slept in three days. I fight to stay awake, but the heaviness of this pine scent makes me drunk and sleepy. I fight to not feel hungry, to not think about food or water. We trained for this time, the difficulties of war. We knew there would not be food or water and that we'd have to be strong, but imagining is not the same as doing.

I was supposed to learn how not to be afraid of people from the city, but I see now that I am still afraid. I remember when my mother and I went to live in Ocosingo. Everything scared us. There was so much noise from cars and trucks and the sound of hammers and machines, and the place was dirty. It smelled nothing like the forest. In fact, it was hard to smell anything because dust clogged my nose. Pieces of paper and colored plastic, pink and blue, rolled around the dusty streets, but people didn't seem to notice the dirt or the garbage. I was afraid in Ocosingo because they looked at me in a way that made me know I was different. And I was different.

The first day I went to school, my mother brushed my hair and wove two long braids for me. They were heavy and pulled on my head, but she said this way I would look more like the other girls. At school, the children my age knew much more than me. They could hold a pencil and write their names and anything else they wanted to write. They read books and counted numbers. That first day, I sat in my chair and listened to the teacher and tried hard to understand what she was saying in Spanish. I had learned some Spanish with Marcos, but this woman sounded different and she spoke fast. I didn't look up once and at the end of the day, she took me aside and asked me to write my name and read a book, and when she realized I couldn't do these things, she got mad. She asked me where I came from, but I could not tell her so I didn't say anything. She asked me my mother's name, and I said nothing. She asked me where I lived and I realized that I must tell her something. I said we lived with Doña Graciela. The teacher followed me home and spoke with my mother. She was angry because I was big, but I didn't know the things I was supposed to know. My mother didn't care that the woman was mad at her. She told the teacher to put me in a class where I could learn and so I was moved to first grade. I was the big girl with the little children, but really I liked it more. I wasn't so afraid with the little children.

My mother worked and studied a lot; she was always tired and didn't have time to talk with me. I got used to Ocosingo, but I never liked it there. I missed my friends. Even today, now that I'm older, I still don't feel right here; I am too alone. I wish I were in the forest where I could sleep unafraid. I would close my eyes and lose my body for a time. Nothing would weigh me down.

I am with my mother. She says, "Now I will tell you your

story. I tell you so that you will understand why you are pulled toward darkness when you stand at the forest edge." She whispers, "You were born the old way, without pain. It was before the time of outside noises. There were no loud machines cutting down the forest, few planes, no roads, no trucks. You decided to come at the right time, when the moon was still small, which is the best time for birth. I felt you inside wanting to come out. You had already been kicking and pushing for many days, but that day you'd been quiet. My stomach got big and hard. You pressed out and then stopped and then you pressed again. I knew then the time had come. I walked away from the hot sticky air towards the coolness of the forest, past the *milpa,* newly planted with cassava and beans and corn. I walked down the path that followed a stream and I knew it was getting late because I could hear red and green macaws screech as they landed in their nighttime trees. I walked until I found the tree, an enormous ceiba with three strong, smooth roots. They were taller than me where they came out of the trunk and traveled into the dark forest getting smaller all the time until they disappeared under the black soil far away. I made a broom from palm leaves and began to clean the ceiba's roots. I swept spiders and leaves, dirt, ants, beetles and mushrooms. The tree was big and it took a long time to work my way around it, and when I arrived back to the spot where I had begun, I found you there. That is when I knew that life would be different, that you would be a mix of the old that we are losing and the new that we try to ignore. These days, when a woman feels her first pains, she goes to sweep, but there are so few ceiba trees, she may choose a papaya, or a mango tree, and we never find our babies there anymore."

I am awakened by voices below me on the road. The two *campesinos* who passed earlier are back, but now their hands are tied behind their backs and their heads are bent toward the ground. I sit up straighter and peer around the branches to see. Two men dressed in military green, machine guns slung across their shoulders, follow them. My heart bangs against my chest. I wish I had my gun. The military men point to the felled tree and yell in Spanish. "Who did this?" The *campesinos* shake their heads, but do not lift them. I can tell by the way their shoulders curve in that they are very afraid. Again the soldiers yell the question. The *campesinos* don't look up. They know nothing. They are not Zapatistas. One soldier knocks the smaller man with the butt of his gun. He falls and cannot brace himself because his arms are tied behind his back. His chest hits first and then his head. He moans. They order the other man to the ground, face down on the road. The first soldier starts yelling. The men on the ground say nothing. Their mouths fill with dirt and their bodies hurt against the rough road. They are as quiet as the tree, as innocent, and like the tree they offer nothing but mute resistance.

Bam, bam, noise blasts from their guns, first one, then the other. No time to scream. Their bodies jerk, twist, raise up and thump down, but they stay quiet. Blood sprays up and speckles their clothes. Still, they do not yell. What were their last thoughts? I want to believe that the body takes over and you don't have to think anymore. The soldiers light cigarettes. Why did they kill them? I try to imagine how they can kill and then smoke. I can't. I try to believe what I see, but I can't. My stomach jolts, but there is nothing to discard. I taste something bitter, like uncooked cassava, and warm bile trickles out. My stomach feels raw and my throat burns as my stomach cramps and shudders. I hear a woman scream far away. A familiar voice. She screeches and cries. Her screams become louder. She is coming closer, coming towards me. Suddenly, she is above me, behind me, right next to me, but I can't see her. I whip around trying to find her. Quiet! I tell her. You have to hide from the soldiers. Quiet! I tell her, but it's too late. The soldiers have already started up the hillside towards her.

CHAPTER TWELVE
Amy

She heard horns and car engines outside, the sounds of people moving around Tuxtla. Inside the hotel room, the air smelled of diesel fuel and fried food. She was hungry, but she hadn't wanted to go to dinner with Pablo, César and Parker. She didn't want to be around César. She didn't want to be around anyone. Parker said they might see a movie afterwards, but she couldn't imagine sitting through a film. She showered, put on clean clothes and lay on the bed. Being clean felt good.

The day seemed impossible, but she knew she had lived it. Here on a bed in Tuxtla, in the middle of Mexico, she realized that she knew nothing of the forces that ran the world, nothing of these people or this revolution, or of a million other things that might be happening at this very moment. She was as ignorant as any insect she would have sampled from the *Acacia* trees.

She felt pangs of hunger and realized she hadn't eaten all day. In fact, she'd hardly eaten since New Year's Eve. She remembered a plaza close to the hotel; she'd seen it when they checked in. She would find something to eat there. She left the hotel and walked down the poorly-lit street toward the plaza. At the corner there was a kiosk and a café. She didn't want to expend energy trying to communicate with a waiter in a restaurant and she preferred to be alone; a candy bar would do. She stood in line at the kiosk. The plaza was full of people. Tables and chairs from a café spilled out onto the sidewalk. The men drank beer, the women cola. In the dark, underneath a ficus trees, a young couple sat on a bench and kissed. Couples strolled by. There was music playing. No one seemed to be bothered by the war going on just a few miles away, acting as if nothing out of the ordinary was happening. When she approached the kiosk window, she saw a newspaper that said something about the uprising. She bought it and two candy bars. Back in her room, she ate the candy bars and stared at the newspaper. She couldn't understand the words, letters combined in new ways, but she spent time on the article anyway, picking out the words she had heard before. *Neoliberalismo*, NAFTA, *ejidos,* Tzeltales, *criollos, caciques.* What did all those words really mean? She needed to make sense of this. She had to understand. Exhausted and still hungry, she put the paper away, crawled under the sheet, turned out the light, and fell asleep.

* * *

The next morning Pablo drove them to the airport.

"You missed a great love-comedy," Parker said.

"I don't think I could stomach Hollywood humor right now. Too much contrast," she told him. She was anxious to get on the plane, feeling that as soon as she was air born, she'd be safe once again.

"You'll call me next week?" Parker asked Pablo.

"What? You're not coming with us?" she asked Pablo.

"No, I'm going to wait to see what happens."

"There are precious data waiting to be collected," Parker told her.

"You're the comedy act," she said. Parker smiled at her and she couldn't resist smiling back. His sarcasm was infectious.

At the airport, Pablo waited inside with them until their plane was called. When it was time to board, she hugged him goodbye and stood to the side as he hugged César and Parker. They boarded the small plane and she took the window seat. Parker sat next to her. As the plane took off and circled around she looked out at the green valley and mountains and felt regret. Parker looked over her shoulder.

"Not exactly the trip I planned," he said.

"No. Me either."

"Not the trip I would like for us."

139

* * *

After one short plane ride she was even further away from the conflict, removed to safety, on her way home. Since the arrival of the reporters in Ocosingo, time had sped up and she had been quickly removed from danger. *Her* life was somewhere else and, unlike the people in Chiapas, she could leave the poverty and war behind. Still, the fog had followed her so that now, in the airport in Mexico City, she felt as if she were in another world: stylish, rich, modern, but instead of feeling comforted she felt confused. She walked past a newspaper stand and stopped in front of a colored picture of three young indigenous men. The words Chiapas and *guerra* were written in bold letters across the headlines. She bent to look closer at the picture and then straightened quickly. She knew one of the men! She peered down again. He was the boy with the large mole above his eyebrow, the one with the fake rifle, who was part of the group that had stopped them on the first day. In this picture, he was lying on his stomach with other men and their hands, with bloody wrists, were propped limply over their backs. A pool of blood surrounded each man's head. She bent down to look closer at the legend. It read "Mercado. Ocosingo, Chiapas." She recognized the market from the day she went there with Pablo and César. She bought three copies of the paper and a copy of every other newspaper with headlines about the war in Chiapas.

She stuffed the newspapers into the front of her cart and pushed it toward the check-in counter. She felt dizzy and hot and then suddenly full of energy. As she walked along, she noticed the other people in the airport. Women clicked by in high heels, chic clothing, perfect makeup. Other people sat in bars, laughing, smoking and drinking. She wanted to go to them, shake them, yell at them. Didn't they understand what was happening? People were dying. There was a war going on. How could they ignore this? She pushed her cart to the ticket counter to check in. She wanted to sit down as quickly as possible as her legs felt shaky. She couldn't think standing up, and she needed to think. The ticket agent took her ticket, read the name and then looked up, surprised, "Amy Hill?"

"Yes."

"One moment." She typed on the computer keyboard. "Window or aisle?"

"What?" Amy said.

"Would you like a window or an aisle seat?"

"I doesn't matter." Suddenly, things that would have been important a week ago, seemed unimportant now. What could it possibly matter where she sat? She was going home and that, as well as the newspapers clutched under her arm, were all that mattered. The woman printed out the boarding passes, but didn't hand them back.

"There is a gentleman here from the American Embassy who'd like to speak with you," she said. "I'll call him."

A moment later, a man walked swiftly through the door behind the ticket counter, accepted Amy's boarding pass when the agent handed it to him, and came around the counter, a smile on his face. He held out his right hand to Amy, and his left hand rose to squeeze her shoulder.

"Hi, Amy. I'm Simon. I work at the American Embassy in traveler safety. We're so *relieved* you're alright."

"I don't *feel* alright," she said. She relaxed into his physical contact, the first since Parker had placed his hand on her that evening. With his hand on her back, Simon directed her to a café.

"I'm sure you don't. Come. Let's have a coffee, something to eat."

He took charge, seated her at a table, and then went to the counter to order. He was in his early forties, with flecks of gray in his short dark hair. He was beautiful, almost movie-star-like. His skin was golden, but at the same time, in his gray silk shirt, blue tie and conservative-style black jacket, he didn't look like someone who spent time relaxing at the beach with American tourists. She guessed he visited a

141

tanning bed. He returned to the table with coffee and food, and sat down. He looked earnestly at her. "You've been through a couple of rough days, huh?" His eyes were kind. She liked him immediately.

"Yes. It hasn't been fun," she replied, with a nervous laugh. "And it's so odd to finally be here now, away from all of that. We left suddenly and already I'm so far away and this doesn't seem part of that world." She knew she was blathering, but it felt good to talk in English without having to measure her words so that Spanish speakers could understand, and he didn't seem cynical like Parker, so she didn't have to protect herself that way.

"And this." She pulled out the newspaper out and showed him the colored picture of the dead indigenous people. He took the newspaper and stared at the picture for a while. She could tell that he was saddened by the picture.

He reached over and touched her hand. "Tell me what happened."

She began to talk, thankful to have someone to listen, for the opportunity to unburden herself. He was genuinely interested in what had happened, particularly her feelings, and he seemed to understand her trauma.

"We drove down the road and the *guerrilleros* were there," she began.

"Who first noticed the *guerrilleros*?" he asked.

"I think Pablo did."

"Wow, that must have been scary. How did Pablo know that they were *guerrilleros*?"

"I guess it was obvious. They had red bandanas across their faces."

"Did Pablo talk to them?"

"Yes, both Pablo and César talked with them."

"Who is César?"

"Another ornithologist."

"And what did they say to them?" His eyes sparked with interest.

"I don't know. I don't speak Spanish. I know I ought to."
She was embarrassed that she didn't speak Spanish, given
the fact that she was traveling in Mexico.

"Oh, don't worry. I've been here for two years and I
hardly speak it myself," he said. "Do you think he knew
them?"

"Who?"

"Pablo."

"I suppose he could have. Everyone there seems to know
everyone else. I don't know."

She told him about waiting in the house, not knowing
what was going on, but she didn't tell him about the walk
they took. They had been stupid to go out walking in the
middle of something like that and she was embarrassed by it.

"Pablo listened to the short-wave radio," she said. "He
got international stations from France and English and the
U.S. and that was the only way we knew what was
happening."

"Pablo listened to French, English *and* Spanish radio?
He speaks three languages?"

"Amazing, isn't it? I only speak English."

"Yes, it is," he laughed. "Does César also speak those
languages?"

"No. I mean, he speaks some English, more than my
Spanish, but not as well as Pablo."

"Did César listen to the radio?"

"No, well, yes, we all did sometimes."

She told him about the military's arrival and how they
weren't allowed to leave.

"They suspected us! Isn't that absurd?"

"Absolutely, but their military isn't like ours," he told
her.

"I know! The privates didn't seem the least bit
professional, not like at home," she said. "My father is in the
Air Force, so I've spent time around the military, and I can
tell you, I wouldn't feel safe if I lived here with this military."

"Yes, they're not well trained," he said. "Makes you glad to be American, huh?"

"Yes. I guess. I don't know, I mean, of course I am. " She wasn't usually this indecisive in her answers, but she couldn't answer anything for certain right now; what she'd seen and felt and experienced the last few days had shaken her up and she needed time to think about it all again, to decide what she thought. Simon didn't seem to mind her ambiguous answers. He was warm and attentive, and for the few minutes they spoke, Amy was able to relax. She had even begun to think about which insect he might be, but couldn't get a good fix on him. He seemed indescribable. Smart. Kind. Beautiful. Too good to be true. Was he some sort of undiscovered species? The thoughts relaxed her and for the first time in days, she felt a moment of relief.

"Thank you, Amy," he said. "You've been very helpful." He handed over her boarding pass. As he stood to leave, he held out his hand once more for her to shake and placed his other hand on her shoulder. "We're *thankful* no Americans were killed."

The statement was odd, but she ignored it. He must have meant that he was thankful that she wasn't harmed.

* * *

By the time she reached Phoenix her body was shaking uncontrollably. She called Christen's house, but he wasn't there and so she tried the coffee shop, but they said he was out buying supplies. Too tired to talk, she didn't leave a message. Her arms and legs continued to tremble and her teeth knocked together even after she'd boarded her final flight. The flight attendant noticed her, and brought blankets. Amy draped the thin blankets tightly around herself, closed her eyes and tried to sleep, but she couldn't. She kept seeing women carrying wood, barefoot children, boys with bandanas over their faces, army men with suspicious expressions, and especially, the young men whose open eyes swam in pools of blood. She realized that they were murdered. It must have been that night she heard the single gun shots, but she didn't understand why. She thought of the boy with the fake rifle. He was so small, so young and thin. Knowing that she would never be able to forget him, she was absorbed by the memory of his glossy, vacant stare.

Finally, she arrived at St. Paul and took a taxi to her apartment, not even caring about the extra expense. She let herself in, locked the door and then took a long shower. Her only desire was to feel hot water on her body, to wash herself, to be clean. After the shower, she wrapped herself in a blanket and curled up on the couch. She was still shaking and cold even though the room was warm. She was barely asleep when she heard the click of a key in the door, like the setting of a gun, and suddenly she was awakened with fear as Christen walked through the door.

CHAPTER THIRTEEN
Mario

Anything to stop the screaming. I almost shot her to make her shut up, but she quit on her own. And I wouldn't kill a child. Funny how the other two wouldn't talk and this one wouldn't shut up. But when Javier yelled, "Shut up!" she stopped screaming and stared at us with those crazy eyes. We stared back at her in the silence, a silence so sudden it seemed loud. Her dark eyes sat in two deep pockets on her face, half-closed in a wild stare. A black knit hat covered her brow, and below the hat her cheeks were broad. She was small and really skinny.

"Shit. She's just a kid," Javier muttered. "Twelve or thirteen. What the hell is she doing here?"

"Maybe she's one of them?" I asked him.

"Nah, too young, and she doesn't have any kind of weapon." He laughed. "Not even one of those fake guns carved from wood that some of them are carrying around."

I wondered what we should do with her. We couldn't just leave her the way she was. When we'd walked up to her she was bent into a nook in a tree, folded up on herself with her arms clutched hard around her bent legs, like she was holding herself together, and howling all the while. I couldn't figure out how such a loud noise could come out of something so small. When she stopped screaming, she stayed bent like that, shaking and shivering like a scared rabbit. Her eyes had the look animals do when they know you've got them in a perfect line of fire. Paralyzed, just waiting for it to be over. That's what she looked like, but there was something else, too. She was scared, but her eyes were dark and deep. When she looked straight at me with those dark eyes, I felt like she was seeing into me. It wasn't a look you normally get from a kid, more like I feel in church when the priest looks at me.

"Let's just get rid of her. We fucked them and she saw it," Javier said.

"We can't," I said, my eyes still locked on hers.

"Why not? What if she talks?"

"Who would care if she did? I ain't doing no kid," I said.

"Come on, man. I don't want more shit."

"Look how young she is," I said. "She's not going to say anything."

"Well, you know the saying: nits make lice."

"Forget it, Javier, okay?"

"What the fuck! You losing it, man?"

"Jesus. Shut up, Javier."

"Well, then what?"

"It's just that we can't do it. We'll take her back and let them deal with her."

"What the hell is your problem?"

"My problem? My problem is that she looks kinda like my sister," I finally blurted at him.

"Awe, shit," Javier said.

She did. Something about her eyes and her little hands made me think of my sister, Julia. She's five. Skinny legs, bony knees. Number thirteen in the family, the one who broke the spell. Before her came two boys, who were killed. I'm the oldest, and I remember when most of them were born.

The day Julia was born, my mother went about the morning like always. She was big with the baby, but still strong. The night before I'd heard her up and walking around, sweeping out the kitchen, shucking corn into water. By the time I got up at sunrise, she was grinding corn for tortillas. After she got the *masa* done she wrapped it in a damp towel, then she boiled some water with a knife in it, and told me to watch over the little ones for a while. She let down the curtain when she went into her room. I thought maybe she was sick because she never sleeps in the mornings, but she didn't seem sick. After a little while, she came out again, and said, "Go see your new sister."

I went into her room. Wrapped up in the blankets on the floor was a baby. Only her face showed. She looked at me. Her eyes were glassy and dark. She was so tiny. I got this feeling that she liked me. When I went back out to the kitchen, my mother was rolling and cooking tortillas.

"What's her name?" I asked her.

"*Si Dios quiere*, we'll call her Julia."

All in all we were thirteen. Eleven of us are still in this world. The two before Julia were killed, but Julia was strong and the spell didn't work. The spell happened because of a woman who was jealous of my mother, jealous because God had given my mother so many children, and she didn't have even one. So she went to visit another woman, who we all know is a *bruja*, and the *bruja* put a curse on my mother so that her next two babies got sick after they came. My mother cried and prayed for each one, but when she gave them the breast, her milk spilled out of them as fast as they sucked it in. When they were too weak to suck, she knew it was over and started to cry. They shriveled up like old men and after that, they died pretty quick. My mother mourned for a long time, but she knew God would take care of it. He would punish the woman and the witch too. When Julia came, her soul was so strong, the *bruja* couldn't do anything about it.

The day after Julia was born, the *bruja* sent a cat to our house. The cat was pure white; from head to tail there wasn't a speck of color on it and its eyes were see-through blue. That cat was full of black magic bad luck. We could tell it was possessed by the way it crouched down in the dirt yard, then stood and turned in circles and then crouched again some more and watched us with those mean blue eyes. My mother screamed for me to get Julia as soon as she saw the cat. I picked up Julia while my mother went crazy trying to kill the cat. She chased it around the yard with a stick, screaming for it to go away. The cat acted afraid and crouched lower whenever she got close, but instead of running away, it just jumped to one side or another. There was no way my mother was going to catch that cat. Pretty soon Julia started to cry really loud, and so my mother came inside and took her from my arms. She went back outside and held Julia out to the cat. "You can't have this one!" she screeched. The cat looked at her with wild, blue eyes, sat back on its haunches and then lay down and died. Just like that. We thought it was faking dead, but after it didn't get up for a long time, I went over and saw that it was really dead. I went to pick it up, but my mother screamed for me not to touch it. She told me to go get the priest. I walked the hour it takes to get to the church, but when I got there they told me the priest had gone to another town, so I had to wait for him to return. When he came back the next day, I explained to him what happened; he didn't want to come, but when I told him about Julia just being born and the other two dying, he understood how important it was. By the time I got back to our house with the priest, that white cat had been lying there almost two days, and it didn't look so white or scary anymore, not with the black flies buzzing around. The priest called all of us out to the yard and we stood while he said some prayers that took all the bad away from the cat. When he was done, he said some more prayers for us and for Julia, and then he told me that I could bury the cat. We haven't had any more trouble since then.

* * *

"Let's get walking then," Javier said. He motioned for her to get up, but she stayed crouched against the tree. He told her again, but it was like she couldn't hear him, so he pulled her up. She stood and I could see that her pants were wet and there was a sour smell coming from her.

"Shit. She peed her pants like a baby." Javier lit a cigarette and didn't bother to offer me one.

After Javier pulled her up, she obeyed. We got back down

to the road and started walking again down towards Ocosingo. Her eyes kept that weird glassy look, almost dead. She stared out and walked, and it seemed like she was in a trance. Her head bobbed up and down as her legs wobbled. At least she's got a hat, I thought, which is more than we have. I felt the thick, white mist more now and it was cold. Cold and wet. I hoped the sun would burn off the fog soon. I wasn't walking too good either. It was getting to me. The cold night, the wet morning, the two motherfuckers, and this girl. I was so damn hungry, too. For a while I thought about what I might eat. I thought about a nice piece of chicken and some warm tortillas, but all we ever got these days was dried, tough horsemeat. Even that would be okay right now. Just thinking of food got the juices going and my stomach started aching and begging too much. I tried to think about something else.

Her eyes reminded me of my father's before the last time he went to *el otro lado,* to the other side. He'd had a bad trip the time before that. Seems like he forgot about it while he was up there in the U.S., but when he came back to spend time with us, he started to talk. I don't think he'd talked to anyone for the ten months he'd been up there because when he came home, he kept talking and talking, mostly telling us about the last time he crossed over.

He'd taken the bus to Mexico City, and from there another bus further north to Chihuahua. That's where he always met the *coyote* who helped him across. Usually they went from Chihuahua to Ciudad Juarez, right on the border, and he'd cross over by train, hidden in a car. Only something had gone wrong, and the train wasn't possible anymore, but the *coyote* said it was alright because there was another way.

There were two other men going, so with my father they were three. The *coyote* told them there'd be food and water along the way. It would take two days and they'd have to walk the second day at night. The *coyote* had a priest's robe and he wanted my father to wear it, saying if someone saw them, they'd be less suspicious of two guys traveling with a priest, but my father wouldn't put it on. "Those clothes are sacred. It would be a mockery," he said. One of the other guys said he'd wear it.

The *coyote* drove them northeast of Chihuahua and left them in the desert. He unloaded their supplies, three small bundles of food, three large jugs of water, a flashlight and a compass. He showed them how to use the compass, saying the needle should point northeast, and he told them if they kept walking like that, they'd find food and water along the way. They paid him and he got in his car and drove away.

The other two laughed as one man put on the robe and collar and the other man helped him, but my father still didn't think it was a good idea to wear it, and he told them. They laughed at him for not seeing how funny it was. They walked together, but didn't talk much, not only because they didn't know each other, but because no one was happy to be going back. There was no choice but to go. They knew that much, so with each step they hardened themselves for another ten or eleven months of loneliness, of being quiet and staying in the shadows, of trying to remain unseen in the gringo world.

The three men walked through the desert. "A thirsty place that drinks from you all of the time," my father had said. There wasn't much there, white dirt hard as cement, prickly cacti and thorny bushes. The sky was deep blue and very far away. Everything looked white in the light. He could tell other men had crossed this way because the trail was marked by little piles of rocks and arrows carved into small trees. Like the *coyote* said, they found food and water along the way, some nuts and raisins, left by who knows who. They walked the whole day under the burning sun. Thirst scratched at their throats and tongues and they drank too much from their water jugs. At dusk the sun was soft and that felt good, but they were still thirsty and tired. They walked toward a thicker bunch of small trees with tiny leaves, and decided to stop for the night. They lay down and slept, and then like the *coyote* had told them, they stayed in the trees all the next day until evening time, only starting to walk again when it was dusk. They had to cross the border at night.

They walked through dusk and into the dark. When they stopped to rest my father took the flashlight and went into some trees to pee. He found a spot, turned off the light and opened his pants. Everything was quiet and when he looked up he saw that the sky was huge, dotted with more stars than he'd ever seen, more than he could count, single stars, clusters of stars. He said he never knew the sky was so big, or so beautiful. It held him and he stayed looking up, not thinking anything at all. He didn't know how long he'd been staring up, but suddenly, it was like he woke up and he felt he'd been standing like that for a long time. He turned away from the sky. When walked back to where he had left the other two men, they were gone. A breeze picked up and he felt cold air on his arms. He was wet, sweaty. He thought they'd left him, but then he saw the water and food, and he still had the compass. He called out to them. No answer. He told himself that they were playing a joke, so he tried to laugh a little, but even as he called out again to them, he knew they wouldn't hear. They had disappeared. His lips began trembling and his teeth clicked together, so he sat down and tried to think. He told himself that he shouldn't panic, but he felt a rushing in him and he had no way to stop it. He decided to wait for light. Maybe they'd walked off while he'd been in the trees and gotten lost. In the morning, he'd find them and they could cross over the next night, and it would be over. He lay down on the ground and listened to the night too afraid to let himself fall asleep, but he must have slept because when he opened his eyes, the sky was beginning to lighten. He looked around. There were groups of small trees and not much in between. White rocks, sandy dirt, a few dried up leaves. No tracks. Not a single footprint. It didn't look like the same place he'd been the night before, but it had to be. All of their things, the food, the water, were still here. He walked five minutes in each direction, afraid to go much further, but there was no sign of the two men. He was alone and they were gone. Again he waited for dusk. When it came, he continued on. There was no choice. There wasn't much water left and he was afraid of this place. Something was wrong. It was the robe. He'd never liked the idea of the priest's robe.

After he told us the story a few times he seemed okay, but when it came close to the time for him to go back, he started to get funny. He quit talking. He couldn't sleep. His eyes got a glassy look, and he seemed more dead than alive. He was still like that when he left to meet the *coyote*. After he crossed, we got money for two months, and then all of the sudden the money stopped. They said he died of a sickness with a complicated name, but we knew it was the robe. He died of fear.

I don't miss him like my mother does. I never saw him anyway. He was gone eleven months out of every year and home for only a month. I know he didn't like it much up there. He didn't talk about it like Domingo does. He never got lucky like Domingo. He didn't have a car or any extra money. He said people were cold and mean to Mexicans and that everything was confusing because he couldn't learn to speak their language. He told me he had tried, but it was too hard. The words felt funny in his mouth and when he tried to spit them out, they didn't sound right. No one understood him. He said work days were long and he was tired all of the time. He said he lived thinking of home. I guess I'm glad that he doesn't have to go back there anymore, but I miss the money he sent. It was enough to help us buy food and clothes and I was going to finish high school.

* * *

Thirty kilometers is pretty far, especially without food, but at least up here the air is better, thinner, and we walk on asphalt. Down there, in the jungle, it's hot and sticky and cold all at the same time. Down there you don't walk, you

153

drag yourself forward through the muck. Red and sticky, like pine sap, but worse, too. It holds you back. Slurp. Slurp. The mud sucks you in. It tries to keep you down. I don't want to go back there. I want to stay where I can see what's behind me and where I'm going. It's colder up here, though. It's like you can't win in this damn place. It's either too hot and heavy or too cold, wet everywhere all of the time. And never enough to eat. Chiapas is all fucked up. It's like everything got turned up side down, and now they can't set it right. No one can make it right.

CHAPTER FOURTEEN
Pablo

Pablo called home to Mexico City. It was the middle of the day. Siesta time. His mother answered the phone and then called his father to pick up as well. She cried. She had imagined the worst.

"You must come home," his father said.

"There really isn't any danger. I don't know what you're hearing in the news, but it's fine. I'm still working with Parker."

"You shouldn't be there while a bunch of crazy men in ski masks try to hold up the country," his father said. "It's nuts."

"They're not nuts, *papá*; they just want a better life," Pablo said.

"That is ridiculous, Pablo," his father said. "Armed rebellion is no way to get anything done. We're not living in the past. This isn't the era of *caudillos* and Pancho Villa!"

"Well, they're destitute and desperate."

"They can't be too desperate—somehow they got enough money to buy machine guns. Obviously, they're working with drug money, part of the Colombian FARC."

"I haven't seen many machine guns. I think what they really want is for the government to respect the laws and the constitution."

"Pablo," his father said. "There are laws, like the constitution and they're important, but there is also reality, and that is more important."

Pablo disagreed. He thought this uprising was something new, with potential. Their leader was eloquent, articulate, passionate. His father had no idea how much the people in Chiapas suffered.

"In any case, I still have work to do."

"Whatever you're doing there, you can do in Mexico City. I'm sending the company plane and I expect you to be at the Tuxtla airport. Call me at ten tomorrow morning and I will tell you when it's due to arrive."

Pablo had never defied his father so blatantly, but he was twenty-five, an adult, and he didn't want to leave. He thought about going to fight with the Zapatistas. The thought came to him in a flash and he felt the hair on his arms stand up. He would be doing something good. The idea thrilled him. He admired the man they called subcomandante Marcos who had been sending out press releases, which had been read on the radio over the past few days. He was eloquent and poetic, and what he said rang true. Marcos had given these people the right to fight for a better life, but Pablo knew he'd be a useless fighter. He couldn't carry a gun, and he didn't know anything about shooting or fighting or how to live in the forest. He didn't even speak Tzeltal or Tzotzil. Still, he knew he couldn't leave. He wouldn't leave. There might be something he could do to help this movement. They will teach me and I will learn, he thought. I'll live with no possessions, live in nature, be part of the Earth. I will no longer be someone feeling sorry for the poor, I will live poor and fight poor. I'm tired of my father always deciding for me, telling me what to do. I can't go back to that.

"Listen, *papá*, don't send the plane because I won't be there to meet it." His father knew the threat was real because instead of arguing, he had simply hung up the phone. Pablo talked to his mother for a few more minutes and reassured her.

"Pablo, you are making us worry. Will you at least call again tomorrow?"

"Yes, I'll call again when I can. In a few days."

"And you won't stay any longer than necessary in Chiapas?"

"No, I won't stay longer than necessary."

"You will be in San Cristóbal de las Casas, right? Promise me you won't go back to Ocosingo."

"No, *mamá*, I won't go back to Ocosingo."

"*Te amo, hijo.*"

"*Si, mamá.* I know you love me. *Mamá*, I love you too. Goodbye." He heard the click of her phone. He stood there for another second listening to the hum, listening as his promises went dead on the line, and then he hung up.

* * *

Pablo drove the car back to Ocosingo, in part to retrieve the hidden computer, but also because he wanted to see what was going on. Parker hadn't wanted to lose anything, and so before leaving, he and César had dug a hole in the back yard and buried the computer and copies of disks with data. They had been afraid to take the computer out of Ocosingo when they left because the military had a history of taking advantage of chaotic situations to rob people, but they also knew that if they left it at the house, it would be stolen. Pablo planned on getting the disks and mailing them to Parker in the States, and storing the computer at a friend's house in Ocosingo, but he knew he couldn't return to Mexico City just yet.

His was the only car on the incessantly curving road. He pulled the wheel left, right and then left again. There were no planes or helicopters in the air. All of the days had been like this since it started, quiet during the day with a complete lack of normal rural sounds, and then at night, the fighting again. Shots. Blasts. The drone of planes and then silence again.

The only person he saw on the four hour drive was a dead man lying next to the shot-up bus thirty kilometers outside of San Cristóbal de las Casas, the same bus he,

Parker, Amy and César had passed on their way to Tuxtla. Without thinking, he stopped the car at the edge of the road and got out. He walked toward the man, but before he arrived at the body, the smell of decay overpowered him and he turned away. When he had passed the bus three days ago, on the 4th, there were four dead men. He wondered where the three had been taken and why this man was still here. Taking a breath and holding it, he turned back to look at the man. He stepped closer. This was the first dead person Pablo had ever seen up close, and he didn't know what to think. He had dissected countless birds. As a boy he hunted them with a sling-shot from their wire perches in the city and opened up every one that he managed to fell. Later at the university, he and his classmates scavenged for freshly dead dogs, rats, cats, pigs and chickens to dissect for anatomy class. Dead animals were opportunities to study for real as opposed to only seeing things in textbooks. This was different. This man looked real and unreal at the same time. Passive, resigned, but not peaceful. Pablo turned his head away, took another breath and then looked back again. The man's skin was greenish and his body was swollen fat. The tight skin had cracked open on his fingers and toes. Flies jockied for spots, buzzing up and landing again, lapping at yellow juices as they oozed out, before they dried. Spots of blood had soaked through his shirt on his chest and stained one place on his pant leg. Pablo didn't want to look at him, but he couldn't help it. The man looked empty. Pablo knew that there had been fighting and that people were being killed, but so far, it had all been hidden in the forest, or obscured by the darkness of night.

He returned to the car, got inside and took a couple of deep breaths to settle himself. The foul odor remained in his nostrils, making him queasy. Perhaps he should do something with the body, but what? There was no one to call for help, but he was sickened by the thought of simply leaving the man to rot. His hands shook slightly; suddenly, he felt claustrophobic and he was overcome with the urge to flee.

He started the engine, rolled down the car window and drove back onto the road. He would try to contact someone to come for the body from Ocosingo.

By the time he neared Ocosingo, heavy afternoon clouds had replaced the white clouds of midday, making their way down from the highlands in the southwest. Masses of dark gray moisture touched the green rolling horizon, the hills black in shadow. Like a spotlight, the sun shone on Ocosingo. Within an hour, the wind would pick up and then it would rain. This much he knew.

He didn't need keys when he arrived at the house. The door had been forced open and everything was turned up side down. He stepped in and looked around. A wooden chair had been broken. Books were ripped apart and crumpled and torn pages were littered across the tile floor. The paper bindings of books had been torn half way down the back, exposing the glue and threads that had once held the pages together. His first impulse was to clean it up, to try to put everything back in order. Instead, he went to the window and looked out at the valley. He watched cattle skirting small thorny *Acacia* trees, eating concentric circles out from under them at the right distance to avoid the pain of thorns. They munched mouthful after mouthful of grass. In a while, they would relax under the larger *Acacias* and chew their cud away from the afternoon sun that burned through cracks in the clouds after the storm passed. Oblivious to the rebellion, just as in more normal times, they would be oblivious to the fact that in a few weeks the *finca* owners would come and order them slaughtered, their meat sent north to the U.S., the largest and best-muscled for *gringo* boys and girls, the old and tough for *gringo* dog and cat food.

He thought about how fast things could change. Just a few days ago, everything had been calm and sweet. For most of three years, he and César had gotten up at five in the morning, drunk their coffee and gone out to survey birds. They had competed for who could identify each species fastest, who was right more often, who could recognize the most songs and calls. César was better at identifying the warbler calls, but Pablo was an expert at the owls and resident birds. Working with César, he had known what the future looked like, at least for a while, but that had all changed. Already, he missed this house that he had called home for three years.

In the afternoons Pablo had liked to sit on the veranda, his back against a cement pillar and watch the drama. César would usually come out too, and prop himself up to read, more interested in literature than the sky. Black Vultures, dark with a white band on each wing tip, came off a carcass in the valley, rose with what appeared to be two or three arduous wing beats, and circled on the invisible columns of rising, warm air. Their gliding looked effortless. Pablo watched clouds build in the southwest. By one o'clock during the rainy season, they were huge and rolling, exploding over the highlands. From the ground they looked substantial, weighty, but he knew that up there, they were intangible masses of water and particles, dust and energy. By two o'clock they became gray, only their edges were white where the sun reflected. White fluffy clouds on a gray background. A troubled sky. A tormented sky. And although it rained every day during the rainy season, each day the clouds were different. He would watch as rain started in the highlands, a white sheet flung out over the darker background and then carried by wind over the valley, and usually he would hear the rain before he felt it. In the distance it sounded like a rushing stream. But before that, before the rain actually made any sound, grumbling thunder would announce afternoon's arrival. Pablo and César took the thunder as their cue for an afternoon beer, but they never actually went for them until the third significant thunder clap. Of course, significant was always up for interpretation. At the first thunder clap, neither commented. On the second thunder, if it was small, César would look up from his reading. They'd look at each other and then one of them would say, "Too small to be number two." They'd silently note number two as it came, loud and worthy. Then on the third major thunder of the afternoon, one of them would rise, go inside and get the beers. He didn't know when they'd started this ritual; it had developed slowly over time, part of their rhythm of being together.

Pablo loved this place. Topographically, it was complex, the old mountains broken up by time. Hilly, not jagged, but still rugged. The sky was wide and clean, not obscured by civilization and, as far as he could see, the hills were green. When gray clouds moved over, the green looked brighter, banana green. Or the hills could look black, sometimes even blue. Some days the thunder crackled. Other days it sounded like a jet taking off. Lightning drew perfect lines of light in the sky, separating north from south.

He thought of what he knew about the people of this place. There was so little trust—people were divided by ethnicity, economics, religion, and they all wanted the same thing. Land. A better life. But they spoke different languages, and couldn't understand each other. How could people come together when they couldn't communicate? And Parker was right; there were too many people vying for the same space, and they kept coming, from all the different ethnic groups, looking for a little place to farm. Before the Spaniards came, the groups had been small and separated from one another and there was plenty of land, but that had all changed with time. The Spanish explorers had come and they'd been quickly followed by the Catholic Church with its promises of salvation. Now there were new churches—Pentecostals, evangelicals, and they all promised the same thing—the way to a better life. And so now the *guerrilleros* were trying the way of guns, but of course, coming up against the Mexican army was akin to mass suicide. Pablo wondered how this uprising could possibly make anything better for anyone.

Standing at this window now, he knew that life as he had known it was over. His world had come undone, and he felt a loneliness unlike any he'd ever felt. César had gone to the city to wait it out, happy to take the forced vacation to work on his screenplay; Parker returned to the States; and he was here. He sensed that nothing would ever be the same.

Pablo left the living room window, stepped through the kitchen and went out the back door. Behind the house he spotted where Parker and César had buried the computer. He couldn't find the shovel; it must have been stolen. He went back into the house to look for something to dig with, but the only thing left was a large metal soup spoon. Outside again, on his knees, he scraped the spoon across the dirt, but it was worthless as a shovel, and he began to dig with his hands. Wet, cold soil coated his fingers, lined his fingernails and cuticles. The soil wasn't hard and they hadn't buried the computer deep.

He had just gotten to the plastic bag covering the computer case when he heard men behind him. He turned around quickly, probably too quickly he realized when he saw that they were military and heard the safety of one gun click off. He learned at this moment that moving too quickly could be dangerous, and told himself that he must remember to slow down. There were three soldiers standing above him with their guns pointed at his head. Three men, three guns. One would be enough. He looked at them and they looked at him. He tried to seem friendly, but guilt took over his face as he realized what they must think. Guilt and fear.

His legs shook as he stood, saying, "*Hola chicos*, how's it going?"

They ignored his greeting and one of them said, "Go on. Finish digging your treasure."

"It's a computer," he told them, but they seemed dubious. He bent over again, scraped the last bit of dirt away and lifted out the heavy plastic bag. He untied the knot and extracted the computer case. He unzipped it and showed them the computer, praying all the while that none of these guys had a fast trigger finger. Their faces looked confused and perplexed by the computer and he thought it was possible that they had never seen a laptop computer before.

"Come with us," one soldier said and he followed them, computer in hand down to the Pemex station, the same place they had been taken the first day the military arrived.

"Wait here," they told him. "We'll call Sergeant Alvarado." He sat on a curb by the side of the building. The mist had burned off and the sun was now hot. He heard thunder over the highlands, and wondered if the rain would come this far, usually only teasing the valley during the dry season. By the time a fat sergeant ambled out to talk to him, Pablo was sweating. He was disappointed to see that the sergeant was not the same man he had talked with before.

"What's your name?" the sergeant asked.

"Pablo Garcia de Lopez de Perez."

"What are you doing here?" he asked.

"Studying birds," Pablo told him.

"Birds?"

"Birds."

"Birds?" The sergeant was incredulous.

"*Si*, migratory birds."

Pablo answered all of Sergeant Alvarado's questions, explaining the migratory bird research in the different kinds of coffee plantations.

"We left a computer with some data and I've come back to retrieve it," Pablo told him. He started up the computer to show the sergeant the files, but the sergeant got caught up on the fact that the documents were in English.

"You speak English?" he asked.

"Some."

The sergeant seemed suspicious. "Stay here. I'll be back." He walked quickly back to the station. In a few minutes he was back. "You speak French?"

Pablo thought it was an odd question, but answered anyway. "Yes, I've studied French. I went to a boys preparatory French school in ...."

"Follow me!" the sergeant grunted, cutting him off.

They entered the Pemex station and approached a door with a padlock on the outside. The sergeant extracted a set of keys from his pocket, unlocked the door and stood back, implying that Pablo should enter.

"Stay here. I'll be back," the sergeant said.

Inside the room, there was no furniture. Pablo was immediately aware of a sharp, almost fetid odor in the air, much like the smell of the dead man on the road. He was not alone. There was a young indigenous woman in the room as well, cowering on the floor in the corner with her head resting on her bent knees. Her long dark hair hung over her face and legs. She didn't pay attention to them coming in and the sergeant didn't look at her or make any reference to her.

"Let me call my parents in Mexico City," Pablo appealed to the sergeant once again.

"We'll see," the sergeant replied. He left the room and Pablo heard him replace the padlock on the door. Pablo sat on the cool, cement floor, relieved to be out of the sun. He tried to imagine what was going on. Who cared if he spoke English and French, or Chinese for that matter? Of course, everyone was on edge, but why hold him? He was tired, sweaty, dirty. He had never been locked up before, and the sensation of being kept somewhere by another person was hideous. He thought of the dead man by the road. He felt vulnerable and threatened, and a sense of drowning in his feelings of anger, fear and hate for the military. It was all so very clear, he thought. They have guns and we don't. No one pays attention in this country unless you've got a gun. And because people are either too desperately poor to think or too rich to care, everyone has amnesia. Memory is a thing of the past that no one wants to remember.

Like a torrential downpour in the rainy season, emotions rushed over him. He stood and paced back and forth, trying to calm himself with movement. The image of the man on the road, lying there, days after having been shot, continued to replay in his mind. That man is enough to keep me a coward, Pablo thought. That could be me. I could be shot here and thrown out into the forest to decompose and no one would know. I wouldn't be the first person to have been disappeared in this country. But no. That's ridiculous. They wouldn't arrest me and then shoot me just like that. Would they? In all the time he sat and paced, the indigenous woman in the corner didn't look up once. Six hours later, another man, someone superior to the sergeant, came in. Pablo stood and the man stopped directly in front of Pablo, close to his face.

"You're smaller than I thought you'd be," he said.

Pablo replied with a nervous little laugh and a smile. He was hungry and tired and he had no idea what the man was talking about, but he wanted to get the hell out of this station, as fast as possible.

"So, you are who they call Subcomandante Marcos," the man stated.

"What?" Pablo began to laugh and then quickly repressed it. This man couldn't be serious, but he was.

"Please, sir," he said. "There is a misunderstanding. I'm a biologist. You can check my name, my address."

"Sergeant Alvarado has reason to believe that you are a *guerrillero* and you have trained people to kill."

"Where could he possibly have that information from?"

The man got angry at that question. "It's not your right to question our sources. If what you say is true, it will be apparent when we do a search. If not, you will be held as a traitor."

"You haven't checked my name yet?"

Pablo wrote down all of his information, including his father's company and telephone number. The man left and Pablo sat back down on the cement floor, incredulous. What a farce! But he was also afraid. His stomach ached, but they didn't bring him any food or water. What had they been doing all of these hours? Why hadn't they checked his name before?

He didn't try to talk to the indigenous woman and she still didn't lift her head. After three more hours, the man came back. Pablo picked his stiff body off the floor.

"Well, Pablo, you're not who we're looking for. You can go. I suggest you return directly to Mexico City. Good luck."

"Thank you, Sir, and good luck to you too," he lied.

"We don't need luck. They're going to die, one by one." The man gestured with his head toward the woman in the corner. "Do you speak their language?"

"No," Pablo responded. What he wanted to say was that *they* speak many different languages, you stupid idiot, but he kept it to himself. Mostly he just wanted to get out of there.

"She won't speak or eat. She hardly drinks anything, and she smells bad," he said.

At that moment, the woman looked up at Pablo. She looked up through a mess of long black hair, and he saw her oval face, her wide-set eyes small, dark and strong. A young Lacandón woman! What was she doing here? She looked straight into him with an unbroken stare and suddenly, he felt a weight on him. It was a look he couldn't deflect. Her mouth didn't move, but he swore he heard her whisper, "We're a long way still."

"What?" he asked her in Spanish.

"What did you say?" the officer asked him.

"Nothing," he quickly answered. Maybe she hadn't said anything. Perhaps he imagined it. He was so hungry, perhaps he was hallucinating, but he could have sworn that he'd heard a female voice speak that phrase to him. He'd heard it clearly in his head.

"I'd like to get rid of her," the officer said. "I don't have anywhere to put her, and I think she's sick, but I'm afraid to let her go. She's so young."

"I'll take her with me," Pablo blurted out, not thinking.

"With pleasure," the officer said, as if she were his to give.

Pablo approached her. She was still staring at him. He

held out his hand and she took it and stood. She was short and petite, and extremely young. Her dark hair hung half-way down her back and chest. He could see from her glassy eyes that she was more exhausted than frightened. He didn't know if she could understand him, but he spoke to her anyway.

"It's okay," Pablo told her quietly. "You can trust me."

She didn't let go of his hand and together they left the room they had shared for nine hours at the station. He wondered how long she had been there. Outside there were five helicopters circling, each touching down in turn in a level field behind the Pemex station, and dropping more men. Three bombers flew in from the east, circled the valley. With their oblong gray bombs hanging below, they resembled pregnant cows with twins, big and ripe, just waiting to be dropped, waiting to suck the life out of everything.

Pablo assumed that she didn't speak Spanish and so he gestured to her that they would get something to eat. She nodded her head. She stumbled a bit and he reached out to steady her. Together they walked down to the plaza in Ocosingo and went into a restaurant that had re-opened for business. Without even sitting at a table, Pablo called out an order for food and water to the waitress and led the young woman to the restroom. She was obedient, following him when he gestured, allowing him to lead her. He wet a paper towel and washed her face and neck, as if he were washing a child. She stood still, making no effort to stop him or take over and wash herself. He washed her hands and her arms. She was dirty and bloody. He could imagine too well. She was so small, so young, so bruised.

When they returned and sat at table, Pablo saw that a group of reporters had stationed themselves at a table by the door. Pablo recognized one from the day they left Ocosingo with the press. He thought he was from *The New York Times.* Pablo invited him to join him at their table and told him the story of how he had been detained for nine hours because they thought he was Subcomandante Marcos simply because he spoke English, French and had green eyes.

"And they stole my computer," Pablo added. The reporter took notes like a madman, following up every question with a new question.

"They make up their lies," Pablo told him, "and afterwards they have to go and find something real, something tangible to validate the lie they just finished creating." While Pablo was talking with the reporter, the young woman hovered in her chair, her head down like before, hair covering her face. Pablo considered telling the reporter about what they did to her, but he thought that somehow, it would be a violation. He told the reporter once more, "Be careful of the lies." After the reporter left their table, Pablo and the young woman finished eating, stood and left Ocosingo.

As they walked east, there was rapid gunfire on the northern slope, maybe a kilometer away, and then everything was quiet. The storm was approaching; across the valley it was already raining, the black streams of water coming down like a veil. He watched dark lines mark the sky and was happy for the rain that would give the Zapatistas a reprieve from the army. Just as the veil completely covered the sky in the east, the clouds above him broke and the sun raced through revealing an enormous rainbow. For a few seconds, colors stretched across the sky, uniting the forest with the highlands. He pointed the rainbow out to the woman, but he didn't think she could see anything because her eyes had gone hollow again. It didn't matter. He saw it and he knew what it meant. He was walking in the right direction. There was no doubt now.

* * *

By nightfall they reached real forest. She still had not spoken a word and Pablo had said very little to her, but he knew she could understand him. When they arrived at forks in the trail and he asked her in Spanish which direction they should walk, she answered with a small lift of her chin, and they headed in that direction.

They had been crossing settlements, small plots of land carved out of the forest for most of the afternoon, but as they neared the forest, the trail became narrow and rough, the simple corn fields gave way to mixed-crop *milpas*, and there were more large trees shading the crops. The entrance into forest wasn't abrupt; at one point he simply noticed that corn and coffee had fallen away, and there were just trees. She took the lead then. Together they crawled under fallen trunks, crossed streams, searching for the path of least resistance through the leaves. They walked for an hour and then the forest opened into a small clearing and he saw a hut, roofed with palm-leaves.

They approached the hut and she motioned for them to stop, her eyes saying she was too tired to continue. He could tell the place was newly-deserted, the firewood still stacked in a neat pile in a corner. Pablo made a fire on the dirt floor and they sat next to it warming themselves. He wished there were tea or coffee, but they had nothing to drink. After a while of sitting there together, watching the angry flames, she lay down circling her body around the warmth, her arms forming a blanket for her head.

She lay her head close to where Pablo was sitting. He wanted to reach out and touch her, to tell her to put her head on his lap, but he didn't. He lay down as well and stared up at the thatched roof above them. He noticed that her breathing had quickly become steady. She was asleep. He could hear the breaths taken in and those released, and for the first time he became aware of his own breath. He was suddenly conscious of the fact that he was alive, and that he had been petrified at the military barracks. The military men, especially Sergeant Alvarado, didn't seem particularly clever, his only power coming from bulk and rank rather than ability, and this thought frightened Pablo even more. He hoped that they hadn't phoned his house in Mexico City. His father would be livid. He inhaled hard, filling his chest to the point of pain. He held the breath there, stretching and pushing his lungs. He let it out slowly, feeling it move through his nose and mouth, feeling the pain lessen. Again he took in air. Again he released it back into the night. Over and over, slowly, until eventually, he fell asleep.

CHAPTER FIFTEEN
Chan Nah K'in

They said the scent was always here, just covered up by innocence. I know otherwise. It came that day on the hill. I'm sure of it. I saw it rise from the two *campesinos,* like smoke from a fire. The death-smell left their bloody, useless bodies. Left their mouths in a last, quiet breath and rose into the air. The soldiers smelled it too, and turned away. It floated up the hillside and entered me. The worst kind of smell imaginable, stronger than peccaries moving through the forest. A foul smell that got down into my stomach and made me sick, took me over, possessed me. Now I sense the world with the nose of death, and it is a cruel smell. A world that stinks with lies, and I alone here, trying to make sense of the senseless. I couldn't be strong. I failed and gave myself away. I was stupid. Now the fight is dying and I am left with a useless life that is worth nothing.

When the soldiers came up the hillside and saw me, they thought I was a child, no more than thirteen, they said. My size and young looks helped me, and for the first time, I was grateful that I didn't have my gun. They didn't push me to speak like they had the *campesinos.* They ran up the hill and then stood above looking down, dark eyes and big guns pointed at me. Thick men, muscled, army-trained with belts of ammunition looped around their chests. One soldier lowered his gun, but the other one kept his pointed at me, ready to shoot. Sweat poured off his hair and neck. He wanted to shoot, but he didn't. They picked me up, my body shaking and limp, and walked me back to the barracks in Ocosingo.

They took me to the market building and asked me if I knew the five men lying on the cement floor. Álvaro was on his stomach, his feet dirty and bare. They had cut the ropes, dyed red with blood, from his wrists and ankles, and they lay on the floor beside him. His bruised face was turned toward the door, toward me, one eye swollen shut, the other staring past me. I recognized Luís and José too, but the two others were turned away, their hair fallen over their faces, and I couldn't be sure. The soldiers asked me again if I knew them, but I didn't answer. I stared at Álvaro and watched flies buzzing around his head, lapping up the last of the blood before it dried. I flinched when I saw my friends like that and I was afraid that the soldiers would know who I was. It's hard to stay calm when you're looking down at dead friends and you can see exactly how they died.

"You think she knows them?" one asked.

"No, she's just a scared kid. Let's go up to the station."

From Ocosingo I made it home, but still it was like a dream. There was a man, a nice white man with true green eyes who helped me. As soon as I felt his presence and saw his eyes, I knew they were kind and I knew I could trust him. For the first time since the soldiers got me, I felt hopeful. The white man took me away from the fat soldier, who thought I was younger than I am, and liked me better because of it. The man with green eyes washed the blood from my thighs. He washed my swollen face and my dirty hands, and then he walked me away from that horrible town, eastward toward forest, to my home. He started out leading, but later when we got to the forest, I had to take over. He didn't know where to go. I showed him the way. He couldn't have known where the different paths led, and then sometimes, when the forest got thick, it was hard to find any path at all. I had to slow down so that he could keep up. As we walked, I heard him behind me, tripping when it got dark, snapping branches, making noise. White people are big and clumsy. They don't really fit in. They seem to always be fighting their way through. When we got into a clearing and stopped at a house, I could see that he'd gotten all scratched up. He looked tired.

We stopped for the night there. I slept, really slept, for the first time since it started.

When I arrived at my village with that smell and the green-eyed man, no one but my mother recognized me. There was no escaping the odor of death. It had followed me. I returned home, but it was not the village I had left. Houses made of balsa wood and palm leaves blended among the trees like always. Chickens scratched hard dirt in a pen at the far edge of the village. Men and women swayed at mid-day in hammocks under new palm roofs, watching the leaves dry a little bit more every day. They would be dry and ready before the rains came. Small trails led to the lake, to the forest, to the corn fields. Like always, men worked at planting and fishing. Women cooked. But the place was now dotted with white flags. People had ripped their long white tunics into pieces and then tied these to sticks. There were small flags stuck in the ground in front of houses, large flags hung above roofs. White flags surrounded corn fields, and they'd been woven into the mesh of chicken pens and attached to the canoes drifting at the lake. As if enough white flags could keep the conflict away.

My first morning back I sat half-awake in front of our house and watched a skinny dog scratch fleas. Without getting up, or even raising his head, he scratched a series of spots on his stomach with a hind leg. Tiny clouds of dirt and fur formed in the air above him and settled back onto him. Word got out and before long old Nuk came at me shaking a white flag in my face and holding her hand over her mouth, "You are with sin."

Then Koh came, followed by Nah Bor. Both women stopped a ways from the house when they smelled me and spoke from there.

"You bring trouble," Koh told me. I had nothing to reply. They had never supported the Zapatista movement, and they'd always been resentful that my mother and I had joined.

"We already made agreements with the foreign men.

We've got land, and they gave us good money for our mahogany," Nah Bor called so that everyone could hear. "We don't need your group of rebels."

"Ha, and where is that money now?" my mother asked, coming to my side. "You put your fingerprints on paper, mahogany trees fell and then the true people up the river got all the money. What will you do now? Carve canoes from balsa trees?" She laughed.

"But we were given the land we live on. These Zapatistas are trying to move onto the land given to us."

"Either way people are coming, Nah Bor. We have to help them get their land back. We can teach them what we know and learn what they know."

"But they know nothing of this place! They've just arrived. They're worse off than we are!"

"Which is exactly why we must help them. Otherwise, they'll destroy the entire forest."

"I help my own," Nah Bor said.

My mother led me away, replying over her shoulder as we left, "You know, Na Bor, you've become one of those dolls you sell to the tourists. A little Indian to buy and play with."

At home I began to smoke tobacco. I thought that the smell on my fingers would mask the smell of blood, the odor of death. It didn't. I showered with soap, rubbed frothy suds over my body turning my brown skin white, and then rinsed with hot water that burned me red. My knees and elbows and hands bled for the trying. I washed and washed and smoked and still the smell was with me. Despite my efforts to rid myself of it, I know it will never go away. Now that I have smelled death, the scent is with me, inside me. Now I smell like death. I am death and death is me.

My mother baked bread, hoping the perfume of rising life would overcome me. It did not. She rolled *xate* leaves and wound them together. She collected *pom* and put the resin on top of sacred stones in her father's incense burner, and when the *xate* leaves had dried, she blackened them with copal smoke from the burner. They burned and I walked through their incense. At night she rubbed the black leaves over my body and hung the bunch above my hammock as I slept. She thought the fumes from the leaves would enter my skin, cleanse me, but the plant's perfume went away after a day, and I was left smelling rotten again. I can't escape the smell of death that has overtaken me, clouded me, soaked into me. It is choking me. The scent of death kills everyone it enters, from inside out.

My mother went into the forest and collected strips of bark from the *ba' che'* tree. When the strips had dried, she soaked them in water and honey for a day. After it was tart and ready, we drank *balche'* together. We prayed to the gods to take the smell away, but they did not listen. Or maybe they wanted to help, but couldn't.

I was afraid at home. Afraid because no place can be home to one who smells like death. Afraid because the other Hach Winik people knew the smell for what it was, and shunned me. I feared they would not believe what I had seen and felt, and how the scent had come to possess me. I was foul, not only to myself, but also to them, a reminder of the decay that is our fate. Guilty of my fault in this.

"Perhaps Nah Bor is right," I told my mother. "We were wrong. What has changed? The country didn't rally behind us. The government only responded with the guns, and it's not just the Hach Winik who shun us. There are lots of Tzeltzales and Choles too, who have been given guns from *ladinos* and the military. They are fighting us too." I didn't mention that without their love-pieces our soldiers, brave or not, were being killed the same.

"But some people are paying attention, and we have pushed some finca owners back," she said. "It takes time."

"Well I can't stand it. I've become a messenger for everyone who thrusts his way into the forest, into our lives, into me."

"Ha! So now you know! You were raped once; the forest is taken every day. Think about that when you're fighting again."

"You're saying I should go back?"

"Of course you'll go back. Think of the forest."

"But as the Hach Winik, we have forest. The government gave us thousands of hectares. All we need to do is take care of it."

"Papers are meaningless. The forest can't survive so many foreigners. Do you think they're going to stop moving here because of a few papers from Mexico City? You must help them to fight so that they get their land back and then they will leave our forest alone."

I'd been sacrificed. The realization came fast and mean. She'd trained me all of those years to deal with pain, violence. In her mind, Álvaro dead, me and the fat man were nothing. It didn't matter if I couldn't survive the foreigners either. She didn't care that I'd never talk to Álvaro again, that we'd never have the chance to laugh together, or dance. She couldn't see that his death was the end and that I'd never be able to forgive myself for not protecting him, for leaving him there in Ocosingo. She couldn't see that the loneliness was too much. She didn't care about how I'd been crushed and broken open by the fat man. For the first time, I believed the other Hach Winik. Perhaps she truly was crazy like they said. The stories she'd told me had been creations of her mind, crazy talk. How silly I'd been to believe her when she said, "Everyone has a mother, but not everyone has a father. I found you at the ceiba tree." No wonder the other Hach Winik didn't like us. She had taken me away and told me stories that made me feel different, stories that made me want what she wanted. The forest, always the forest.

I couldn't live there, not with my mother, or the other Hach Winik, so I left home and came here. I stay hidden in this cave, in the moist darkness where I am alone with my death-smell. There is a heaviness that makes it hard to do anything but lie here. Everything takes so much effort to move, my arms and legs don't work right. It only feels okay if I stay still and don't try. It's cold and still I sweat, the sweat of fear that reminds me of everything I want to forget. I remember Álvaro coiled around himself when we ran away, and how still he was when I saw him later, no longer impatient. I keep seeing his eyes alive and then that one eye dead. I remember the fat man and the rough floor scraping against my back when he pressed me under his heavy body. I try not to think about how I cried out on the hillside, calling the soldiers to me. Mostly, I try to keep back the memory of the man I was too afraid to shoot before I lost my gun.

It had been the second day in Ocosingo and the military arrived from Palenque without warning. Trucks, tanks, helicopters and planes all moved in at once with the noise of thunder. Hundreds of soldiers came toward us and we had to run. We ran and hopped like insects escaping army ants, trying to cover each other as we ran. Pacho ran first, and then watched out while I followed from the back of the municipality building to the corner. Pacho ran on down the sidewalk toward the police station. I followed, stopping halfway down the sidewalk behind a column to cover Álvaro, while Pacho looked for our next move. That's when I saw him hiding behind a column on the other side of the plaza. He wasn't military. He was *ladino* and he held an old hunting rifle. I watched them both. With one eye I saw Álvaro sprint toward me before I had given him the signal. With the other, I saw the *ladino* raise his rifle. I took aim and I had a clear view. I was ready to shoot him. In the head, the chest, the leg. I could have shot him anywhere. And then Álvaro fell, shot in the calf. He yelped and crumbled to the ground, grabbing his leg with his hand. I screamed, dropped my gun and ran toward him, but at the same time Pacho returned and grabbed me hard on the arm. He screamed, "No!," and pulled me away. I left Álvaro and my gun behind.

* * *

During the day I pace around inside the cave, blindly touching walls, feeling where rocks are jagged and where they are smooth. At dusk I peer out of the opening into the forest below. With one turn of my head, one sweep of my nose, I take in the bodies scattered across the landscape. Boys shot down in the forest smell fleshy, like rotten fruit. Those in the town, who have fallen on the concrete, smell odd. They don't mix with soil-smells. Their bodies take up the cold mist at night, bloating like some infected limb. During the day, they heat up, drying in the sun, and the fumes drift into the sky. Up, up, up, calling out. To the vultures these dead boys are sweet, and now at dusk, the birds come circling down low.

I am becoming used to the smells inside this cave, knowing which ones come from each part, which are mine and which are not. I use the far corner for my waste, but now with no food, I don't need to go there anymore. I have nothing left to get rid of. When I have to pee, I squat down over the pile and a stream hisses out. I wait for the last drops to drip. I am careful to find the right place. My sense of location is better each day, so I can find the spot without going in circles like before.

On the other side of the cave I sit and smoke and sleep. I strike a match against a rock. It lights a bright flame. I raise it to the tobacco and inhale the musty flavor. For a few moments I am better, but the tobacco always burns too quickly and the cold returns like before, only worse. I am a little more alone with the short, dead cigar in my hand.

I listen for noises, for those who might come to find me. I listen and remember. The animals keep me company. They let me know if someone is coming. With them I am never as lonely as I was out there. During the day, wind rushes the tops of trees close above me, otherwise, it's quiet.

Yesterday I heard a troop of monkeys pass over. I heard them across the way so I went out and watched them in a fruit tree. They popped small brown fruits into their mouths, sucked and spit out the seeds. The seeds made music when they fell through the leaves to the ground. I watched as their nervous heads twitched left and right, keeping each other in sight, cackling in their secret language. They jumped and leapt with no fear of falling. They know they'll never miss. I noticed a female with a baby. She sat away from the others, eating with one hand while the other arm hung over the tiny dark baby feeding at her breast. The other monkeys twitched and jumped continuously, but she remained calm. A male came toward her. She screeched at him twice, baring white teeth, and he turned away. Like a good mother, she protected her baby.

I watch and listen. I sleep and I smoke. This is how I pass the time, while I wait for the death-smell to eat me up. I remember the missionaries who came to teach us in the forest camps when we first began to train. The catechist said, "There is a God." What kind of craziness lets a person believe in a god? What kind of god would allow this cold death-smell, the disgusting fumes to attack me, to make *me* the messenger of the smell of death? No. God is a lie like this world is a lie, like love is a lie. Rotting lies. They filled me up, the lies. I ate them up, got fat on them. I believed we would succeed. I believed we would get the land we need. I believed my mother. I hoped. What good was it? What good was trying if it ended so quickly and in so many deaths? That Chol woman was wrong. Cutting out the love-part did nothing. We died just the same, or worse than during all those years before.

When I saw Álvaro and the others, I understood what had happened to them. They had been picked up from wherever they fell in Ocosingo and put in the marketplace so that everyone would see them. Their hands were tied behind their backs so tight that their wrists bled. They were hit and kicked, first with fists and sticks and then with gun butts, tortured into speaking, but nothing they said was good enough to save them. After some days, they were lined up on the ground and shot one by one in the head. They died like the *campesinos* died, only worse. Now with Álvaro dead, we are no closer to justice. We are no closer to land, or education. All lies. The lies burn layers of skin off my body, wasting me away until there is nothing left but the smell of death. When I breathe out for the last time, this spirit of death will leave me to go out, just like it left the *campesinos*, to enter and eat up another fat life.

But ha! I have found a way to cheat the smell. I can't escape the odor, but I will stay in this cave. I hunker down in darkness where there is no wind, no breeze, no way for the smell to escape. Every breath I set free sends a little more of the crazed death-smell into the air, and the smell is taken by pools of water on the floor. I will decay in this stinking hole, in this death drenched air, and the rocks will take up the smells. And this smell will die here with me, or because the death-smell never dies, it will stay here forever, locked in the dark, damp rocks of my cave.

CHAPTER SIXTEEN
Mario

There's a stink in the air. Like a whorehouse that's had its windows closed. This whole jungle smells like a bitch, and I'm inside her. She's fat and pumped full of semen and blood, and she's sweating it out at me. The hole in my stomach fills with smoke. Emptiness eats me from inside out. I crouch down, thinking my stomach will smash in on itself and I won't feel so hungry. I wish the aching would go away. I'd be happy if I got a piece of horsemeat now. It would feel good to chew on something besides the inside of my mouth. Something salty. My mouth is dry too. I wish I had some water. I crouch here, resting on my heels, and I try to think. I wonder if they will come back for us. How long will it take them?

Last night we were sent out into the jungle again. It was the same as always, cold, damp and dark. Can't see a thing. There was supposed to be a camp where they hide out. We were going to attack and get a bunch of them all at once. The sergeant told us to spread out, make a half-circle and move forward like that. "Like a net," he said, "we'll drop around them, surround them and swoop them up."

Javier and I went off to the east, to be the outer-edge of half of the half-circle. We moved slowly around plants, pushing big wet leaves out of the way, trying not to jump when branches snapped at our backs. It was black. How do they expect us to know where to go when we can't see? I couldn't tell if we were going east, north or what. We just more or less picked a line and walked into it, entering black hell.

We were turning in, trying to see that net the sergeant told us about, trying to imagine pulling it in on them and swooping them up, when we heard someone close by. It sounded like they were right in front of us, but we couldn't see anything. Javier stepped closer to me and touched my arm. This is the only time he's ever quiet—in the forest at night. He touched my arm and then I knew we'd both heard it. We held our guns ready. They'd been ready all night. He lifted my arm and pointed it in the direction of the sound. I squeezed his hand to let him know I'd heard it. We stood still and kept our bodies like we were taught in training, keeping our feet planted hard into the ground, like a statue, and our upper-bodies easy. Don't lock up, they taught us. Keep your arms loose, ready to move the gun, ready to fire. We stood like that, trying to see something, listening hard with our ears, but not knowing what any of the sounds were. We're such dumb fucks out here. We jump at leaves. We shoot at sticks falling through branches, the sound of water dripping. Maybe that's what it was, I was saying to myself, just a bunch of sticks or some ugly beetle or something, when all of a sudden, Javier shoots off a round. I hear his shots ripping through the black green trees in front of us, and before I know it, they're shooting off some rounds back at us. I feel my gun explode and lift away from me, like the forest is pulling it away, like the forest is trying to steal it from me. I stop shooting and squat and feel around for Javier, who was standing right beside me a second ago. I can't see him and I'm too scared to move, too scared to talk. I just crouch there trying not to make another sound, hoping they'll go away. Silent bastards. You never hear them. I stay like that for a long time, feeling my heart banging in my chest and the sweat pouring down my face. I'm crouched and my knees scream for me to get up, but I'm too afraid to move. I don't hear anything, and there's no more shooting. And then I hear Javier start to moan softly. I'm afraid to let him make all that noise and so I move toward the sound. I do a squat-walk towards him and before five or six steps I bump into him. Funny, he wasn't really far from me at all, but with the dark and his low moans, it sounded like he was further away.

"Javier, are you okay? You hit? Can you get up?" He moaned in response. I felt his body to see how it was. He was lying on his side, one arm underneath and the other over his chest. His legs seemed all twisted up and I wanted to make him more comfortable, so I took hold of his arm and rolled him onto his back to try to straighten him out. He screamed. I didn't try to move him anymore.

He started mumbling, "*Dios, déme la paz, déme la paz, no me deje, por favor, no me deje.*"

I knew he wasn't talking to me, but I answered anyway. "Don't worry, Javier. I won't leave you." I didn't know what to do. "You're going to be okay," I told him. I reached over to his shirt pocket for the cigarettes. His shirt was sticky and he was shivering and that made me worry. I took the cigarettes out. The pack was damp, but not ruined. I lit one and in those few seconds of light, I saw Javier's face and it looked like the face of an old man, and I knew he was shot really bad and that he wasn't going to make it. I began to smoke the cigarette, switching between my lips and his. He couldn't inhale very well, but I knew he'd want one if he could. Fuck. I wished I could see better. I wished I knew what to do. I wished I could stop the cold. I stayed next to him and tried to think.

"You're going to make it, Javier," I whispered. I knew he'd want to hear a voice, that he'd want me to talk now that he couldn't. "You know, Javier, when I get out of here, I'm going to go north, up to *gringo*-land and get a job and when I get some good money, I'll send some down."

His moans told me he was listening.

"We'll go to a warm place, just warm. Some place that's never hot and never cold. There's got to be a place like that."

He moved a little and made a small sound.

"You can come up and we can work together and we can

buy cars—shiny new cars and drive around all of the time and maybe even find some women."

He moaned again.

"Not *gringa* women; there's got to be Mexican women up there too. Some nice pretty plump girls. We can even get married and they'll have babies and you'll be Uncle Javier. I'll be Uncle Mario."

And then I didn't hear any more moans. I didn't think he was with me anymore. I kept talking for a while, but then it seemed stupid to be sitting alone talking, so I stopped.

* * *

When the rain started a little while ago, I didn't know what it was. It started so quiet, without thunder. First, there was a light sputtering in the trees way above us, a kind of music as the drops made their way down through the leaves. And then almost as soon as I felt them on my back, everything was drenched, soaking wet. I put out my tongue and drank. Now it's been a few hours since Javier quit moaning, quit breathing. The rain must have stopped because it's just dripping slowly down here. Loud, single drops that don't sound like music at all. His body is getting cold and stiff. I'm shivering. There's not much difference between us, only that I breathe and he doesn't. I guess I'm lucky. A meter either way, me or him. It was him this time. Only I don't feel lucky. Fuckers. If I got close to one of those boys now, I'd drop my gun and kill him with my hands, strangle him until his tongue hung from his open mouth. I would. I know I would.

I thought someone would have come by now. They'd notice us missing when the half-circle closed in on itself, and they'd come for us when it got light, but it has been getting lighter in shades, black to black-green and brown, and I haven't heard anyone. I can see Javier now. They got him in the chest and stomach. Black blood has soaked his shirt, and now he just lies there, not feeling the cold at all. It makes me sick to see him like that. He looks like Javier, and then he doesn't. Every time I look at him, he seems less like Javier.

I don't think our group is coming back for us. We've been deserted, abandoned. They've left us for dead. I bet they're chalking us up on the dead list right now. Javier's gone. I'm gone. From person to number. Soldier to corpse. Easy as that. Fuckers. And Javier really is gone.

Jesus predicted this. They read us his words in church, "*La maldad sigue veniendo.*" He was right about evil coming; I guess he was always right. Everything gets worse and worse until the end, when we're dead. And so what if I am dead? What then? I don't know, but I know I don't hate enough to do this. This place, this fighting, this forest—it makes you ugly. Not just Javier and the way he looks now, but me too. I know what I could do. Clear as ever. I could walk. I could walk away from this place, back to Guerrero. I could go some place where the sun shines and you feel it, where there is space to move, where you're not always bumping into a plant. I want to be someplace where you can see the sky. Here I look up and see spots of light above the trees, and I can tell it's full of life up there with air you can breathe. I wish I could get up there, but it's such a long way. Down here there's nothing but rotting leaves and wet death. I want to be someplace where I'm not tired, where I'm not afraid. Since I'm dead, and Javier's dead, I can go any place I want. They won't miss me or look for me, because I'm already gone. I've got nothing to lose. I can leave this smelly place. I can get away from this pregnant whore who's swollen with the stink of death.

CHAPTER SEVENTEEN
Amy

It couldn't be true. It must be a coincidence, or she had become paranoid, but it was too unlikely not to be real. Just three days back from Mexico, she sipped her coffee and paged through *The New York Times*, hoping to find something about Chiapas and then she saw his picture. Pablo, his blond curly hair light gray in the grainy black and white photograph. An interview accompanied the picture. He had been detained by the Mexican army and told he was Subcomandante Marcos—the leader of the uprising, their similarities being green eyes and the ability to speak English, French and Spanish. He said the military suspected him because local people had seen him talking with *guerrilleros*. It was ludicrous. She realized what must have really happened and her hands began to shake. She grabbed her parka, not bothering to put it on, and ran outside.

Cold morning air cut her face and froze her hands, but she welcomed the pain. Tears were impossible in freezing air and after so many days of crying, the sting of cold was better than the burn of tears. By the time she arrived at the coffee shop, her lungs were burning. Christen saw her come in, flushed red, her chest heaving with lack of breath, and he rushed around the counter to meet her.

"Amy, what's wrong?"

"It was my fault. I sent them to get him." He put his arm around her shoulder.

"Slow down. What are you talking about?"

"This." She handed him the newspaper. Christen scanned the article.

"I don't understand. It says this Pablo guy is okay. He was released."

"Yes, but *I'm* the one who said he was talking with *guerrilleros*! At the airport. I talked with a man, his name was Simon somebody and he said he worked at the American Embassy in traveler safety. He had a nice smile and I talked with him, answering all of his questions, and I mentioned Pablo's name a couple of times. I still don't understand how he knew I was at the airport, how he could have been waiting for me to check in at the airline in Mexico City.

"Jesus, Amy, you were tired and in shock. Give yourself a break," Christen said.

But she knew there wasn't any excuse. She was responsible for what had happened to Pablo. It was her fault.

"And do you know what else he said? He said, 'Thank goodness no Americans were killed.' Can you believe he said that? I should have thrown my coffee in his face! If I had known why he was asking me those questions, I never would have talked to him."

"Of course not, Amy, but you were tired. How could you know?"

"I think the American Embassy sent my information back to the Mexican military. Simon whoever. I bet they don't even *have* a department of tourist safety. He must have been CIA!"

"Don't blame yourself. It's not that big a deal."

"Not a big deal? Christen, don't you understand? I was an informer!"

"You weren't an informer, Amy. They took advantage of you, and it says right here that Pablo is okay."

"What scares me is that what I said in Mexico City got back to Chiapas."

"Come on, Amy," he said. He led her to a table.

"I have been so naïve. So stupid. I unfolded my innocence and laid it out for that guy, like a huge white dinner napkin."

"Come on, honey. Let's take a break." Christen was pleading now. "I'll bring us something to eat."

She couldn't eat. She had hardly eaten anything in the

three days she'd been home. The process of preparing food was impossible. She couldn't muster the energy and even when Christen put something in front of her, she couldn't make the motions of fork to food to mouth. She became nauseated imagining the feeling of metal on her tongue and the soft, warm food in her mouth. Her stomach and digestive tract had just shut down. Christen came back to the table with two scones and some cheese. She shook her head, sat back and watched him eat.

"Knowing more makes life harder," she whispered.

"Amy, you've had a lot of life thrown in your face," Christen said. "A better perception of reality. You've learned something from the experience."

"Come off it, Christen. I refuse to intellectualize this."

"That's not what I mean, Amy."

"It's only easy to talk about all of this globalization stuff when you're here."

* * *

In the first days after returning home, Amy had clung to Christen and he was there for her. She didn't want to be alone, and so she went to the coffee shop with him in the morning and they talked whenever he wasn't busy with customers. She was grateful that she still had ten more days before the semester would begin. It was impossible to imagine teaching. Being in Christen's presence calmed her. He was attentive and caring. As soon as he had opened the shop, brewed coffee and settled her into a booth with a cup, he went out to buy *The New York Times* for her. Later during the morning lull in business, he searched the internet for articles and printed those he thought she would want to read. He brought her hot, soothing teas with just a touch of sugar and lemon; he made sure the candles on her table were always lit, and when he was too busy at the counter, he sent over one of the servers to see if she was hungry. She read articles, sipped tea and watched people in the shop, mostly students. They chatted and laughed, pulling their chairs up to make larger and larger groups, or they studied at corner tables with headphones shielding their ears. She didn't feel as though she were part of their world, more like an observer, only a poor one at that. An observer in a daze, she thought. Still, the clatter of dishes, the bitter smell of coffee, the sound of voices rising in volume with the morning rush and softening afterwards, reassured her.

Christen scheduled fewer late shifts for himself in order to be with her, and she was grateful for his company. In the evenings at her apartment, he put on music and cooked dinner. She knew cooking gave him something to do and helped him relax. He liked to be busy, and he didn't mind whether she ate or not. She didn't want to be alone, but she didn't feel like talking either. Understanding her need for silent company, Christen didn't initiate conversations about Chiapas. He let her be and listened whenever she spoke.

The first day, when he'd come in to her apartment to water her plants and found her at home, she'd told him almost everything that had happened, but now she didn't have much to say, at least nothing new. Her mind repeated the same images and questions, and none of the reiterations of the experience did anything to relieve her confusion.

Christen busied himself with cleaning, humming to music as he went along, squirting blue fluids onto everything and spooling through roll after roll of paper towels. He'd stand back and admire his work and then continue cleaning.

"You don't have to do that," she said. He was taking apart the stove and scrubbing it with cleanser.

"I know. I want to. It's good for me," he said.

Already, in the first three days since she'd come back, he'd emptied and scrubbed the refrigerator. It was now spotless. He'd moved on to the cupboards, the floor, the bathroom. The entire apartment smelled of disinfectant and the fumes made her a bit ill, but she didn't complain.

She wished there was someone who could explain everything to her in a way that made sense. She wished that

Pablo and Parker were here and the three of them could figure it out and understand it together. They knew so much more about Chiapas than she did. Her thoughts and emotions remained half-formed in her mind.

Love-making with Christen was imbued with a new passion and urgency. She desperately wanted to connect with him, and through him to the whole world. She reached out to him and he responded. She undressed him and kissed him frantically and when he moved to caress her in return, she said no. Wanting to feel his weight, she slid underneath him and pulled him down onto her, holding him there with all of her force, feeling him moving inside of her, wanting him to come as soon as possible. She was only able to feel pleasure through him, and the rare times she did come, in that moment of release, she felt nothing but sadness and shame, her pleasure juxtaposed with images of the boy with the mole. She burst into tears and cried in Christen's arms until she fell asleep.

With every passing day, Christen became more and more interested in the Zapatistas and what Subcomandante Marcos was saying in his speeches. He checked out books from the library about Mexico and Mexican history, and his philosophy group, which had been suffering a loss of momentum, was revived. They decided to read Mexican writers, such as Carlos Fuentes, Jorge Castañeda and Carlos Monsiváis. They were newly invigorated by the current events, but Amy only felt exhausted.

* * *

She had anticipated the beginning of the new semester, hoping she would think less about what had happened in Mexico because she'd be busy reading and preparing lectures. Her time would be filled with students, laboratory exercises and grading, but it hadn't worked out that way. She thought about Mexico just as much as before the semester started. The experience had become an entity; images and thoughts of Chiapas refused to conform to her schedule and came whenever they wanted, beyond her control.

She lectured to her entomology class. "Today we'll review insect development. Unlike mammals, insects go through many free-living stages of development before they come out as adults. There are basically two kinds of development: Hemimetabolous and Holometabolous. Hemimetabolous insects have incomplete metamorphosis. There are only three stages: egg, nymph, adult. Examples are grasshoppers, the bugs, mantids, walking sticks and dragonflies. Holometabolous insects, on the other hand, have complete metamorphosis, which means they go from egg to larva to pupa and then come out as adults. Flies, ants, bees, wasps, butterflies and moths are all holometabolous."

As the words formed and exited her mouth, her mind jumped and she remembered the sound of shots, the green valley, and the feeling of mist and cold. How could insect development be relevant anymore? She brought herself back.

"Taken together holometabolous insects are much more diverse than hemimetabolous insects; evolutionarily and ecologically, holometabolous development has been very successful. Perhaps you'll want to devote some time to thinking about why that might be the case."

Amy noticed a student raise his hand to ask a question. She knew him from the previous semester and ignored his hand.

"That was a huge hint and if anyone raises a hand to ask if you need to know insect development for the test, I'm going to cut his arm off."

The young man lowered his hand. Her comment must have come out sounding serious because none of the other students laughed. She knew her nerves were sensitive right now, but she couldn't cope with such questions, with this level of immaturity.

She heard a helicopter fly over the college. She shivered and saw the black helicopter rising above the Pemex station

as they had walked down the road in Ocosingo. She heard
the machine's rumble and felt the grating sound enter her
body, shaking her inside and scaring her. Her body was here,
but her thoughts jumped back and forth, north and south
exhausting her with their constant travel. Her head felt heavy
and thick, as if her brain were swollen and pushed up against
her skull so tightly that nothing could work right.

After class, she sat in her tiny office and looked out the
window. Simple things were strange now, like the fact that
here it was winter and snowing and yet she felt warm, almost
too hot, and there, in tropical Mexico, she had felt nothing
but cold. Everything was upside down.

The sky was gray and bleak. She watched a group of
house sparrows flit around on the ground looking for seeds.
Above, starlings in winter plumage, whistled in the bare trees.
She ought to remember to buy bird seed next time she was at
the store. She could bring it to school and scatter it on the
ground in front of her window. The birds needed energy now
to maintain themselves in this cold. They seemed so hungry.

Weeks had passed since she'd heard anything about the
situation in Chiapas in the news. For the first few days after
she came home she could be sure to garner more information
every time she turned on the radio, but now there was
nothing. She spent her first days home reading newspapers.
She bought them all: *The New York Times, Los Angeles Times,
The Christian Science Monitor.* She read and read. January
1st, January 2nd, January 3rd. She knew that most of what she
read wasn't true, especially articles published in the first
days. She had been there. She had seen and heard the things
that were never reported. On the 3rd, the Mexican presidential
spokesman stated that the army was still in its barracks and
force would not be used to quell the insurrections, but from
the minute they arrived, they had shot the automatics like the
finale to a fourth of July fireworks show. She thought of the
bodies she had seen when they passed the bus on their way
back to Tuxtla, and now here they were again on paper, their

faces blurred by the graininess of the photos. Some colored. Some black and white. There was also a photograph of the young boy with the mole. She knew now that he had been shot that night when she woke to the sound of single gun shots, the night Parker had slept next to her.

She had joined Christen's philosophy group and listened to their discussions. At first she was jealous of their ability to delve into the situation, even when they hadn't ever been to Chiapas, and come up with a sophisticated socio-economic-political analysis. They talked for hours about the rebellion, its significance, its potentials for failure and success, but then she became frustrated with them, almost offended by their analyses and questions.

"The meaning of this is potentially catastrophic for indigenous peoples around the world!" one member said.

"You were there, Amy, tell us about it," implored another.

"I'm not all that interested in talking," she told them. "I'd rather just listen."

"But it's one of the great movements of our time!"

"She's more interested in insects than people." Christen said. He wanted her to speak, to tell them everything she'd seen, especially the part about Simon from the American Embassy, but so far, she'd refused.

"Listen," she told them. "I saw a bunch of super-poor people go up against the Mexican military and essentially, they got stomped on. You call that a great movement?"

"But the symbolism and energy of it must have been immense from that perspective!"

Later, she realized that part of her frustration was the inability to tell them what Chiapas was like because she didn't really know what it was like. She'd only been there for a few days, and she couldn't say what had happened or how the people felt, or what they should do. She couldn't tell the story, not really, not truthfully because she simply didn't know it, and it frustrated her that they were inspired by it. She wasn't inspired. She was reeling with the images and confused by her inexplicable sense of guilt, and she felt embarrassed, especially when they expected her to provide insight to what was happening just because she'd been there. She couldn't understand where her guilt was coming from, but she knew it had something to do with having met Pablo, César and Parker. She felt watched from their eyes, and how she responded to Christen and his philosophy friends was somehow a reflection of who she was. If she engaged them, she felt guilty. If she got angry with them, she felt impotent.

The birds outside her office window made her think of the migratory birds she'd hoped to see in Chiapas, species she knew from the Minnesota summer that wintered in Chiapas. She thought again of a conversation she'd had with Parker and Pablo in the house in Ocosingo. They were talking about the Lacandón Indians.

"I wonder why the Hach Winik, the Lacandón Indians, aren't part of this rebellion," Pablo said.

"Why should they be?" Parker said. "They've got a huge forest preserve where they can live as the 'lost Mayas.' Tourists come to take canoe rides around Lake Lacatum and then they pay them good money to take their pictures. What else do they need?"

"I don't see why you come here," she interrupted him. "You're so cavalier and cynical."

"No," he said. "It's not cynicism. It's just that the Lacandones aren't all that special in my eyes. They might be related to the original Lacandón people, who were here when the Spanish arrived, but they might not be either. No one knows. Nonetheless, they shouldn't be held up and worshiped."

"It doesn't seem like you could worship anything," she said. He ignored her comment and continued.

"I think it's our inability to accept the past, to get past the guilt of what our European ancestors did here. Look, let's face the facts. Europeans came. They converted everyone they could to Catholicism and then killed those who resisted.

Some people didn't die or convert but lived by hiding in the forest, more or less isolated. When they were "discovered" by modern anthropologists, they were touted as the lost Mayas, the direct descendents of ancient Mayas, who everyone knows deserted this area long before the Europeans arrived. The reality is that the Europeans caused lots of groups of people to die, their languages and customs to go extinct, but we want to believe that some survived, that there is the possibility for redemption, that we could right those wrongs now and resurrect a symbol of the mythical past. In truth, the Lacandon Indians are just people doing life and the only reason they haven't wrought havoc on the forest is because their numbers have always been too low to make a big ecological impact. You know," he continued, "what really pisses me off is that we're fucking up the environment right now, but no one talks about that. No one wants to fix that because it interferes with capitalism."

She couldn't help but think of the holometabolous insects she'd just lectured on. She thought of herself as a butterfly, newly transformed from a caterpillar. Perhaps this was a new stage in her development—from terrestrial caterpillar to aerial butterfly. She could fly now and the world would never look the same, never be the same, but she knew this thought was a cop-out. She was at fault, and not just for what she did to Pablo. She felt guilty for having known so little, for having been interested only in the insects of the world, for thinking that was enough. Before, newspaper articles had never meant much, just stories from another world, far away. Now every report of an uprising or war brought the same image: the man, face down on the side of the road, and the two soldiers holding rifles above him.

She considered the military in a new way as well. Up to now, the military had simply been part of her life, just as her parents were part of her life, and she'd never thought past the obvious fact that they both represented security to her. Her parents protected her. The military protected her. Yet, in

Mexico the military hadn't protected her or the people around her; instead they frightened everyone. She wondered how the U.S. would respond if the Navajo people suddenly took up arms and declared true autonomy. Surely, they'd have as much right as the Indians in Chiapas, but she was certain that the U.S. military would react in the same way as the Mexican military. None of these thoughts comforted her.

She wondered about Parker. She hadn't heard much from him since they parted in the airport in Mexico City when he'd gathered up his luggage in a hurry. He had needed to run to make his flight. After pulling his baggage off the conveyer belt, he'd turned toward her. They'd hugged in an awkward way and then their hands had found each other. Neither of them said anything about it, but it was clear that they both had wanted to touch. He smiled, squeezed her hand and ran off.

He was back at his university in Texas. He had called a couple of times in January and she hadn't returned his phone calls. What would she say to him? She was both attracted to him and angry with him, and then she'd had so much to do between work and Christen, and every thought of Parker reminded her of César and Chiapas and she was trying to avoid those thoughts. But when she didn't answer his calls, he'd emailed instead. She'd written him back and agreed to read over, and as it turned out, rewrite, a section of a grant proposal he was working on. She remembered their touch and she smiled.

She thought of César, too. She tried to forget that moment with him on the day the military arrived, but she couldn't help but think of it, and every time there was the same tightening in her chest. She knew it was irrational. She was safe and at home, but the fear surged through her so fast that it couldn't be controlled. Her palms sweat and there was the sense of being overcome. She couldn't understand what had made him so angry, but she could still see his eyes, dark and enraged, staring at her and she could feel his fingers clenching her shoulders.

Christen had asked, "Where did you get those bruises on your shoulders?"

"Probably from sleeping on the hard floor," she lied. She'd followed that up with a quick question to distract him. "What should we do tonight?"

She expected him to realize it was a lie, and ask her again, but he didn't.

There was a knock on her door.

"Dr. Hill?" A young woman stood before her. "I was wondering what I should focus on for the exam? And uh, how in-depth should the lab reports be?"

Another student poked his head behind the young woman. "When will we start collecting insects for our final projects?"

She answered them, hiding her resentment. Their bright-eyed innocence reminded her too much of herself. This thought presented itself suddenly to her and she felt closed-in, encompassed within the cloud once again. She wondered if the students standing in front of her, soliciting guidance about class, could see it.

"We'll begin collecting as soon as we get three or four days above forty degrees," she told them. "Don't worry. I'll plan a field trip and we'll collect together the first day."

The invisible cloud had been with her since she returned home; it had followed her from the Ocosingo valley. She didn't know how to describe it otherwise, even if the cloud image seemed silly, reminding her of a cartoon character followed by a dark cloud. After the students left, she went to the women's bathroom and stood in front of the mirror looking for evidence of the envelope she felt, but couldn't see. Maybe it was more like water, like touching water. It moved away as her hand ran through it, but immediately came back to fill the space left free. She wished it were like a curtain that she could part and walk through. She stared at her face in the mirror and looked, but there was no evidence of anything unusual. The image she saw was the same reflection as always. Nothing to mark the change. This must be how it is, she thought. Life puts layers and layers of sadness over us until finally one day we just drown, too tired to swim our way out for a breath.

She found her notes for the next day's lecture, but didn't open the folder. She looked outside. The day had not lightened at all. The gray clouds hadn't shifted, and the sky was dreary and impenetrable. Two hours later, as she still staring out the window of her office, she had an urge. She gathered her things and left school, stopping on the way home at an upscale paper and printing shop to buy a museum quality scrapbook.

At home she leafed through pages of the newspapers she had collected—the American ones, the ones she'd bought in Tuxtla and those from the airport in Mexico City. She clipped every picture and article relevant to the uprising and arranged them in chronological order, those that appeared on January 1st, 2nd, 3rd, 4th, 5th. After the 5th, there were fewer.

She needed to decide among the photographs, some black and white, some colored, which to save. Should she save all the pictures or perhaps, only those of the dead? How did one do should such a thing? She smoothed a crinkled piece of newspaper with her fingertips and looked closely at the picture. A man was stepping out of the frame, right hand over his mouth, left hand in his jeans' pocket. She couldn't make out the expression in his eyes, but she could see that he had just passed four bodies scattered on the street in Ocosingo. The bodies lay ten feet from one another, in disarray, arms and legs going every which way. Each had been hooded, facing a different direction. One man was barefoot. What had happened to his shoes? Were they stolen? Did he not have any to begin with?

Another photograph. The shot-up bus. The black and white picture had been taken from the ditch, below the road.

The two bodies, one on top of the other, looked as if they'd rolled down the hill. At first glance, they could be college students, lovers, lounging drunk after an all-night party. A few feet away, another man lay head down toward the ditch, legs higher above, arms spread, positioned as if he was about to begin making the perfect, upside-down snow angel. She felt the urge, even at this impossible distance, to reposition his arms so that they looked natural. There was a news reporter in the picture as well, walking on the road above them, next to the bus. He was changing lenses on his camera, not looking at the bodies.

The worst was the colored picture of the dead Zapatista boy with the mole by his eye, the way his head was turned, left ear against the cement, his right eye staring into nothing, the black puddle by his head. Other men, whom she didn't recognize, lay next to him. All of them had bloody wrists and ankles. The colors red and black had never been so grotesque.

There was a small black and white photograph of two Mexican soldiers with white handkerchiefs tied over their noses hoisting a large white bundle into a truck. One soldier, using two hands, had lifted one end of the bundle off the ground. The other soldier, holding the heavier part, had not yet moved his left hand onto the bundle, exposing one end of the sheet, soaked with blood. The truck bed was filled with similar bundles.

She clipped and stacked and stared at the pictures. Using glue, she fixed them to the pages of the scrapbook. She labeled the photos, printing the time and place where they were taken in small black letters along the sides. She would remember them, keep them safe. She finished pasting the last article into the scrapbook and returned the book to its felt-lined box. She went into the bedroom and slid the box under her bed.

CHAPTER EIGHTEEN
Pablo

He had entered another country. Of course, it was still Mexico, but it felt like another world. Except for the young woman he came with and this older woman, no one spoke Spanish. In the days after he arrived, people came to the house and talked with the two women, but they didn't come into the house or sit down. They talked from the dirt yard, and the older woman responded from the house. The young woman never said a word. He listened to their voices, but he could make nothing of the words. There was no relation between the sounds their mouths made and Spanish. His ability to speak English and French was useless here. When the people left, the young woman and older woman didn't say much between themselves. They cooked, ate and slept in a silent way.

When he and the young woman first arrived at the small wooden house, it was late afternoon. No one was there, but it was clear that she knew the place. In an easy Spanish, she told him to sit down, and he realized then that she could speak. She went to the kitchen hut, poured water into a pan and crouched near the fire to wait for it to boil. A few minutes later an older woman walked into the house. She saw Pablo first and seemed surprised, but not alarmed.

"You want something?" she asked him in Spanish. When the young woman heard the older woman speaking, she called out in her language from the kitchen hut and the older woman went to join her there. They spoke in hushed voices for a few minutes, and then the young woman brought Pablo a cup of bitter coffee and a bowl of cold rice. After an entire day without food, the rice was delicious, and as his stomach began to fill, he was overtaken with exhaustion. He propped himself against the outside of the house and spent the remaining hours of light listening to the two woman speak and thinking about the rebellion and the short time he'd spent in custody. Within a week, Ocosingo had turned into a city of policemen and army soldiers, black boots covered in dust, guns, radios with antennas, and helicopter landing pads. There was no longer a market for local produce or open storefronts, only deserted streets and military patrols. There had been only that one restaurant open near the plaza where he'd gone to eat with the young woman, and they were open to serve reporters. It was uncanny how fast Ocosingo had gone from small rural town to military center, and seeing the change had disoriented Pablo.

When it was completely dark, the young woman approached him again and gave him a warm tortilla and some water. "Tomorrow there will be more food," she said.

"It's fine," he said. At the moment, he was too tired to think about hunger. "I'm very tired," he told her. Hearing him, the older woman strung up a hammock and pointed him toward it. He'd never slept in a hammock before and until he tried to get in, he had no idea how difficult it would be. He opened the roughly woven material and tried hopelessly to flatten it out. Realizing that it was impossible to enter forwards, he put his back to the hammock, took a piece of the weave in each hand, set himself down in the middle, lay back and swung his feet up. The hammock rocked on its hooks making it impossible to position himself in the middle. He scooted and rolled until his body was entirely wound into the hammock, and finally, feeling foolish and noisy, he stopped moving and accepted the position. He was wrapped in rough fibers, much like a larva in its cocoon. His left shoulder stiffened and his right hip ached, but he could not move or reposition himself. The night was painful and so when he heard the howler monkeys roar out the morning just before sunrise, he was grateful to get up.

He rose hungry and fatigued. The last few days of

returning to Ocosingo, being held by the military, and then walking here, were taking their toll. He couldn't remember ever feeling so displaced. At least in the morning light, he could better see the surroundings of the young woman's place in the forest village. There were two buildings, a sleeping house where they had all slept in hammocks, and a kitchen hut. Both were made of light balsa wood and palm roofs; the kitchen hut had only one wall and was open on the other three sides. The two woman were already awake and in the kitchen hut, so he went and sat there with them. Scattered on the dirt floor were gourds, brown and black from fire, wooden bowls, spoons, and water jars. Hanging from the low thatched roof hung nets and skulls of deer, peccaries and monkeys. Lined up along the one wall were a number of gourds with lids, and next to them were small piles of bird feathers, some brown, others green and blue, a spindle of cotton thread and a few white bones. The back corner of the kitchen was used for grinding corn, the grinder fastened to a pole with a container on the floor where pulverized kernels could fall. A trail led from the kitchen hut to another group of houses close by where other Lacandón people lived.

* * *

Three days after he arrived, he woke and rolled out of the hammock to find that the young woman was gone, and he was alone with the older woman. He didn't know what he should do.

"Where is the young woman?" he asked. At this moment, he realized that he did not even know her name. He had spent four days with her, and he hadn't asked her name and she hadn't asked his.

The older woman lifted her chin and pointed toward the forest. Her reticence made him hesitant to ask more questions.

"I want to stay," he told her.

She shrugged her shoulders and handed him a warm

tortilla. She was not old or young, but somewhere in the middle. He couldn't tell. Her hair was black and long, and fell down along her face like the young woman's. She was small like the other woman too. He watched her form tortillas, slapping the dough between her hard and callused hands to thin it out and then placing it on the hot metal griddle.

"Do you know the Zapatistas? Maybe there is something I could do."

"There is always something to do," she answered.

Again, he felt that he should not ask too many questions and so he left her and went to sit on the stoop of the wooden house. He chewed the burnt-flavored tortilla and watched a bird flit in the high canopy. He heard its high sharp zeezee call and presumed it was a warbler. If he had binoculars, he could tell which species it was. Lowland rainforest had its own array of species that, except in migration, didn't occur in the Ocosingo Valley. Instead of coffee, cattle ranches, Acacia trees, here the vegetation was huge and complicated. Vines entwined, climbed and sprawled over the tops of trees thirty meters above, and every space between canopy and ground was filled with plant life. He recognized none of the plant species and he knew the birds only from books.

"I don't want anything to do with them anymore," she said.

He turned toward her, not knowing exactly what she was talking about. She was crouched next to the fire looking into a black pot, and so he was unsure if she'd actually spoken or if he'd imagined it.

"They're trying to take our forest, the Zapatistas. I thought I'd made them understand, but they're talking again about building settlements in the reserve."

"The biosphere reserve?"

"Yes, that one, and our land, Hach Winik land too."

Pablo waited for her to continue, but the silence stretched and he realized she wasn't going to say anymore. Before he finished the tortilla, two men arrived and stood in front of him. They wore shorts and rubber boots, but no shirts and they both had machetes. The woman said something to them from the kitchen and then she walked toward Pablo, handed him a machete, and spoke to him in Spanish. "Go help them."

Pablo followed the men down a well-trodden trail of hard red dirt, passing a group of similar houses with balsa wood sides and thatched roofs. In front of every house, a stick had been pushed into the earth and a white piece of cloth tied to its top. Behind the houses there was a wire enclosure for chickens, also adorned with white flags, and on the other side of that, a trail entering secondary growth forest. After a few minutes of walking through the secondary forest, they emerged into a *milpa*, a field of corn, yams, cassava, beans and fruit trees that didn't look anything like the organized fields of corn in the highlands. The red-brown soil was high in clay, uneven and strewn with remnants of burned forest. No effort had been made to completely clear the land or even-out the soil. The men crossed the field and he followed them, looking at the mix of vegetables in all states of growth as he passed. Tiny bean seedlings, with no more than four new leaves, grew right next to mature corn and tomatoes.

The men ignored him and gave him no directions. They began to hack at weeds surrounding the far end of the field and so he stationed himself along with them and cut at the weeds and bushes as well. The sun heated the morning and before long he was soaked with sweat and suffocating in the stagnant air. The men worked at a slow, regular pace and did not stop to rest or speak, the whack and slash of their machetes against vegetation taking the place of conversation. Pablo tried to keep up with them, but he could not and had to continually pause to rest.

* * *

That had been his first day in the field, and now every day since he'd arrived the week before, had been a repeat of that one. There was little talk, just the zing and whack of machetes and when the men did say something, he couldn't understand them. When Pablo could slash no more, he rested and watched birds. At this low elevation, there were so many new species that he'd never heard or seen before. Tiny hummingbirds, green violet-ears, and lucifers zipped through the *milpa*. Warblers sang their dulcet songs. Loud, obnoxious parrots came to eat fruit and were chased away by the men. And trogons, the most quiet of creatures, were a special treat. So far, he'd seen both the eared trogon with its gray head, bright red chest and green-blue back, and the simpler elegant trogon. He watched one perched silently on tree branches, with its head tilted. Suddenly, it would fly out to catch an insect and quickly return to its perch. And the day before, at dusk, he'd seen a spectacled owl, a rare bird he had always admired in books: large, chocolate brown with white brows over its eyes. When he noticed it, the owl was perched in one of the enormous uncut forest trees that stood like lonely soldiers at the edge of the *milpa*. The owl's body was immobile, its giant, clear eyes fixed on Pablo's movements.

With the squawk of parrots flying to their night perches in the late afternoon, the men would stop working and head back to their houses. He followed them and returned to the woman's house, which sat away from the others. She said little and he was so tired, it was enough to eat tortillas and beans and then sleep. He'd never been this spent before. Exhaustion took over as soon as he climbed into the hammock making his dreams as opaque as the foggy highland mornings, but he welcomed the tiredness. Being tired made sleep possible in the constricting hammock and heat.

The woman was conscious of him, but unconcerned. She occupied herself with her work. In the mornings she let the chickens out and threw them a handful of seed. In the evening, she rounded them back under a set of large baskets. When he went to bed at night, he left her crushing corn or stirring her pots over the wood fire. At sunrise, when he rose sore and stiff, she was already crouched next to them. Often if he woke during the night, he heard that she was up, working, moving logs around, blowing on the embers of the fire, keeping things alive.

This morning when he woke and rolled out of the hammock, he saw another man in the kitchen hut, sitting by the fire, talking in low tones with the woman. Outside, tied to a tree stood a saddled bay horse. The man's presence surprised him. In the week he had spent with the woman, since the young woman left, no one had come to talk with her. As Pablo approached the kitchen hut, he heard that they were speaking in Spanish. She noticed him and handed him a warm sweet potato wrapped in a banana leaf.

"This is Jorge," she told him.

Pablo knew that Jorge, in western clothes and speaking Spanish, was not Lacandón. Jorge stood and smiled at Pablo. His eyes were black, his smile white and he had a beautiful face. His handshake felt warm and firm.

"Nice to meet you, Pablo. Can we talk?"

"Of course," Pablo said. The sound of his own voice was odd after so many days without speaking.

They sat on the stoop of the kitchen hut and Jorge spoke in a quiet voice.

"I'm a Zapatista. We have been told that you would like to help, and we have a request." He paused, Pablo nodded his head, and Jorge continued. "We want to send communiqués to the newspapers stating our cause, why we have taken arms, what we want, but we need people to deliver them. You, because you are white, can do this without risk. Our people cannot."

Pablo nodded his head. It was true. He could walk on the roads without suspicion. The military wouldn't suspect him, not outright, not if he was just walking along. "Yes, of course, I would be honored to deliver the messages."

"The communiqués must be taken to the cathedral in San

Cristóbal de las Casas. From there, the bishop will make sure they are delivered to the newspapers."

"Yes, of course."

"It is an important job. We want people to understand. This woman says we can trust you."

Pablo nodded.

"I have a communiqué with me. Will you leave now?"

"Of course. I'm ready."

Pablo collected his backpack and followed Jorge outside to the horse. From a sack tied to the horse, Jorge pulled out a roll of paper wrapped in plastic and handed it to Pablo.

"*Suerte*, and the faster the better," he said. He shook Pablo's hand, mounted the horse and reined him away. Pablo looked back at the house. The woman was standing at the edge of her kitchen hut, watching them. She nodded to Pablo and then returned to crouch next to her pots. Pablo stepped onto the path that he now knew would lead to the muddy road. If a truck happened to pass him somewhere along the way, he would hitch a ride to Ocosingo. Otherwise, he would walk.

CHAPTER NINETEEN
Amy

Warm spring rain. Minnesota awoke from winter and everything living was getting ready to try again. Birds, just back from the south, were thin, their fat reserves burned off in migration, but this didn't stop them from beginning each day with frenzied singing, courting and nest building. They tugged worms from damp soil, pecked at larvae just under bark, and waited for adult insects, newly pupated and slow, to emerge.

Amy took the entomology class to a deciduous forest to collect insects for their final projects. Violets, claytonias, and mustards pushed up through brown leaves and flowered under the still naked trees. In a few weeks, at the end of April, their world would be shaded by the trees above, the opportunity for growth and reproduction lost until the next spring. Using Winkler Funnels she helped the students sift through leaf litter that lay still undecomposed under the snow. She knelt, measured out a one meter squared area and then gathered the cold, wet leaves inside the square into a small pile. She transferred a portion of them to the sieve and shook the green nylon back and forth. When her arms tired, she gave the students a turn and watched as they shook the sieve, urging any insects hidden in the leaves down through the mesh. They discarded the leaves from the sieve and added more. Dirt and insects fell into the bag below the sieve, tied shut at the bottom. Later, they would transfer the sieved soil and insects to mesh bags and hang those within a muslin tent. As the soil dried, the insects would crawl out looking for moisture and drop into the cup of alcohol tied to the bottom of the muslin tent. Shake and wait. It was a great way to survey insects in leaf litter.

She watched the students at work on the task of sieving and collecting insects. She was grateful for their focus. Teaching, and this entomology class in particular, was helping to bring her back.

When she had returned from Chiapas in January, she had been relieved to be in a familiar landscape once again. She understood the cold of winter, the white snow, the dreary sky. She knew the names of the trees, birds, and insects. She knew where they could be found and how they lived, what they were up to.

Yet in the last few weeks, she had begun to feel that there were shortcomings to predictability, to knowing. You stopped looking when you thought you understood, when you anticipated what you were going to see, and although she knew that there were always more layers of details to discover, it was hard to remember to look.

* * *

At home in the late afternoon she sat at the kitchen table surrounded by insect identification books, pinning blocks, pins and small white labels. Her eyes rested against the oculars of the dissecting scope. Without lifting her eyes, she felt for the lamp and positioned it to better illuminate the inert insect lying on its side in the petri dish. She peered down at a slender, dark ant. The ant's waist had one segment, so its subfamily was either Formicinae or Dolichoderinae. She consulted the key for the next step in identification. Ants were not her forte, but she was patient. The next question in the key asked about the anal acidopore. Gently, she took the ant in forceps and turned the ant so that she could see whether the pore was oval with hairs or a slit. It was an oval, so it must be in the subfamily Formicinae. How beautiful and complicated the ant was when seen up close through the microscope. She worked her way through the key and at last decided the ant belonged in the genus *Camponotus*. She then glued its thorax to a paper triangle attached to a pin. She pressed the pin into styrofoam and scribbled the identification on a piece of paper and started on the next insect. She didn't know how long she had been working, but when she looked up again, she noticed that it was dark outside.

If Christen were around, he would want her to stop working for the evening, clean up the table and eat dinner with him. It was convenient that he was at the coffee shop, talking with his philosophy group. She was glad to get a break from discussions about Chiapas. Christen had become an expert on the situation, and at first, it was fine because she had needed to talk and try to understand what was going on there, but she had tired of constantly analyzing the situation and so she had closed herself off. She was naturally protective of her emotional experiences, but now, even when she tried to share her feelings about Chiapas with him, it didn't work. He understood everything too well, but only intellectually, and he couldn't feel what she felt. And he wasn't right when he'd accused her of forgetting about Chiapas. In fact, she had thought of little else throughout the winter months, but spring had brought insects, new lives, new hunts. The students were enthusiastic and she was eager to add to her collection and begin new research projects. In keying out insects, she could lose herself for a while, enter another world, remember that humans were just one of many species; she could remind herself to look.

The truth was, she was sick of Christen's philosophy group. Since January, they had progressed at double speed, and now in April, the group still met three times a week to discuss the situation and organize their efforts to maximize their coverage of Mexico. One read history about the 1500s, another contemporary history. They gave each other tutorials. They searched the internet and downloaded Marcos' speeches. They read newspapers from around the world, each of them translating from whatever language they could, relating to each other what the French, Germans and Italians were saying. They had become experts about current events in Chiapas, the names Salinas and Zedillo rolled with ease. Oppenheimer had written such and such in his latest column, and was Camacho Solís really mediating or just pandering? Within the first few weeks they had brought each other up to speed on the PRI, PRD and PAN political parties. Over coffee they discussed the reports, marches, speeches, and the military repression. When Colosio, Salinas' choice for the next presidency, was shot in late March, they debated who had done it, what should happen, and how the country would respond. They spoke about the closing of the stock market and reports that people were changing all their money from pesos to dollars. Would the economy collapse?

In the beginning, just after she'd returned from Mexico, Amy had enjoyed sitting with them because they were so well informed and through them, she was learning a lot about Mexican history and politics, but with time, she began to feel increasingly offended. Their analysis of the situation struck her as almost perverse, a sort of political voyeurism, which did nothing to help her understand. In their presence, her confusion only deepened.

The last time she attended the group, she watched Christen as he compared the reality of landless peasants in Mexico in 1994 to that of Russian peasants in 1904. As he spoke, his eyes grew wide and excited. He paced back and forth as he explicated. His comrades nodded their heads; they hadn't made the connection and they were impressed. They thought he was brilliant. The more he talked, the more his curly bangs flopped over his forehead and into his eyes. He brushed them away, only to have them fall again. When she'd met him, she thought this blond lock of hair was hip and sexy, but now it looked affected and ridiculous.

"The way you talk," she said, "you seem happy that there are peasants in Mexico who can live out your revolutionary fantasies."

He stopped pacing, stared at her and walked away.

"That wasn't fair, Amy," one of the others told her.

She knew it hadn't been fair, and she didn't mean to attack him so hard. Christen meant well, but even the earnest way that he looked hurt bothered her. He didn't defend himself as Parker would have; he just lumbered away to sulk like a child.

That evening she had apologized to him. "But don't you see, Christen, how odd it is?"

"No," he said. "I don't."

"The strangeness of the situation, the fact that their deaths have revitalized your philosophy group?"

"It's a call to action," he said.

"Action?" She exploded as she said it. She was angry now. "What are you going to do?"

"Do?"

"Yes, this call to action must mean you're going to act, doesn't it?"

He didn't respond, and so she continued. "You talk and talk, but you never *do*."

He waited before he answered her and in that time, nothing, not even the air between them, moved. He looked directly at her. "You would never know what I do because you have tunnel vision from your microscope!"

He quietly left her apartment and when she saw him a few days later, they both apologized, but after that conversation, Christen began to work the afternoon and evening shifts at the coffee shop. He still came by her apartment on the way home, only not every night like before. She was uncertain about their relationship, but also tired. Sometimes, even when she was awake, she turned off all the lights when it was time for the coffee shop to close so that it would look as if she were asleep. After enough time had passed, so that she could be sure he'd already driven by, she'd go back to the living room, click on the microscope light and work. She knew Christen was upset because she no longer wanted to talk about Chiapas, or, really, anything else. He

212

thought she was a career-hungry academic who was too focused on science. But, in secret, she still collected every new article about Chiapas that she could find. She cut them out and pasted them into the scrapbook, allowed the glue to dry and replaced the book to its green, cloth-lined box and pushed it back under her bed. A couple of times, she had taken it out, planning to read through the whole book, beginning to end, but so far she hadn't.

Tonight, she didn't miss Christen and felt a bit bad about not missing him, but it was true. Without him, she could spend the entire evening pinning and studying until she was tired and ready for bed. Look at how many ant species she had found in just one day. The sheer diversity! So many ways to make a life. She'd collected an ant in the genus *Acanthomyops*, the first she'd ever seen. They were subterranean ants that only came above the surface occasionally, surviving by farming root aphids, tiny sugar sucking insects that latched onto roots and funneled the plant's phloem through their system. Much like the ants on that plant she'd shown Parker in Chiapas, these ants drank the "honeydew," from the aphids' anus, only this time it all happened underground. This species of *Acanthomops* was beautiful, almost yellow, with a citronella scent.

She thought about the aphids that held their babies and grandbabies, perfect clones, inside of them. To carry an exact copy of yourself. She knew it was the best strategy, getting all of your genes to the next generation, but something about the idea repulsed her. Besides, clonal organisms did really well if the environment was relatively constant over time, and in truth, the environment was rarely constant.

There were others: carpenter ants, myrmicines and formicines. Without Christen she could work as late as she wanted, until she was totally exhausted. She could focus her attention entirely on insects and their lives, all other emotions held at bay by the incomparable and exquisite pleasure of pinning.

* * *

The next morning she awoke disoriented and afraid. Her dream had scared her, especially because the images failed to fade as she showered and made breakfast. In the dream, she had seen the six Zapatistas from that first day, when they'd been stopped in front of the rocks. Pablo and César were there too. They stood in a row, Pablo, César and the six Zapatistas, but now they were on pedestals. Their hair had been trimmed, the bangs cut short and straight across the front revealing high foreheads. The red bandanas, no longer covering their faces, lay in circles at their feet. Behind them she could make out a vegetation-covered hill, and there was the suggestion of an old building, a ruin, off to one side. Erect and still, the men stood like soldiers with their shoulders square, collar bones prominent. Their bare arms hung down, elbows bent, their own severed heads held lightly between their hands. She could make out every detail. She saw the young one with the mole. He was conscious. They all were, but now there was no fear, no pain. One Zapatista had a wide scar across his chin. The cut had needed stitches. Except for these details, their expressions were identical: even Pablo and César looked resigned and calm. Eight pairs of eyes stared straight ahead with passive expressions, intent on the sacrifice they offered. Mouths parted slightly, on the verge of speech, they were suspended somewhere between death and life.

She tried to shake the image as she hurried across campus to the lecture room. She picked up the dusty chalk and wrote while forty heads, eighty eyes, watched her. Three words: diversity, speciation, extinction. The students copied the words.

"Question," she announced. "How many species are there on earth? Humans are one species. How many more do we share the planet with?"

"No one knows," offered a young man.

"Right, we don't know the *exact* number, but there are estimates," she told him. "So how many?" she asked the class again.

"A million," ventured one student.

She wrote the number on the board. "Others?"

"A billion," another student suggested.

"More guesses?"

"That's too many," said another student. "It's more like three hundred thousand."

"Okay," Amy said. "We have estimates that span quite a range here. How would we go about figuring out which estimate is best?" She worked them through various estimation methods for determining species diversity, and they discussed the pros and cons of each.

"Now, another question," she said. "How many species have lived on earth through its entire life as a planet?"

Amy lectured about extinction and speciation events throughout the earth's history, and then moved on to present-day extinctions. "Today's rate of extinction is one hundred times that of any extinction episode in the past." She turned on the slide projector. "Here are examples of some of the species that have been driven to extinction by humans in the last four hundred years. There are, of course, many more that are less photogenic.

"The dodos were large, flightless turkey-sized pigeons that used to inhabit the island of Mauritius in the Indian Ocean. They were hunted by sailors to replenish food supplies on ships. Since these birds evolved without humans, they didn't have appropriate fear, and because they didn't fly they were easy to catch and kill. The dodo went extinct in the 1600s.

"This bird, the passenger pigeon, occurred in enormous flocks." She projected a drawing of the bird, a slender pigeon with a gray head, rust-colored breast and long tail. "In the early 1800s an ornithologist reported seeing a flock of more than two billion migrating pigeons in North America. Think about that!" As she spoke she felt a tightness in her chest and her hands began to shake. She continued, "The passenger pigeon's demise is attributed to deforestation of habitat and commercial hunting by colonists, who unlike Native Americans had gun technology." She couldn't gain control over her feelings. The dream must have upset her more than she thought. Her eyes filled with tears and in a thin, trembling voice she said, "In 1914, this species was declared extinct." When the second tear rolled down her cheek, she could no longer retain any semblance of composure, so she dismissed the class. She sat down. She'd never lost control during this lecture before, but this time when she'd seen the slide of the brown pigeon with its reddish chest she'd thought of the boys with their bandanas. Once again, as had happened so many times since she returned from Chiapas, she was crying, and she felt afraid.

* * *

Back in her office she flipped through the phone book until she found what she was looking for. It had been two, maybe three years since she'd shot a gun, but suddenly, she had the urge to hold a gun, shoot, to take control of her fears. She left the university and drove to the range on the edge of the city. The man inside insisted on a lesson.

"I know how to shoot," she told him.

"I believe you, but we've got to protect ourselves. Rules of the range."

"Fine," she said.

"What do you want to shoot?"

"What do you have?"

He raised an eyebrow. "Whatever you want."

"I doubt that," she smiled, knowing that he was probably telling the truth. Most ranges had everything, even illegal weapons, which were kept hidden away for special customers. "How about a rifle, something simple to begin with."

"What kind of target: human or bull's eye?"

"Bull's eye is fine."

Inside the booth he handed her the rifle and stood back while she loaded it. She lifted it to the arm rest, positioned her ear plugs and took aim through the site, lining the two marks up. She pulled the trigger, putting three small, clean holes into the target and then she glanced back at him. He acknowledged her skill with a nod of his head, left the booth and returned with a hand gun.

"Try this one," he said. "It's super sweet."

She took the gun from him and felt the worn wood of the handle, doubting that his callused hands could appreciate its softness. The gun was heavy but not more than she could handle. She steadied her right hand with her left, aimed at the target and pulled on the trigger. The first shot went wide, barely hitting the target. She adjusted. The second was better, but still not very good. "It shoots well, but I'm out of practice."

"You're not bad," he said. "That one is mine. Seventies model. You thinking to buy? Pretty girl needs some defense?"

"Thanks, but it's just a sport," she told him.

"Sure," he said, "but you get used to carrying it around. Feels good."

"I believe that," she said. "Do you have another pistol I can practice with? Something lighter?"

"Sure."

He brought her another pistol and then left her alone in her booth. She loaded the gun, took aim and fired at the target. The shots weren't perfect, but they were decent. She was reassured that she hadn't entirely lost her skill, but the shooting wasn't doing what she'd imagined. Coming to the range was supposed to make her feel powerful and secure, but as she held the small pistol, shot and heard the muffle of the gunshot through the earplugs, she realized she wasn't feeling better. She could hurt and kill someone with the gun, but it couldn't ever defend her from real fears. She continued to shoot, but now her hands had a slight tremor and it was difficult to steady the gun. She lowered the gun. Nothing protects us, she thought. Not guns nor the army nor fathers, nothing except perhaps ignorance, in an ironic sort of way, and now she no longer had ignorance either. The question was how to live inside this new state, how to accept the vulnerability without collapsing from fear. Like with guns or identifying insects or anything in life, it must be a matter of practice, she thought. She took aim and fired the gun again.

CHAPTER TWENTY
Pablo

The full moon cast a bright shadow illuminating his path so that there was no need for a flashlight. In the soft light, vegetation appeared blue-black, and without its daytime harshness, the world welcomed him. Pablo was two people walking with a message, and he didn't feel lonely anymore. In the three months he had been working as a courier for the Zapatistas, he had begun to enjoy his own thoughts and the night birds that kept him company as he walked. At first he had walked during the day, but he had passed too many of the same people, becoming a familiar face. The military didn't suspect him outright because he wasn't indigenous, but if they had seen him coming and going, he wouldn't have lasted long. Being detained once by them was enough, so he switched to sleeping during the afternoons and walking in the dark. He had become of the night, just as the Zapatistas said they were, and this new schedule—to be awake while most people slept—liberated his thoughts and imagination.

He took the communiqués from someone at the edge of the Lacandón Forest. Hand to hand, the pieces of paper were passed, rolled up like ancient scrolls, stuffed in a cardboard tube and placed in a plastic bag. Each one was a separate treasure for him to protect and deliver. Local people on the route knew him, and if they could, they gave him tortillas and beans to eat; otherwise, they gave him a small piece of *marquesote*, sweet cornbread, and a cup of weak coffee. Mostly, they gave him warmth, a blanket if they had one and a place by the fire next to them. The cathedral in San Cristóbal de las Casas where he delivered the communiqués always had a hot meal waiting, a warm bucket of water to wash himself and a real bed. In the first two months of the uprising, there had been constant correspondence from the Zapatistas to the Mexican people and he had trekked back and forth between the Lacandón Forest and San Cristóbal de las Casas many times, but now the flow of communiqués had slowed.

Just that mid-morning, Pablo had learned that there was a new communiqué coming, the first communication from the Zapatistas to the press in weeks, the first one since Colosio was shot. A child in the village was sent to tell him in the *milpa*, at the edge of the forest where he helped to weed and care for crops. The day had begun like most days since the frequency of communiqués and the need for his services had diminished. He had risen and gone out with the others, machete in hand. He was becoming better at wielding the machete so that now he could almost match the other men, who kept perfect time as they cut back the vegetation that threatened their crops, their machetes making a zing-zing sound as they sliced through plants. But he could never cut as fast as they could because he wasn't as strong, and also the birds distracted him. Parrots, warblers, trogons. He learned to recognize their calls and songs, the rhythms of their flight and the way they moved in vegetation. Birds were the only thing that relieved the monotony of hot, oppressive days when he cut and sweat and planted without sharing a single word with the other villagers.

He had no idea how people in the village were notified when there was a new communiqué, but everyone seemed to know more than he did. He was constantly amazed. They knew what was going to happen hours or days before he did. He had come to believe that there were two simultaneous universes, the one he lived in and the one they lived in, and that these universes or states met only infrequently at points where they crossed, points that were fleeting and unpredictable.

After the boy gave him the message, he left the men working and went to his hut to sleep for the afternoon so that when evening arrived, he would be fresh to travel. The Lacandón people knew that he would be gone for a few days, and although they didn't like the Zapatistas, the war or anything to do with outsiders, they'd never said anything to him. In fact, no one ever spoke to him, and he wasn't sure it was a language problem. They simply tolerated him without offering themselves.

Just before sunset, he went into the forest. Usually Jorge was the one to deliver the communiqué to him and Pablo hoped he would be the one this time as well. Pablo knew the communiqué would comment on Colosio's assassination and he was anxious to see what it said. As he hoped, Jorge was waiting for him at the meeting spot. Jorge was Tzeltal, but he spoke Spanish well. He had finished high school and then continued his education with Marcos, and he and Pablo always had good conversations. He was a bit shorter than Pablo and his body was perfect; Pablo envied his natural strength. His shirt was unbuttoned and Pablo could see sweat collecting on his hairless chest, wetness over the soft, cinnamon color of his skin. Pablo felt the tingling of arousal and tried to divert his thoughts to something else. Jorge greeted him by reaching out and holding his shoulder. "Hola *compañero*. How are you?"

"Fine." If Pablo were braver he would tell Jorge that he liked him. Who knows? Pablo didn't know the cues down here, and he wondered how gays met, how they let each other know, but he knew it was a silly thought. The rules of romance were the same everywhere, weren't they? He'd know if Jorge were interested. Pablo pulled out tobacco, rolled two cigarettes and they smoked together.

"How is life in camp?" he asked Jorge.

"Hot and wet. We're tired and hungry, but morale is pretty good. We have patience."

"I guess it is a matter of patience, but it's hard for me," Pablo told him.

Jorge shrugged his shoulders. "There's not much choice.

We can't take on the military. Our biggest offensive is the internet."

Pablo watched the way Jorge held the cigarette in his hand, gently, with his wrist slightly curved up, making little circling motions with his wrist as he spoke. It wasn't the tough way that most men smoked with cigarette between thumb and forefinger. Pablo resisted the urge to reach out and touch Jorge's smooth, muscled forearm. The tingling began again and Pablo tried to concentrate on something else.

"What do people think of Colosio's death?"

Walking now in the moonlight, he realized he hadn't paid much attention to Jorge's answer. Jorge had said that Colosio's death didn't mean any more or any less than any man's death. His murder was just more evidence that the government was corrupt, and maybe now the Mexican people were moving closer to change, to new leadership. Pablo had spent the moments enjoying the way Jorge spoke, the quietness of his voice and the weight of his words, his deep-set energetic eyes, the movement of that wrist, the forearm. Watching Jorge, Pablo had also felt pain—the horrible and deep-rooted tension was the same as always. An intense desire to touch and caress and make love to Jorge and to be touched back, to come in each other's hands or mouths, to be united, connected, desired for that one moment. All of that stood up against the cruel awareness that he must resist his needs.

When he'd finished smoking, Jorge had given Pablo the communiqué, and each returned to his world, Jorge to his in the forest camp, and Pablo to his on the hillside trails. In the beginning, Pablo had wanted to follow Jorge into the forest. He wanted to know that world and he hoped he might get a glimpse of Subcomandante Marcos, the man who penned these works of art. The way everyone talked about him, he must really have a special energy or magnetism. Pablo wanted to be near that, and closer to Jorge.

If time permitted, Pablo always stopped outside of San

Cristóbal de las Casas before reaching the church, pulled the communiqué from its tube and read Marcos' words. He felt special, being the first to read the new message, poignant and lyrical, full of wisdom. Sometimes, Pablo imagined Marcos wrote directly to him and he was overwhelmed with a sense of admiration and faith. Of course, he immediately felt embarrassed for having such thoughts about Marcos. He should know better than to succumb to superficial admiration and make Marcos into a celebrity. Still, the man's words drew him in just as they'd drawn in so many others in the world.

"For years and years we harvested the death of our people in the Chiapan countryside...Our men and women walked in the long night of ignorance that a shadow threw over our paths; our people walked without truth or understanding. Our feet moved without destination; alone we lived and we died. So we directed our blood and the path of our dead to the road that other feet walked in truth. We are nothing if we walk alone; we are everything when we walk together in step with other dignified feet."*

Pablo wondered how anyone, including even people like his father, could be immune to the poetry. Reading the communiqués was his incentive and the anticipation of them was what kept him walking through the cold nights.

Life came into perspective on these journeys. Food, water, shelter took over as the most important things. He had very little money, so he ate only when people gave him food. Already he had lost many kilos and his jeans hung on him and wouldn't stay up without a belt. He could make out the bones in his hands and his feet, and he was developing the same hollow indentations below his cheeks as everyone else. It wasn't that people were stingy with food, only that no one had much and with all of the walking he did, the energy

---

* "We are Nothing if We Walk Alone," *Shadows of Tender Fury: The letters and Communiqués of Subcomandante Marcos and the Zapatista Army of National Liberation*; *Monthly Review Press*, Feb. 1994.

burned off fast. Being thin, he felt vulnerable, and it was a new and unsettling feeling, as if he were never truly safe. He felt the cold more, too.

When he left the forest in the lowlands and climbed up the steep canyons he sweated hard, so that when he was at the top and the wind blew, he shivered with cold. He put on his sweater, but the wet seeped in through his clothes, through the wool sweater and cotton shirt, all the way to his sweaty skin and into his bones where it stayed locked up. There was no keeping it out. Forever cold inside, he would be grateful to arrive at the church. The warm food and bath helped cut the cold, and for a while, he would be insulated.

He had started out three months ago with a pair of almost new leather boots, and now they were in tatters. He had learned that leather wasn't the best material for this climate. The sticky red mud in the *milpa* worked its way into the boot's seams, and since it was always damp, the leather never completely dried unless you left it in the sun, but if you did that, it cracked so that next time, your feet suffered more. His feet were always cold and wet, wrinkled like when, as a child, he'd spent all day in a swimming pool. Fungus now grew under his toenails making them black and blue and one was almost green. It was better now, because his feet had become hardened and callused. At first, he got blisters, huge swellings on his heels and toes. Each step was a separate torture, but there could be no stopping. He learned that if he kept going and walked through the pain, the blister would eventually break and the skin underneath would get hard and scaly. He learned that if he kept walking, he never got a blister in the same place twice. In time, the body created its own protection.

He thought about the night shortly after he started as courier when he learned a new sound, the call of agony. He had already been walking for many hours, and when he approached the highland village and heard the commotion, he was so tired he wasn't sure what the noise was. He heard a whining crescendo as he neared the plaza and when he arrived, he saw a mass of people standing over four bodies— two men, a woman and a child. The people moved around the bodies like bees in front of a disturbed hive, the women letting out low painful sobs, praying and consoling each other. The men talked fast, in Tzotzil, which Pablo couldn't understand, explaining to each other what they already knew. Pablo asked a man what had happened and the man told him in Spanish. A paramilitary group, made up of both Tzeltales and Tzotziles, had come through earlier that day and killed this one Zapatista family. The man told Pablo that the paramilitary men were local, but they had sophisticated guns, the same kind as the military. He said that there were more and more of these groups now who attacked Zapatista supporters. They used military weapons and received payment from landowners who had lost land because of the uprising. Pablo saw the house burned black, the wood still smoldered into the night air. He didn't stay long at the plaza. There was nothing for him to do and he needed to keep moving to deliver the communiqué by the next day. He walked on, planning to carry the sad news to the next village, but when he arrived he realized they already knew about the men, the woman and the child.

* * *

He usually stopped for a short rest at a couple of *campesino* houses on the way. There was one he especially liked. The young couple had a little girl with lively brown eyes. Eyes like stars. Her eyes were the kind that the young Lacandón woman should have had, the young woman who had looked straight at him and without speaking had said, "We're a long way still."

Pablo had told Jorge about that experience, of how she had spoken to him without sound and what she'd said, but Jorge didn't seem surprised. "The Hach Winik are different, older." Pablo wasn't sure what that meant or what to think.

He didn't usually believe in anything supernatural, but still, he had no explanation for what he'd heard. Mexico was a place that defied explanation, a land of inexplicable happenings, and Chiapas stranger still, and this was one of the reasons he loved his country. So much was unknown, unpredictable, open to interpretation. He enjoyed the contrast of studying biology and understanding the world in a scientific way and, at the same time, allowing himself to feel that nothing he figured out through science would ever be more than a meager approximation of reality. There was too much to understand.

One time, when Pablo was at that house, he called the little girl with star eyes to him. He wanted to give her something so he leaned down and whispered that same phrase, 'We're a long way still,' in her ear. She giggled and ran away.

Pablo had seen amazing things walking the footpaths between the Lacandón forest and San Cristóbal de las Casas. Night birds accompanied him. He and César had always limited their point counts to daytime, so these night birds were new to him. The buff-collared nightjar, whose call sounded nothing like a bird, announced itself with a rapid series of sounds that ended in an upward shrill, and then its cousin, the spot-tailed nightjar joined in with its high pitched sibilation. They would sit on the trail and then explode in silent flight away from him, landing twenty meters further along. As he approached again, they would repeat their song and dance. He wondered how they achieved these odd calls, and thought once again of continuing his studies. He missed research, the excitement of the questions, the daily rhythm and monotony of data collection, analyses and then answers. With science, at least, you had the option of asking questions for which there were answers.

He remembered the night he had urinated on the trail, next to a rock where he normally sat to rest. The next day, as he passed on his way back from the city, the spot was filled with butterflies. Big butterflies, tiny butterflies, two kinds of *Heliconius*, a brown *Artemia* with white and red stripes, yellow sulfurs, white sulfurs. After the initial scare from him, they settled back down to lap at the moist soil. It was the ammonia they wanted. When he began to walk again, they fluttered up, casting their colors into the misty morning. Colored butter that flew. Soft. Delicate. Vulnerable. He knew that if you caught them, the scales of their wings would rub off on your fingers and they were left more vulnerable than before. He wanted to be that colorful. He wanted to move with the same grace, to flutter up into the sky and get a proper view of the world and to fly down again, to sip nectar from flowers. He also was attracted to the concept of transformation. To spend half of one's life, or more, as a toxic caterpillar, worming one's way across leaves, feeding and growing fat on the juices of the sun. Later, to make a cocoon and hide away for a while, and then to emerge as this gorgeous other being, this creature of color and light and butter. To fly away, enlightened in the last days of life.

There had been a *Morpho* in the group of butterflies and this made him think of Amy, the American entomologist. He assumed she had arrived home to the United States and had settled back into her life. He had been to the States various times and was always amazed at how easy life was, everything from driving to shopping to paying bills was simple. Gringos were funny people. One thing he noticed was that they were constantly apologizing for things they did. If they coughed or sneezed or burped, they apologized, as if those were acts they could control and take back. More than once, in the supermarket or standing in line for a movie, a person had casually bumped him. Pablo hadn't even noticed it until the person began to apologize profusely. Did they think space could be owned? Funny that they acted like that with each other, but they didn't seem to have a problem invading the rest of the world.

He hadn't thought about it before, but it must have been

a radical change for Amy to come to Mexico, much more foreign than it was for him to travel to the States. He felt sorry for her too, especially for how César had treated her. She had been naïve, but before she left, he sensed that her eyes had begun to open. Still, it would take more than a few days in Chiapas to make someone like her see. He suspected that the United States put blinders on everyone, the kind of leather flaps they put on horses so that they couldn't see what was in their peripheral vision. Only most Americans didn't know they had them on, and so they never knew they could take them off.

Pablo had also learned that nothing stays the same. The house he and César had lived in, their home for three years, was now a brothel. The people around Ocosingo told him the military always set up such houses close to barracks so that soldiers would stay satisfied. Their house was perfect because it was close to the Pemex station and well-kept. The roof didn't leak, there were rooms with doors, a kitchen, and a toilet that worked. Those who paid more, got one of the beds and a private room. Those who didn't care just did it in the living room, while the other prostitutes sat around and waited for customers. The military would hire any woman they could, anyone who was desperate, which Pablo knew meant a lot of women. Probably they would have put that young Lacandón woman from the Pemex station there. The men would have liked her. They said that young girls brought double money.

* * *

Pablo arrived at the outskirts of San Cristóbal de las Casas in the hour before dawn and walked narrow, cobblestone streets up toward the cathedral. He delivered the communiqué to the bishop, bathed and ate, and by the time he finished, the city was bustling with morning. Storefronts opened, restaurants began serving breakfast and lines formed in front of the bank. He went out to buy a phone card, knowing he needed to call home, but not looking forward to the call. There had been a cease fire since the twelfth day of the uprising and his parents had calmed, but then Colosio, who was supposed to succeed Salinas as President, was murdered. Pablo knew his parents, like the rest of the wealthy PRI and PAN supporters, would be distressed. He knew that the communiqué he had just carried from the Zapatistas commented on the assassination and that it would be published in the newspapers the next day. He dialed the number.

"No one can know what this means," his father said.

"Maybe it means it's time for the PRI to go," Pablo said.

"And what instead, Pablo? The Zapatistas?"

"Well, no, not the Zapatistas, but maybe a real democracy, like the Zapatistas are calling for, something other than PRI." The phone provided a distance that gave him liberty to speak more freely with his father than he ever could do in person.

"Zapatistas!" his father yelled. "Salinas has been too easy with those imbeciles. Instead of real bombs, he's dropping cotton balls and talcum powder!"

"They are people, *papá.*"

"What kind of people? You can't think much of someone who won't show his face." His father was referring to Marcos who always dressed in green pants, a black jacket and a black ski mask.

"*Papá*, the mask is a costume."

"Well, life isn't a mardigras festival."

Pablo heard the familiar click that announced his father was done with the conversation. His father didn't understand. Marcos was a superb manipulator. Flirtatious, brilliant, magnetic. A great actor. He knew how to create images and put on a performance that lasted like a movie you couldn't forget. Marcos had raised reality to a fiction and people were paying attention, and not only in Mexico, but all over the world. His father would never understand him or his view of the world, and the realization made him sad. Pablo hung up the phone, walked to the main road out of San Cristóbal de las Casas and thumbed a ride back toward the forest.

CHAPTER TWENTY-ONE
Chan Nah K'in

My mother knew where I had gone, she knew the exact location of the cave, but she didn't come for me. Not at first. She let me go with the death-smell. She let me live it out as long as possible. She knew I had to get close to the smell, and then she came. She didn't just pick up my thirsty, hungry body and carry me back to the village. She stayed in my cave with me for three days, giving me bites of monkey tamale and all the water I could take. I didn't speak to her, and she didn't try to make me. On the second day she told me a story.

"Chan Nah K'in," she said. "This is the story of my mother's mother. She was alone when they came. A young woman, maybe your age, she was in her father's house, grinding softened corn kernels in the stone *metate*, making tortillas for when her father, brother and husband returned from the hunt. She heard a rustling of leaves, her dog jumped up, and then she saw them standing at the edge of the clearing. The dog cowered back behind her. There were three men. Two *Ts'ur*, men she had never seen before, but the third she recognized. He had come many times before to talk with her father. After this man visited, her father always laughed and told her how the man talked of a strange god and all sorts of crazy things about life, what people were supposed to do and how they were supposed to pray.

"The three men came closer and now they stood before her house. The two *Ts'ur* held funny sticks in their hands. They should not have come this close. They should have waited for her father and husband to return. They should have waited to be invited, but they kept coming still, closer and closer until they were below the edge of the palm roof. They sat on the ground. She ignored them, thinking it was better to not see them until her father came.

"When her father, brother and husband came home, the foreign men stood up and moved underneath the roof next to her. She trembled, but she did not run away. She continued to grind corn and tried to ignore them. The foreign men spoke and pointed their funny sticks at her. The man who had come before, the one who talked of the funny god, translated what the two others had said to her father and husband. Her father was angry at first, and then he looked confused and defeated. She had never seen him with this look and it made her afraid. In the end, she, her father, brother and husband followed the foreign men. The foreign men made them walk very far and put them on a truck and took them away. They had never seen such a machine with big wheels and a loud engine and they couldn't understand how it could move.

"These men had been sent by another man, an important man, the ruler of the country of Guatemala. He wanted to amuse his people, thinking this way they wouldn't feel hunger, and he hoped they wouldn't notice how fat he was becoming. He decided to make a zoo like one he'd seen in another country. He sent workers to collect animals from many forests and strange people, too. And so it happened that she, her husband, brother and father were strange and odd attractions. They were put in a cage. The people of this country came and stared at them through metal wiring. "Keep your eyes down," her father told her. The people looked in at them and pointed and laughed. They watched them as they ate and slept and peed. "The forest will become angry," her father said, "and the animals will hide from these people. They will be hungry in the future." After many months of watching them, the people of that country grew bored. One day, she, her father, brother and husband were let out and brought home.

"My mother's mother was especially grateful to be back in the forest because she was pregnant and she wanted her baby to hear the sounds of the morning, howler monkeys growling, spider monkeys crashing through trees and parrots squawking. She wanted the baby to smell the forest when it was newly burned and ready for planting, to see the way the corn was planted, and how beans, peppers, tomatoes, yams and cassava grew between the stalks. She wanted her baby to hear the rains that made the cornstalks grow and to learn when they were ready to harvest. She imagined teaching her baby about the *päk che' kor*—the fields where they planted tobacco, agave, avocado and cacao after the soil was tired of corn. My mother's mother came home to the forest and she was happy again, and after some days it seemed like Guatemala, the zoo—the people's faces staring at her through wire—was a bad dream. Only her happiness was short. They had missed the planting season, and so there was little to eat. They were hungry and had to beg work and food at another house. Within three months her father, brother and husband became very sick. They were tired and hot, sweating all of the time. She cared for them as best she could, but they could not eat and water didn't stay inside them. Within a few days, they died. The sickness, the memory of Guatemala, had followed them back. And so my mother's mother was left alone with the baby growing inside her. She had no father, brother or husband, only memories and, now, their deaths."

My mother finished the story and then she left me in the cave. I continued to eat and drink until I was strong enough to stand. I didn't know what I would do or where I'd go, but I knew I would get up. Her story had made me see. In some small way, you must be better than history.

* * *

Before leaving the cave, I felt around in the dark and collected three small stones for my incense burner. I stepped out of the cave and the forest took me in. The leaves were darker and greener than before, the bark more red. Water dripped from wide leaves and I opened my mouth and let it roll onto my tongue and down my throat. I was so thirsty. I bent down at a small stream and felt leaves brushing my skin. I cupped my hands and drank the red-brown water. Close to the ground I could smell the wet dirt, ripe fruits, rotting pulp and roots, like the scent of my monthly blood, the blood that no longer came. It had been months since I'd bled. There was not enough food and I was too thin. My body didn't want to let any part go. I drew in air and remembered the forest.

I thought of my brothers and sisters who hadn't lived. They died when I was little, so I don't remember their faces, but my mother told me they died of hunger and I understood. We are often hungry; there is rarely enough. I imagine that when you're little, you're soft and pure and you can't stand so much pain in your stomach, just a little bit makes you die. I thought back and couldn't remember a time when I had not gone to bed hungry, when I had not woken hungry, the aching in my stomach a constant part of life. You'd think that after so long, you'd get used to it, but you never do.

I realized that after my mother I was the only one, and after me there would be no one. I didn't want to be the last one and I decided then, as I walked away from the cave through the forest, that I would have a child. I would go back to fighting, not in the way I was trained with a gun, but I would find some new way. For my child, life would be better. I would work and fight so that my baby never cried of hunger. And I knew that if I was going to have a baby then I also had to make sure she didn't repeat my story. Children must go a little bit further than their parents.

I came across a ceiba tree and stood at its base. I walked around it and climbed over the large roots, thinking it would take twenty people to surround its girth. I ran my hands over rough bark, feeling tree and lichen and vine, and I looked up so far that I got dizzy and stumbled away. I returned to the spot, leaning against the tree to steady myself as I looked up again at leaves blocking the bright sun. Green light. I wanted to catch the light on the leaves. Catch it, eat it, digest and send it back.

The tree must have been very old. Older than my mother, my grandfather and great-grandfather, who had died of the disease of Guatemala. I wanted to know what it felt like to be that old, to have seen so much, to stretch from the dark ground all the way up to the green light. What did it feel like to connect these two worlds? The tree answered, "You must be patient. When you're a little seed and just beginning in the shaded soil, there are lots of dangers. An agouti can come along and eat you in one bite. A branch can fall and smash you. Leaves from bigger plants can cover and block your light. If you're lucky, you aren't found or smashed or choked and you sprout a little leaf. You grow up and up and send roots down. There isn't much to grow on. The sun is taken by tall trees above, the food in soil sucked up by their powerful roots. You do the best you can. If you manage to grow for some years, you stop for a while. You wait. And you wait. You wait for the storm that will one day come. That will be the day when the big tree, which is old, splits in the wind. It will fall and you will be there. Waiting. Ready. Then you will grow. You will take the place of the one that fell."

From that ceiba tree I walked for another two days back to our original camp. I was weak and hungry, but I knew I had to reach that old camp. I found the clearing in the forest where the old man had cut the love-pieces out of the soldiers. Already the forest was growing back, erasing the evidence of our having been there. The huts had fallen, their roofs collapsed underneath the weight of three seasons of rain. Vines reached out and entwined poles that had been used to hold up houses, changing the buildings from brown to green. Small seedlings had rooted in the clearing and were growing quickly there, free from the shade and roots of big trees. I saw how fast the forest could fix itself.

I walked into the forest a little ways because I wanted to see if the love-pieces were still there, or if they'd disappeared when the soldiers died. I found the spot where my mother had left them in the banana leaves. They were lined up in a row at the base of a tree just as before, tiny packages throbbing softly on the ground. Pieces of Álvaro, Pacho, Luís and all the others. I couldn't leave them like that, waiting and beating forever, so I took them. I untied the packages, folded back the banana leaves and one by one, I popped the love pieces into my mouth. Now, with those pieces of love, my heart is bigger than before.

CHAPTER TWENTY-TWO
Mario

I guess sometimes life picks you up and sets you down in another place, and you don't even get to think about it. I ended up in San Cristóbal de las Casas, at the bottom of these stairs leading up to a yellow church. Maybe it's the yellow color, but I feel like this church is the first thing I've seen clearly in months. Something about it pulls me up and so I climb. It's evening. My legs are tired. I stop half way up to buy a thin, white candle from a woman sitting on the steps. She's wrapped in a black shawl with two small children curled up at her feet. She accepts my money, hands me the candle and mumbles a blessing.

Inside the church darkness is waiting for me, but somehow I feel lighter. This is the real church, the true God. I can feel it. Ever since I was little, people have come around trying to convince us to go their way. Pentecostal. Protestant. Mormon. They came from other countries, sometimes alone, or in groups of two or three, young guys with blond hair and new clothes speaking good Spanish like rich kids. They'd sit on the floor in our little house and talk to us about their church, inviting us to come along, but we never went. My mother said that God wasn't something you could choose. He just was, and we'd already found him at our church.

I don't know if I should dip my dirty fingers into the holy water at the entrance, but I do. It would be worse not to. My hands are stained black from working in the amber mines for three months, ever since I left Javier in the forest. Ugly black work, digging out that yellow stone, but I made enough money to get myself here and tomorrow I will sell the special piece I found and then I can head back home with some money in my pocket. I barely touch the cool water and then make the cross on myself, forehead, chest, left and right. I walk along the shadows, the long, thin candle in my hand, passing wooden benches where people kneel, heads bent, praying. No one sees me. I come to a doorway that leads into a small room. I don't know why, but I go through the door. Inside, there is a window cut into the thick wall of the church and evening light seeps in through the bars. I can see that outside the day is fading, giving way to night.

Six people, Indians, on their knees, mumble and whisper prayers to the Virgin de Guadalupe, who is lying on her back on the altar. I walk to the back of the small room and stand underneath the window. The Virgin is small, brown with huge eyes lined in black. A tear is drawn on her face just below her left eye. She lies immobile on a bed of red shiny material, surrounded by blue and pink flowers, the kind that never fade, and hundreds of candles. She looks calm.

A man and his wife, tiny like children, step into the room. Only their faces tell that they are old, perhaps sixty. The man goes toward the altar and lights his candle from another that is burning. He tilts it and lets a few drops of wax fall onto the cement and then affixes it there. He goes back beside his wife. They drop to their knees, faces down, and fall into the same rhythm of whispers as the others.

I watch from the back of the room, and then feel bad that I've been standing there with my unlit candle. I go up to the altar, light the candle, and return to the back of the room to settle onto my knees. I don't know the whole prayer, but I mumble along, whispering what I know for Javier.

I hated to leave Javier in the forest, but I didn't know what else to do. I couldn't carry him and I didn't want to go back to the barracks. I wanted to bury him, but I didn't have anything to dig a grave with, so I left him. I don't want to think about it anymore. I don't want to imagine his body now. From there I wandered to the edge of the forest and then followed the road away from Ocosingo, being careful to always stay hidden in the leaves. When I came to a village, I hid my gun at the edge of the road and tried to make myself look like I wasn't in the army. I unbuttoned my shirt and let it hang open. I pulled my pant legs out of my boots to cover them up, and then I went in search of someone to buy my gun. It wasn't easy. At first no one wanted to talk to me, but after I spent a day just hanging around making chit-chat, they could tell that I wasn't in the army anymore. These people know a lot more than they let on; I'm sure it was obvious that I'd deserted. Still, I took a big risk telling that guy about wanting to sell my machine gun, but I had no choice. He nodded his head and told me to wait. He walked off and about six hours later, he came back and said that he knew someone who would buy it. I sold it to him for only a fraction of what it was really worth, but I didn't care. Probably it ended up with the Zapatistas, but I don't care about that either. With the money, I bought clothes, ate good food and drank some beer. The rest I saved. I stayed in that village for a week or so and asked around for work. I needed to make some money before I could get a bus home. I didn't want to arrive with nothing and I knew I'd need money for my mother and for whatever I was going to do next. Everyone said the amber mines were the best place to find work because it's so bad that people don't stay long and merchants are always looking for new people to mine.

From the village I caught a ride to the mines at Simojovel. I asked around and found a guy who showed me where to go and how to mine. He lent me a hammer, a steel nail and a lantern and told me I could pay him back in amber, half of whatever I found the first week. That's how I got started and after that, every morning I climbed up the muddy hill, through wet, slippery plants to the entrance of the cave. I took off my shirt and ducked my head to enter. Inside I could almost stand up straight but the ceiling was just a little too low. I held the lantern up to the rock wall and looked around for a line of light gray rock and held the spot with one finger while I set the lantern down. Holding the nail, I hammered into rock, breaking off pieces and squinting my eyes so that no little bits could get me. It didn't really matter if my eyes were open or closed because it was so dark, I could hardly see anyway. Once I got a big chunk of rock to fall, I stopped hammering, collected it up and went outside to look. My eyes hurt as I came out of the cave and I had to stand there for a minute until I could see again. Outside the cave I could breath a little better too. Inside there is nothing but heat and dust and I felt like I was going to suffocate all of the time, so I learned it was best to beat the rock for only a little while and then come out and look. I looked down at what I had, to see if there was any amber. It's a rock, sometimes red, sometimes yellow. They told me it came from pine trees, the sticky stuff that comes out from bark and somehow, after a long time, becomes rock. They told me that if people are sick, they think this rock will make them better, so they pay a lot of money for it. They make beads and jewelry and wear it around their necks.

At the end of the week, I went to another guy's house. In his backyard, he worked pieces of amber to make jewelry that he sold to merchants. He looked at what I found and paid me for the pieces. He told me that there were shops in San Cristóbal where rich people bought the jewelry. He wished he could sell his jewelry there because he'd make a lot more money that way. One time when I was at his house selling the red-brown and yellow-brown pieces of rock, another miner came in really excited. He had a big piece of amber and inside the clear rock, you could see a fly. It had gotten stuck. The man who made jewelry got excited too and paid this miner five times the normal price for that piece. The guy told me that people really like to buy rock with insects stuck inside.

One day I was inside the cave, hitting on the hard, gray rock and it came to me. I realized what had really happened that night in the jungle with Javier. I replayed it over a few times in my mind and every time it got clearer. We had been walking deeper and deeper into the jungle and it was too dark to see anything. It was horrible not being able to see. Javier must have gotten scared because when we heard those strange noises that we couldn't recognize, he shot. They shot back and hit him, but now I don't think they were Zapatistas. I think one of our own guys shot Javier. I was thinking about it. If we were a half circle and Javier and I were at one side, then we would've been directly across from two of our own guys, and when Javier shot them, they shot back and that's how he got hit. We were aiming at each other all along.

A few days after I realized what had happened to Javier, I found my treasure. I guess this rock does bring luck. It started out like most days. I was hunched over in the cave early, hitting against rock, the nail making the same ding sound over and over. Dust was floating around and choking me and covering my body, making me dirty and black. The air was hot and sweat was running down my back and chest. Pieces of rock were falling and I was hitting harder and harder until finally a big chunk came loose. I collected up the pieces and took them outside to look. I saw it right away. There was a piece of clear yellow rock, half the size of my hand, and inside in the rock was a small scorpion. I knew that it would be worth a lot of money, more than all the money I'd made so far, but I also knew that I shouldn't sell it there in Simojovel.

I brought the rock back with me to San Cristóbal de las Casas and this morning I walked along the streets where they sell amber. I couldn't believe how much money they were asking for pieces of jewelry. Two hundred times what I got for the same size rock. I knew then that I must be very careful so I didn't try to sell my piece right away. I put my hand into my pocket and felt it down there, warm and smooth. I needed to think and so I left it there and continued walking around the city until I found this church. Tomorrow I will sell the scorpion.

* * *

There is no more day outside, only flickers from candles light the face of the Virgin. It's cold. My knees hurt, but the pain is somehow good. Kneeling here, I see that everybody's afraid. I'm scared to think about what's next. I'll go home and be with my mother. I want to see her and everybody else again, and I'll be happy to give her some money. Then I'll get ready to leave. I'll try to get in touch with Domingo. He said he'd help. It can't be that bad up there. It can't be worse than this, can it?

I look up at the Virgin. We all have different reasons for asking her to care for us, but in the end, they're all the same reason. This is as much as we can do. I don't know where I'll go tonight, or where I might sleep. I pray for help. After a while, I don't even know how long, I look up and I see that the room has filled with people. I didn't hear them come in. People quieter than whispers. Now I smell them, their fear, their dirt, and I don't feel cold anymore. We give each other our heat. I feel a wetness on my face and realize I'm crying. *Pinche* war. *Pinche* country. My knees hurt on the hard floor, and that makes me pray harder. I want to make sure no more tears escape my eyes. I pray for Javier and Julia, for my mother, even for that girl we found on the hill. I pray for *La Virgin* to be with me, to keep me safe when I go north to cross the border, over to the other side.

CHAPTER TWENTY-THREE
Amy

In the past few weeks, Minnesota had become something beyond humid. The heaviness of the air slowed down everything but the mosquitoes, and Amy could not muster her usual energy. She thought of Chiapas. The humidity there had been cool and damp, and she remembered feeling comforted by the misty coating over the landscape, at least when she'd first arrived, before the uprising. She thought of the green there, every shade from light to dark, countless variations on that one color, and once again she felt disappointed that she hadn't gotten to know the place.

Time had dampened some of pain surrounding the experience. Faces had faded and she no longer thought every day of César's attack, the killings at night or the boy with the mole. The confusion remained, but it didn't hurt as much as before. She was returning to a state of desire. She wanted to be engaged in research, consumed by adventure. She'd barely gotten a sense of the tropics, but she longed for it anyway, knowing it was home to so many bizarre insects and unidentified species.

It had been a month since she'd last seen and spoken with Christen. Their last conversation had begun well, but it too, as all of their interactions lately, had ended badly. Christen had spent the night at her apartment and in the morning, they rose together and got ready to for work.

"Let's do coffee at the shop," Christen suggested.

"Sure." Then she started to laugh.

"What's funny?"

"I just remembered my dream. I was in Chiapas again."

"Uh oh."

"No. Not like the last one." In her last dream about

Chiapas, she had been running up the road in an attempt to leave Ocosingo when she was shot by a military sniper stationed on the top of the Pemex station. She heard the shot and felt warm, wet blood soaking her shirt, but she didn't feel pain. She continued running and then hid beneath a bush with massive tropical leaves. Later, when she'd gotten away from Ocosingo and felt safe, she told people that she had been shot and hurt and that she was bleeding. She asked them for help. They turned her around, looked at her back and smiled. "You look *fine*. There's nothing wrong with you."

"This one wasn't bad," she told Christen. "I was in Chiapas, but this time I was in the Lacandón Rainforest." She laughed more. "What a crazy dream! The trees were forty meters tall, the leaves gigantic, as big as umbrellas, but they were heart-shaped, every single one of them a heart. Long, poisonous snakes slithered by, and it was raining and everything was soaking wet because the umbrella-sized leaves didn't work well as umbrellas. I was slogging through the mud."

"Speaking of umbrellas." He handed her an umbrella and grabbed his own. Outside the morning was still cool, but the air could hold no more water. It had begun to rain and the drops made sharp ping noises on their vinyl umbrellas. She had the feeling that it wasn't really going to rain hard. The clouds were going to let out a few drops and by afternoon, it would be unbearably humid and heavy again. Why couldn't the sky simply open up and let it all out at once, unburden itself and give them a reprieve? They opened their umbrellas and walked toward the coffee shop. Christen was smiling. "And?"

"I was collecting data for my indicator hypothesis and so far, the data were looking good. As I walked along, I was writing the award-winning article in my head thinking about how I'd craft the introduction and the discussion and which journal I'd send it to. I knew that what I was doing was significant and there was a feeling of eureka, which you know, you almost never get in real science. It was as if I'd discovered something akin to speciation by natural selection!"

"Sounds like a drug trip." Christen laughed more.

"You know," she said, "I was thinking I might go back to Chiapas when the semester ends."

He stopped walking and looked at her. "Are you nuts, Amy? There is a war going on!"

"Actually, I don't think they're fighting anymore."

"I suppose it's for the research." His face told her he was hurt. His voice sounded angry and resentful.

She waited a moment before she responded. "Maybe."

She hadn't seen Christen since then. They hadn't exactly broken up, not formally, but it was clear to her that they wanted to do entirely different things with their lives. She knew Christen had a good heart, only she'd come to understand that it wasn't an adventurous heart. He bought shade coffee. He contributed to the local house for homeless. He wanted to do the right thing. Indeed, he was the spider she had imagined him to be and he was comfortable in his coffee shop web. At first, when he reacted negatively to her idea of returning to Chiapas, she felt as if he were trying to capture her like prey, bind her up, put her in his web and suck her dry, but as soon as she thought it, she knew it was silly. Even if he did want to keep her there, he wasn't trying to capture her. She knew he really liked her and he wanted her to stay. If he complained about the science, it was only because he couldn't comprehend her focus on an academic career. He didn't understand when she explained to him that she *had* to worry about getting tenure.

"Academia is the only place I can do what I love to do," she said.

"Which is?"

"Figure things out about insects and their worlds, sit over a microscope and marvel at them. Dream of discovering something new."

She knew that the coffee shop and the life he'd built around it were good for him. It was the only place he'd ever feel safe. He could interact with the world, but on his own terms, from his vantage point behind the counter. He served coffee and was pleased if people congregated in his shop to talk and relax. Political science and philosophy undergraduate students came to him for recommendations or they consulted him on their research papers. He read their work, made comments and helped them out. He watched people, chatted with everyone and served good coffee. After he closed for the night, he cleaned up, locked the door and went home.

Amy wanted more than that. She thought about Mexico. As horrible as the rebellion and the experience had been, she'd learned how much she didn't know. That was the first step—realizing how little she knew. Now she wanted to go out and meet the world even more. She remembered that first day in Chiapas when she and Parker had arrived at Ocosingo. The expanse of the green valley, the *Acacia* trees, the walk around the market with César and Pablo after lunch and her visit to the church. The exhaustion and distress at seeing so much new had worn off relatively quickly, and she'd been excited to understand it all better. She thought about the poverty she'd seen and about how shocked she'd been to see barefoot children, women bent in half by cargo on their backs, corn growing everywhere. She now understood the urgency of the situation for those people as well as for the resources they depended on. She hadn't decided what she thought about the Zapatista uprising yet, but she knew that at least it had focused world attention on the plight of those people, and she realized that there were probably many others in the world, like her, who simply hadn't known.

More than ever, she believed that there was a role for her. She had read that the ancient and incredibly sophisticated Maya civilization in southern Mexico and Guatemala had fallen for unknown reasons, but one hypothesis for their demise was that populations had grown so large with the advent of agriculture, they'd run out of wood resources. They'd deforested the area and began fighting the neighbor city-states for access to wood. Perhaps Parker was right. It was a case of too many people in the same place, but people were smart and they could learn how to not abuse resources and live in some sort of balance. She was sure of that.

She still wanted to test her indicator hypothesis, and if it worked she could use it to help governments protect the most diverse tracts of land. There weren't any great solutions to the problems of rainforest conservation, but sooner or later, decisions had to be made and she might as well collect useful data that would help to make better decisions.

* * *

The semester had just ended and now she only had to finish grading and turn in her grades. She sat at her desk and read essays. Without the students, the hallway outside her office was quiet. She heard the phone ring in the secretary's office down the hall and then heard the woman's squeaky voice, "Dr. Hill you say? No, but I can transfer you." When the phone rang a few seconds later in her office, her hand was already on the receiver.

"Hello, Amy Hill speaking."

"*Doctora entomologa.* Such a fast pick-up. You must have been waiting for my call."

It was Parker. She felt her stomach squeeze in on itself. She had thought it might be Christen, and she hadn't expected Parker to call again.

"No. I heard the secretary talking about transferring the call."

"How are you?" he asked.

"Fine. Where are you?"

"Texas, but I'm heading south soon. I got the grant and I'm going to Guatemala. The system is similar so we can continue to collect comparable data."

"That's great."

"Want to come?"

She laughed. She was reminded of his quickness, the way he lacked any interest in carrying on casual conversation. "I remember you saying something about a war there."

"Not anymore. It's calm now."

"When are you planning to go?"

"Now."

"Now? You don't give much lead time, do you? I'm finishing the semester."

"So, you'll come down with me? You wrote the insect part of the grant. You can't really leave that part of our project hanging. And you still haven't told me about your mysterious indicator hypothesis, or how you learned all those details about guns." He was almost stammering now, perhaps having said more than he'd meant to. She was amused. He continued. "I mean, you can collect data for your hypothesis, whatever it is, plus the migratory bird project. I really believe these data might help save a few species of migratory birds. I've got funding to cover your flight, expenses, and ......"

She was laughing again so he stopped talking. There was silence on the phone. It would be nice to see him, but then another thought occurred to her.

"Will Pablo and César be there?" She wouldn't consider going if César were going to be there. She just couldn't.

"No. César decided to finish his screenplay. He says he's going to devote a year to it, and if nothing happens, he'll come back to science, and Pablo is god-knows-where in the Lacandón Forest."

"You're kidding!"

"I spoke with his mother. His father is livid. They don't know what he's doing, but he's living in a little community in the forest without water, electricity or a telephone."

"Maybe he's become a Zapatista," she said.

Parker laughed. "Who knows? Anyway, it would just be the two of us, at least in the beginning."

"Give me a few days to decide, okay?"

He didn't respond.

"Parker, are you still there?" This was oddly speechless behavior for Parker.

"Yeah," he said. "Sure. Of course."

"I'll call you in a few days, okay?"

"I'll wait for the call."

* * *

She really did feel a need to go somewhere, but she knew she couldn't afford time away. She had a paper to write and two manuscripts from her dissertation in need of editing before final submission. She would be teaching a new course in the fall on coevolution between insects and plants and she didn't have a single lecture ready. She had told the department chair that she was going to submit a grant proposal to the National Science Foundation in mid-June, which was only five weeks away, but she hadn't even begun to write. Still, the idea of a research trip with Parker excited her.

She went outside and to take a walk and clear her mind. As soon as she pushed open the door of the biology building, she felt the heavy air engulf her. It was only the beginning of summer and already she felt oppressed by the heat. It didn't rain often enough, and when it did the rain failed to relieve the mugginess of the air. She strolled around the empty campus, exhausted after the end of the long semester and it wasn't over yet. She still had twenty essays to read. And she felt emotionally spent by the tension of the relationship with Christen, everything between them left unsaid or pronounced and misunderstood. Life had become sticky.

She knew that by July, the air would be insufferable and everyone would be shut inside, a sort of summer hibernation in air conditioning until fall. Guatemala. It would also be humid, but she'd be in the forest collecting insects under the canopy of trees. Guatemala. She knew almost nothing of the place, even *less* than she'd known about Mexico. There were a million questions she should have asked Parker. Where would they be staying? What was the political situation? In hindsight, these were questions she should have asked six months ago about Mexico, and now had failed to ask again, this time about Guatemala. Still, it was hard to imagine a situation more unnerving than Mexico. No matter what, Guatemala could only be more positive. Guatemala. She liked the sound of the word, and she liked the idea of being someplace new and unknown.

She remembered the feeling she had every time her family moved. Her parents would announce at dinner that her father had been transferred to another state. Moves were both good and bad. A transfer meant promotion, but moves involved stress, especially for her mother. There were months of anticipation and packing and her mother would invariably break down and cry, complaining that they didn't live like normal people, they weren't ever able to put down roots and make lasting friendships. She always complained to her father about how horrible it was for children to constantly be changing schools, but Amy never minded the moves. Indiana. Louisiana. Fort Huachuca. She didn't care about leaving friends at school because she hardly had any to leave; her real friends traveled with her in insect boxes. Instead of hesitance, she'd maintained an enthusiasm for the new landscapes, new fields or forests where she could watch and trap insects. Much as she had as a child, she still yearned for novel lands, travels and hunts.

She sat on the college swing and rocked back and forth as she thought. She knew that she shouldn't seriously consider the trip. There wasn't enough time. She would be reviewed by the department next year and she ought to have published these papers and secured funding by then. As she rocked, sweat collected under her knees and rolled down the back of her calves. Perhaps she could take her computer and edit her papers in Guatemala. She could submit the grant in the next funding cycle in December; the data she collected in Guatemala would strengthen her proposal. She could even develop lectures for the coevolution course in the evenings down there. She felt her shirt becoming wet, sticking to her back. She rose from the swing and walked back toward her office. Her mind settled on the coevolution course, which she was excited about teaching, and she thought about how she would structure the lectures and which papers she would have the students read. She liked teaching, trying to put things in their simplest forms, but she didn't want to spend her life teaching about what was already known. She wanted to be one of the people who collected new data that ultimately ended up in textbooks.

It was hard to explain to non-biologists. She didn't believe in God or anything supernatural, but every time she was in the field or staring at her insect collection, she felt awe. She watched the little things that most people ignored. She saw magic in the way a jumping spider caught a fly, or the way an aphid pierced into phloem of plants. All of these small species went about their lives utterly unaware of her existence. To them, she meant nothing. To them, she was nothing, and yet she wanted to know them, and the only way to know them was through research. In doing science, she communicated with the cosmos and she found meaning in the world. Science was her fulfillment, her religion, and research was her form of prayer.

* * *

Amy slept late, but she woke the next morning thinking of the gear she would pack for Guatemala. Overnight, the trip had turned into a mandate. It was no longer a choice; she needed to go. She still had twelve more essays to read, but as soon as she arrived at her office, she went to the laboratory and began collecting her field supplies into a pile on the floor. From a top shelf she took down the Winkler Funnel; from a laboratory closet, the delicate butterfly net, the muslin sweep net and the collapsible poles. She unfolded the large duffel bag and began to fill it with the nets and Winkler Funnel. She pulled out her headlamp for late night forays and considered whether she should take a black light. Would there be electricity? She glanced at the clock. Eleven a.m., which meant it was noon in Texas. She could call Parker at work to ask him about electricity and tell him she was coming, but no, it could wait. She opened a drawer and counted out four hundred collecting vials, one large killing jar, three small killing vials and put them into Styrofoam boxes so that they wouldn't break. She placed them into the duffel bag. She found her pinning blocks, pins and labels. Into the duffel bag. She opened drawer after drawer in search of the malaise traps, and then finally found them in a box in the closet. She happened upon a Burlese Funnel. Should she take it? No, it was too big. She packed her aspirator, forceps and ziplock bags. She found pencils, pens, a clipboard and a couple of field notebooks. What else? Binoculars, but she'd take her binoculars in her carry-on luggage. Butterflies! She'd almost forgotten. She needed glycine envelopes for the butterflies and moths. Into the duffel. That was everything, she thought, until she remembered what she'd forgotten. Duct tape. There was none left from Mexico. She made a mental note. She was going to Guatemala. She was going to the tropics to do research. She was going to see Parker, and she must remember to buy some rolls of duct tape.

She sat down at her desk. She was excited and anxious, but she still needed to read the students' papers. The phone rang.

"Hello, Amy Hill speaking."

"Hi." It was Parker.

"I was going to call you," she said.

"I know, but I'm not patient. I was wondering what you're thinking."

She laughed. "Okay. I'm trying to decide whether you would like to clone yourself."

"Clone myself?"

"Yeh, like aphids or plants do."

"Oh god, no. Why?"

"I just wondered."

"You think I'm *that* egocentric?"

"Well, it *is* the best strategy if you are thinking in terms of evolution, getting all of your genes to the next generation."

"I prefer the idea of mixing myself up a bit," he said.

"That's good."

"Was that a test?"

"No, more of a non-sequitar."

"Well, I was wondering more about what you've decided about Guatemala," he said.

"Is there electricity?"

"Yes. The accommodations are better than in Mexico. I rent from a couple who runs a lodge. We don't get the luxury rooms, but it's nice enough."

"Probability of civil war?"

"Remote."

"Remote like Mexico or remote like Canada?"

He laughed. "Not as remote as Canada."

"And is there a clean toilet?"

"I'll clean it myself."

"Then I'll come."

"When?"

"Day after tomorrow?"

"I'll buy the tickets and call you back."

"Parker," she said.

"Yes?"

She wanted to say thank you, but reconsidered. It would sound odd, especially because she didn't exactly know what she would be thanking him for. "I'll see you soon." She hung up the phone and went back to the papers. The sooner she finished the essays, the better. She wanted to pack and then go to the library to find some books. Tonight and tomorrow, she knew she'd be giving herself a crash course on Guatemala.

CHAPTER TWENTY-FOUR
Pablo

The morning after a heavy rain and the forest woke up a little slower than usual. It was already six thirty and he hadn't heard a warbler or a dove. Of course, roosters always called no matter what. Yesterday afternoon it had begun to rain hard. The sky opened suddenly and let go, as if it were angry and forcing out pent-up exhaustion from having held on for so long. Lightning and thunder were close and loud. Sheets of water fluttered in gusts of wind. Pablo swayed in the hammock under the woman's palm-roof hut and watched the downpour. Vegetation cowered under the constant assault of drops. The dry hard clay melted into tiny red rivers that twisted and hurried across the almost flat ground. Water soaked quickly into the soil, forming miniature lakes where before there had been only tiny puddles left from the last rain. And when evening arrived, there was no pause; rain continued to pound the earth, the plants, the hut until finally the thatched roof was saturated. Pablo watched small drops form and drip onto the dirt floor inside. That night his dreams were filled with drumming.

Morning brought drizzle and sun, but lethargy as well. He didn't feel like rising and going out to work in the *milpa*, but when he saw the other men heading toward the field, he rose and followed them. The mud was thick and viscous and with each step, his boots were sucked into the soil. He advanced slowly by pulling on his back leg, freeing the boot and setting it down a bit in front of his other leg where it was instantly swallowed by the sticky muck. Sinking and extracting and sinking again, he finally arrived at the *milpa*. The other men were already at work, but the sight of the *milpa* shocked and dismayed him. Overnight the field had gone from a regular mix of mature corn stalks and fresh seedlings to a mess of standing water interspersed with islands of mud. The larger corn plants had been broken in half and he was depressed to see that so many of the tiny plants, which had just begun to show above the ground, were gone, either washed away or buried beneath water. The other men didn't seem as disheartened as he, or if they did, they didn't show it or speak of it. They worked at trying to fix the damage. They dug canals to drain water. They harvested corn that was almost mature, but had been broken by rain. Carefully, they wiped mud from fragile leaves of the small seedlings that protruded up above the water, and straightened those that were falling by mounding wet sticky soil around them. Pablo set to work along side them.

Slowly birds began to rouse and fly to the edge of the *milpa*. They shook their wings, perched in the sun to dry, and began to preen themselves by quickly running feather after feather through their beaks and pausing in between to keep vigil for predators. It was such an awful lot of work, Pablo thought, this living and maintenance, the daily struggle to make a life in the rainforest. No human should have to live in this place, and likewise, the forest shouldn't have to put up with such abuse. Everything was too hard here. Even the simple act of planting and harvesting corn was more brutal than he ever could have imagined.

At the onset of the dry season, they had slashed vegetation to make the *milpa*; day after day they cut down small trees, vines and bushes. When the vegetation dried, they burned it, knowing that the ash would add nutrients to the soil, and then they planted their crops in the field. Corn, beans, peppers, chayote, tomatoes, cassava and more corn. Always more corn, but now, this deluge. Now, they would salvage what they could.

Even in the best situation, though, when crops and weather were perfect, the amount of work required to eat was grueling. He remembered when he'd first seen the older woman shucking corn and he'd gone to help her. Within a few minutes his fingers ached and blistered from pushing and loosening the hard kernels and the pain forced him to give up. She did not need to pause because her fingers were callused and accustomed to work. She shucked and tossed the kernels into lime water to soak and when they were soft, he watched her grind them with mortar and pestle until she had produced a smooth paste. From that, she made her cornbread. Other times she pounded and ground dry kernels to a smooth flour, which she stored in a beat-up old tin. Later she used the flour to make tortillas. She was stronger than she looked, and her endurance, like that of everyone in this place, seemed endless.

He was lonely, with only birds to keep him company. He yearned for conversations about books and films and science. The people were involved in their own lives and didn't include him. They nodded their heads at him in the morning and made sure he understood what work was to be done. The woman spoke Spanish well, but from the first day she answered his questions with shrugs and grunts. No one really cared whether he was there or not.

The excitement and momentum of the rebellion during the first few months had slowed. Perhaps the uprising was also affected by the onset of the rainy season and the increase in depth of mud. It had been weeks since he'd been asked to carry the last communiqué, the one after Colosio's death. The cease-fire was still holding, but talks between the government and the Zapatistas were stalled indefinitely. The government had quelled the uprising and didn't care to solve the real problems of Chiapas. Around Ocosingo, the poorest *campesinos* had pushed out many larger cattle ranchers and reallocated land for themselves, but then the changes had stopped. Group work and ideology had given way to life. People focused on turning soil, planting crops, playing soccer; no one seemed interested in working together to find lasting solutions to the conflict. Pablo had no choice but to work alongside the others, to plant and harvest and cook, to learn what he could of this place and the people.

* * *

Two days after the rain, a child came to tell him that there was a new communiqué. Pablo felt grateful for the opportunity to do more than work in the *milpa*. He wanted to be going somewhere with a purpose, instead of fighting nature. He went out to meet the messenger, but this time it was Carlos instead of Jorge. They didn't converse long and then Pablo was on his way, walking up canyons on dirt paths toward Ocosingo. Passing Ocosingo this time, he stopped to collect a few books and scientific papers from a friend's house where he had left his things, thinking that after he delivered the communiqué, he might stay a few days in San Cristóbal de las Casas and read.

As he left Ocosingo, Pablo became conscious of the fact that time was of another sort here. Life happened on the order of generations for these people. His whole life could slip away while he worked in a *milpa,* slashing weeds, growing food, and if he had been born here, that would be all he would expect. He wondered whether the uprising had really made life any better for anyone. Deaths could be worth something only if they were followed by real changes, but so far there hadn't been any sign that the government would do the right things. The deaths seemed more like sacrifices than steps forward. The only light Pablo saw was the global attention being paid to the Zapatistas. It was ironic, but Europeans were more interested in the Zapatistas than Mexicans. They flocked to Chiapas, volunteering to act as human shields, bringing money, energy and awareness to the cause. Perhaps, Pablo thought, he just wasn't patient enough. Nothing could change overnight, and in many ways, the Zapatistas were the first real grassroots movement ever in Mexico. Perhaps it would grow and grow like one of the American movements and little runners would pop up in all sorts of places around the world. Maybe, just like the tropical grass that grew as a weed in the city, it would grow and spread and send down roots so deep it could never be killed. Every time a section was cut out or sprayed with herbicide, another would come up in a slightly different place, between beautifully planted flowers, in cracks between the sidewalks, places where it couldn't be totally eradicated.

He arrived at San Cristóbal de las Casas and delivered the communiqué. After a shower and breakfast, he felt renewed and left his room at the cathedral. He walked around the city, up and down cobblestone streets, past tourist shops selling amber jewelry, postcards, Maya-type wood carvings and Tzotzil weavings. He stopped in front of a stand selling little Zapatista dolls. They were new, having appeared in the last month since he'd last been in the city. There were female dolls resembling Comandante Ramona. She wore a traditional skirt and a military shirt and she had a gun slung over her shoulder. There were male dolls with green baseball hats and red handkerchiefs covering their faces. There was even a Subcomandante Marcos doll with two blue-green eyes showing through the black mask and a pipe sticking out of its mouth. Zapatistas had entered the world of playthings, objects for purchase, something to look at, take home, put on the shelf. Pablo felt angry at the peasant woman who was showing him these dolls, egging him to buy one, presenting him with all of the options. Zapatista with machine gun. Zapatista on horseback. Zapatista carrying political banner. Even though he didn't want one, he remained at her table for along time, ignoring her pleas, staring at the little dolls.

Almost a month had passed since he last spoke with his parents, and so he bought a phone card and called home.

"*Hola mamá*," he said. "How are you?"

"Pablo! Thank God you're safe!"

"Of course, I'm safe, *mamá*. What's the news from home?"

"A letter arrived for you a couple of days ago from the

United States. It looked official and I thought maybe it was from Dr. Holt, but I didn't open it."

"Will you open it now?"

Perhaps Parker wanted an update on the situation so that he could decide what to do about the bird project. Things had settled, but he didn't think it was a good idea for Parker to return just yet, and he couldn't imagine the people funding his research would want him to come back to Mexico anyway. Parker had always said they were only interested in results, having the organization's name on published papers. Mexico was risky, their money might be spent on nothing. He heard the sound of paper ripping.

His mother read, "We are pleased to inform you that you have been accepted to begin graduate work in the Biology Department at the University of Utah. We can offer you five years of support with the potential for a sixth year pending your progress. Please inform us of your acceptance within three weeks. What is this, Pablo?"

He decided in an instant. "I'm going to study in the United States. Can you see if there is a phone number on the letter where I can call?"

"A doctorate?"

"Yes."

"In the United States?"

"Yes."

"When would you go?"

"Soon."

"Oh, thank God!"

* * *

Pablo took a bus back to Mexico City. He needed the hours to readjust and become accustomed to the idea of moving to the United States. He knew it would be hard for him there; American students would be different, more like Amy, less like César, but there was also freedom to be who he was. Up there, he wouldn't have to repress or hide his sexuality as he did in Mexico.

As the bus rocked along, he began to read one of the books he'd picked up from his friend's house in Ocosingo. It was about the evolution of bird song, the physiology of how birds made sound and the forms of communication in different kinds of birds. After the first chapter, he closed the book, his thumb marking the place. He looked out the window and thought about birds, constellations, migrations. He thought about the little girl with bright star eyes, and about going forward, about placing each foot a little bit in front of the last. In these months, he had learned that he didn't really move forward in a linear fashion. Rather, it was by circling around on himself that he was spun out in a new direction. To truly move ahead you had to revisit most of where you'd been before and that's what he would do. With the uprising and his role as courier he had forgotten about having applied to graduate school the previous fall. He'd never imagined he would be accepted and so he hadn't thought seriously about going; it had been mostly to please Parker that he had followed through on the application. Still, the decision to continue his studies wasn't hard. With the stalled peace talks, his services were needed less and less so that he spent most of his time farming now anyway. He had wanted to be part of the rebellion and in a way, he had been, but now everything was moving slowly, while the rest of the world hurried on. He missed ideas, books and César, people he could converse with.

A thought flashed into his head. When he got to Mexico City, he would get together with César and tell him that he was gay and about David and all of the things he'd always wanted to say before, but had been too afraid to verbalize. He wanted César to know and he wanted to hear himself tell it out loud. He realized that he couldn't continue to live the way he had for the last three years. He had felt as though he were dying as a man, unwanted sexually, never being touched by another, repressing all of his own desires, or playing them out alone in the dark at night. In a parallel way, he realized the indigenous people of Chiapas had arrived at the same point, only there wasn't really a choice, was there? There was forward and there was death. Between the two, there really was no choice. And he wouldn't only tell César, but now he'd tell his parents. Once he got everything ready to leave, he would sit them down and tell them. He could imagine the scene and it pained him, but he had to do it. He would rehearse what he would say and then he would make them listen. His mother would cry and his father would be angry. It would simply be one more way that Pablo was a disappointment. Pablo knew that, but he also knew that he could no longer continue to live hidden away, always pretending he was something other than he was, always knowing they expected something other than what he would give them. He would tell them and they'd have a few years to think about it, while he was studying.

Yes, Pablo would turn in on himself, go to the United States for his doctorate, and later, see where life cast him out. He would go to the United States, he would survive the Americans, and he might even meet someone. This thought reminded him of David and San Francisco, of the city, the parties, of men living freely together. He felt the familiar heat that overcame him whenever he thought about it and he smiled at the memory. It was crazy not to go. Yes, there were good things north of the border too—the American innocence gave a certain freshness, and the freshness was liberating. He opened the book about bird song again and continued to read.

CHAPTER TWENTY-FIVE
Chan Nah K'in

I am remembering the ways of the forest. I have once again joined the movement, only now I work here in the forest. I have been out there and I have seen what it is like, and I don't want to return to that world. For the last time, I took off the pants, which had always rubbed my legs, and put on my long white tunic. I gave the boots that tortured my feet to another Zapatista soldier who needed them for walking. I am happy to be without them. I don't hide my hair anymore either. It hangs straight down like before, like it's supposed to do. Now, I am like my friends, the *payasos,* the insects who look like the leaves they eat. I work hidden in plain sight.

I work at the forest camp as a cook. Everything I learned about the forest from my mother and the other Hach Winik people serves me now. I built myself a little house, much like at home. Balsa wood is light, the young trees split easily and can be tied together for walls. The roof is woven from palm leaves. My house doesn't stand above the ground like at home. That takes more work. Here this is enough. A good roof means I will stay dry when the rains start again. Inside my house I have a hammock, cooking pots, *comal, metate* and my incense burner. Everything I need.

I said goodbye to my friend Álvaro who was killed in Ocosingo. On the third day after his death, his soul had separated in two. His *ik hach pixan,* his true soul, was sent to Hach Ak Yum's heaven by Sukunkyum. That is where all those who are good in life are sent. His *u wich ik pixan,* the eye of his soul, has gone to Kisin. There the part of him that sinned will be burned.

After I came here to the forest camp and built my house, I remembered him by our ways. Really, it was too late and I didn't have his body, but I imagined him. I thought about it and there, in my mind, I tried to do everything right. I broke a corn cob and put a piece of it in his right hand. In his left, I put a monkey jaw bone for the dogs and a lock of his hair for the lice. Gifts that would help his *pixan* arrive to Mensabäk's cliff. If I had his body, I would have folded his legs at the knees and tied them together, crossed his arms over his chest and protected him with cloths. I would have burned charcoal under his hammock to keep him warm and then dug his grave. I would have buried him, his feet in the east, his head in the west, and given him corn and tortillas and candles for the trip. I'd have built a palm-thatched roof to keep him dry and while I did this, I would have talked to him. "This is what I must do, Álvaro, now that you are dead. Do not come back to me. Do not try to scare me. You must go on." I would mound dirt over him and sprinkle ashes on top to keep the worms away, and then, I would bathe, wash the tunic that smelled of death and put on a clean one. After three days, I would know he was gone. After five, I could burn incense again.

I don't hate the men anymore, the one who shot Álvaro first or the one who killed him later. I know the soul of his murderer will be put in Kisin's fire and as it burns, getting smaller and smaller, it will shriek with pain until it's so small that no sounds come out and then it will be gone forever.

* * *

I greet the soldiers in the morning, "What did you see?" They are learning to pay attention to what their souls see at night. Otherwise, I don't speak much. The women avoid me and I think the men are a little afraid. They're not used to a woman knowing more. Usually they're the ones that have been to school while the girls stay home, but I can read and write. I know things from school and about the medicine my mother learned, but I don't think all that bothers them so much. What they don't like is knowing that here in the forest, without me, they would eat less well. They don't know the trees like I do. They don't know a *huanacastle* from a *bariy*. They tolerate the forest, but they aren't pulled into it; they can't see through the leaves and that makes them afraid. They fight so that they can leave. I fight so that I can stay. This is the difference between us.

If they wanted to learn about the forest, I could teach them how to see and which trees are which, but they don't ask. I could show them what plants to collect, which herbs and seeds are good, how to hunt animals, but they don't want to know. And really, the forest takes a long time to know, and they are without time. They must think constantly of strategy, defense and the next fight. My mother taught me everything she knew about the forest and what she didn't know, we learned together, but that took all the years up to now, and I am still learning.

The women criticize me because I am trained to fight, yet I stay here and cook. I don't talk to them. They chatter like little birds, so fast and high in Tzeltal and Tzotzil, it's hard to follow everything they're saying, but I pick up words. Coward. Old ways. They say I am doing them wrong, proving the men right. They think because I never cut my hair and now I wear this tunic that I am weak. They don't understand. My hair and my tunic make me strong.

I haven't talked to my mother either, but I'm not so angry anymore. Maybe because she's older, she can't see as far as I can. I know we're doing right. The world is listening. Subcomandante Marcos tells us that people everywhere are paying attention to what happens here. Every day. It's slow, though. We're still a long way. We must wait for time. My mother says the Zapatista fight is good, but not at the expense of the forest. She and Marcos had a fight because he complained in a communiqué about the big piece of land the Hach Winik had been given by the government. She was mad.

"The forest is life," she told him. "You're complaining about the Hach Winik because they won't join the movement.

You say the government has bought us off, to use us like indigenous dolls. That's fine. I agree. But now you want our land, our forest. You take the forest and you kill us."

"I know. I know," he told her. "I was just making a point about the way the government has used you people, saying you're a lost Maya tribe, direct descendents of the past. Besides, without solving the people problem, we can't solve the forest problem."

"People problems are never solved," she said. "That's the nature of people." And then she said, "The forest has no problems."

That's when she left camp, but I thought about it later. What she said was right, but then I thought again, and I thought the forest does have a problem and it is us. So we do need to solve the people problem first. In some ways, my mother is no different from the missionaries who came from Spain early on. She wants to kill whoever she can't convert. In the end all our reasons for fighting are the same, but we can't see that. My mother for the forest; women for women's rights; Marcos for indigenous autonomy; men for decent work; me so that my child, who is coming, doesn't feel hunger.

The problem is that there is never enough. Like the other women, I stopped bleeding before it all began; our bodies understood that there was not enough food and we could not think about babies. Not bleeding made it easier for us, especially those of us who fought. We weren't kept back by pains in our stomachs or blood running down our legs while we were on guard. There were no bloody rags to wash and no risk of getting pregnant. I didn't mind before, but when I came to this camp to cook, I knew I needed to bleed to have a baby. I started going into the forest to hunt for myself. I needed meat; cassava and corn were not enough, but I didn't have time to hunt big animals. Besides they are too hard to get without a gun and we cannot risk the sound of gun shots here. I began to hunt, but only for myself. Every day when I was collecting herbs for cooking I watched for tracks of small animals. When I found a little burrow, I returned there in the afternoon and crouched outside until nightfall. That is when the animals come out. I waited and when a mouse or rat or squirrel came out, I trapped it under an old piece of hammock. I stabbed it quickly with a knife, skinned it and cooked it right there in the forest. If I took it back to camp, I'd have to share with everyone, but these animals are too little to share. One day I was especially lucky. I was walking along when I came across a big, black snake. It was as thick as my leg and as long as I am tall, and it was swallowing a large rat. It was the kind of snake that squeezes its food to death and so the rat was already dead—half in the snake's mouth and half out. I saw that snake and I wanted that rat. I made a noise to frighten the snake and it coughed up the part of the rat that was in its mouth and hurried away. The rat was big, the size of a small dog, and half of it had already been skinned by the juices in the snake's mouth. I was so happy. It was the easiest piece of meat I'd had. I hunted as often as I could and finally I began to bleed again. Time had come.

After the bleeding stopped, I waited a few days and then I went to them at night. It was late and I didn't know how they would respond, but I had no need to worry. They all accepted my attention. I think it's hard for men to resist that. The first one thought he was dreaming. He smiled and laughed softly as I touched him between his legs feeling his sex grow. When he was big and hard, he opened his eyes and saw that it was not a dream. I leaned toward him and we could barely see each other's eyes, but we looked at each other, and he didn't push me away. I took off his pants and felt with my hand that he was ready. He grabbed at me and pulled me down on top of him. I lifted my tunic and helped him inside. He didn't hurt like the fat military man hurt, but it didn't feel good either. He flipped me over so that now he was on top, and I pulled my legs up and let him move as much as he wanted, in and out, as deep as he could get. It didn't take long. Afterwards, he fell quickly back to sleep and I left him. That night I went from soldier to soldier, making them all hard, taking them inside me, letting them move fast, letting their juices mix together. One of them will make my baby, and unlike me, with no father, my baby will have many fathers. None of them will own her, but all of them will be responsible.

* * *

When it comes to food they tell me I work miracles. I do the best I can. We have few supplies. Beans, maize, cassava, sometimes dried meat. Everything is rationed, and there is never enough for anyone. They say they never knew corn and beans could taste so good. They tell me they feel less hungry. It's just that I know some secrets. You see, the Hach Winik have lived with this forest for a long time. We know what flavors and cures are hidden in green leaves, hard seeds and bark.

I work all day to make food. There is little time to sleep. In the mornings, the others help me bring water from the stream. We walk down together, fill the buckets and carry them back slowly. Sometimes people from the outside bring us cassava, and we are happy to have the extra food. I take the cassava roots and go down to the stream. I build a little pool with mud and rocks and I set the roots in there. They must soak so that the water can take all of the poisons away. After they have soaked for two days, I return and pick them up. Back at the camp, I set them in the sun to dry. They are ready when they are very white and then I break them up into pieces and set them in water over the fire to boil. Again, the water takes out more poisons. When they have cooked for half the night, I can use them for food.

Tortillas are my daily ritual. They must be fresh and warm for the soldiers. In the afternoon, I strip corn off the cob, twisting and pushing hard kernels against my callused fingers. They sing a music as they fall into the lime water to soak. While they are softening, I go into the forest to find herbs. Herbs must always be fresh or they lose their power. I walk slowly on paths that others hardly see. I am at home here. There is a softness. The forest is gentle. I look as closely as I can. I gather old branches from the *ba'che'* tree for fire. And sometimes, if I'm quiet, I spot a quetzal with its shimmering green feathers and perfect, alert eyes. That bird makes me stop and watch. I pray as it takes in large sweet fruits, swallowing them in one gulp, defecating almost as fast. This green shimmering animal brings movement of wind, which brings rain, which brings life.

When I've collected everything I need, I return to camp and rest for a while. Later, in the middle of night, when there are no planes and helicopters circling above looking for smoke from our fires, I rise from my hammock. I scoop the soft corn kernels into the *metate*, crushing and grinding and mashing them into a smooth *masa*. I do it the old way, with stones, so that the minerals of the rocks mix with the *masa*. Sometimes, I blend in leaves from the herbs. Then, when the tortillas cook, the flavor of the herb comes out with the heat. I pat out the *masa* forming the flat bread with the palms of my hands and then place it on the round, clay *comal*. Heat and smoke from the *ba'che'* flavor the bread. I try not to think about the dead *campesinos* or the fat military man. I don't want their memories put into this food. Instead, I think about the forest, about tall trees, about my ancestors, about the stories my mother told me. Pata, pata, pata, slap. Pata, pata, pata, slap. The rhythm of my hands keeps time to my thoughts. I think about what I learned. You must wait a long time. When it's your turn, you must do a little better than those before you. I pat and cook and pat and cook until there is a pile of tortillas and while they're still warm, I call the hungry to come and eat. Then I return to my pots, to begin the next meal.

* * *

When a group comes back from a fight with the military, I can tell instantly if one is missing. I can tell by the smell of their march through the forest, by the scent on their bodies. Ten pairs of victorious feet make a sweet, relaxed perfume. Nine pairs walk more slowly, the smell full with fear, heavy with sadness. I don't cry like they do when one is missing. I know the missing one has split in two; his true owner has begun a new journey, and the eye of his soul has gone to *Kisin* to be burned. On the days when I smell them coming with the shy death-stride, I go into the forest and gather what I need. I ready the ceremony. I have found only one *copal* tree close by, but that is enough. With a machete I cut a slit into the smooth bark and collect the sap that leaks out onto a palm leaf. Back at camp, I call the soldiers to my house. They kneel before the face on the incense burner while I spoon the sticky *pom*, which has already begun to harden, into the burners until it covers the stones from my cave. When the resin is hard, we burn it and pray through the sweet smell. A true ceremony would last months, but that is time we cannot afford. I must help them become new and fresh within hours. It has to be enough. While they continue to pray, I go to my pots. I add a little bit of this and a tiny bit of that. I save my special herbs and seeds for these moments. Herbs that help dull sorrow. Herbs that revive spirit. Seeds that plant hope. I work the pots, stirring and correcting the flavor. I serve the food, and then I pray for miracles.

Sylvia Torti is the daughter of an Argentine father and American mother. Born and raised in Ohio, she holds a Ph.D. in biology from the University of Utah, where her studies of tropical tree diversity took her to Panama, Trinidad, Chiapas, and the Democratic Republic of Congo. Her trip to Ocosingo, Chiapas occurred on the eve of the Zapatista rebellion, and instead of finding a project, she encountered civil war. *The Scorpion's Tail* is a processing and manifestation of her experiences there, her reflections on the relationship between the U.S. and Mexico, as well as the relationship between humans and the natural world.

CURBSTONE PRESS, INC.

is a non-profit publishing house dedicated to literature that reflects a commitment to social change, with an emphasis on contemporary writing from Latino, Latin American and Vietnamese cultures. Curbstone presents writers who give voice to the unheard in a language that goes beyond denunciation to celebrate, honor and teach. Curbstone builds bridges between its writers and the public – from inner-city to rural areas, colleges to community centers, children to adults. Curbstone seeks out the highest aesthetic expression of the dedication to human rights and intercultural understanding: poetry, testimonies, novels, stories, and children's books.

This mission requires more than just producing books. It requires ensuring that as many people as possible learn about these books and read them. To achieve this, a large portion of Curbstone's schedule is dedicated to arranging tours and programs for its authors, working with public school and university teachers to enrich curricula, reaching out to underserved audiences by donating books and conducting readings and community programs, and promoting discussion in the media. It is only through these combined efforts that literature can truly make a difference.

Curbstone Press, like all non-profit presses, depends on the support of individuals, foundations, and government agencies to bring you, the reader, works of literary merit and social significance which might not find a place in profit-driven publishing channels, and to bring the authors and their books into communities across the country. Our sincere thanks to the many individuals, foundations, and government agencies who have recently supported this endeavor: Community Foundation of Northeast Connecticut, Connecticut Commission on Culture & Tourism, Connecticut Humanities Council, Greater Hartford Arts Council, Hartford Courant Foundation, Lannan Foundation, National Endowment for the Arts, and the United Way of the Capital Area.

Please help to support Curbstone's efforts to present the diverse voices and views that make our culture richer. Tax-deductible donations can be made by check or credit card to:
Curbstone Press, 321 Jackson Street, Willimantic, CT 06226
phone: (860) 423-5110   fax: (860) 423-9242
www.curbstone.org

IF YOU WOULD LIKE TO BE A MAJOR SPONSOR OF A
CURBSTONE BOOK, PLEASE CONTACT US.